The Case of the Reluctant Agent

OSMANISCHES REICH.
SCHWARZES MEER
MITTELLAENDISCHES MEER
Asowsches Meer
Cypern
Candia
Nil Mündungen
Libysche Wüste
Arabische Wüste
Europa
Asien
Adana
Erzerum
Van
Kars
Baghdad
Urfa
Haleb
Damascus
Akka
Beirut

The Case *of the* Reluctant Agent

A Sherlock Holmes Mystery

Tracy Cooper-Posey

The Case of the Reluctant Agent

Published by Ravenstone
an imprint of Turnstone Press
607–100 Arthur Street
Winnipeg, Manitoba
R3B 1H3 Canada
www.TurnstonePress.com

Turnstone Press gratefully acknowledges the assistance of the Manitoba Arts Council, the Canada Council for the Arts and the Government of Canada through the Book Publishing Industry Development Program.

Canada

Cover design: Doowah Design

Printed in Canada
by Friesens for Turnstone Press.

Canadian Catalogue in Publication Data

Cooper-Posey, Tracy, 1962–

The case of the reluctant agent

Includes His last bow by Sir Arthur Conan Doyle.
ISBN 0-88801-263-2

I. Title. II. Title: Doyle, Arthur Conan, Sir, 1859–1930. His last bow.

PS8555.059236C3 2001 C813'.54 C2001-910818-4
PR9199.3.C646C3 2001

To Katherine Rebecca Cooper-Smith.
May you be blessed with Elizabeth's strength.

Acknowledgements

Thank you, always, to my wonderful husband Mark and children, Terry, Kate and Matthew, for loving me despite long periods of being ignored while I, instead, kept company with my computer.

My thanks to Manuela and all the supportive people at Turnstone.

Thanks, Dave, for the advice on horses and horseback travel in inhospitable weather.

Jennifer Glossop, editor extraordinaire, for all her wonderful insights that make a book shine just so and for sorting out my deplorable French.

For all Sherlockian fans everywhere, who demanded the rest of the story.

Table of Contents

His Last Bow

An Epilogue of Sherlock Holmes

(from *His Last Bow* by Sir Arthur Conan Doyle, 1917)

IT WAS NINE O'CLOCK AT NIGHT UPON THE SECOND OF August—the most terrible August in the history of the world. One might have thought already that God's curse hung heavy over a degenerate world, for there was an awesome hush and a feeling of vague expectancy in the sultry and stagnant air. The sun had long set, but one blood-red gash like an open wound lay low in the distant west. Above, the stars were shining brightly; and below, the lights of the shipping glimmered in the bay. The two famous Germans stood beside the stone parapet of the garden walk, with the long, low, heavily gabled house behind them, and they looked down upon the broad sweep of the beach at the foot of the great chalk cliff on which Von Bork, like some wandering eagle, had perched himself four years before. They stood with their heads close together, talking in low, confidential tones. From below the two glowing ends of their cigars might have been the smouldering eyes of some malignant fiend looking down in the darkness.

A remarkable man this Von Bork—a man who could hardly be matched among all the devoted agents of the Kaiser. It was his talents which had first recommended him for the English mission, the most important mission of all, but since he had taken it over, those talents had become more and more manifest to the half-dozen people in the world who were really in touch with the truth. One of these was his present companion, Baron Von Herling, the chief secretary of the legation, whose huge 100-horse-power Benz car was blocking the country lane as it waited to waft its owner back to London.

"So far as I can judge the trend of events, you will probably be back in Berlin within the week," the secretary was saying. "When you get there, my dear Von Bork, I think you will be surprised at the welcome you will receive. I happen to know what is thought in the highest quarters of your work in this country." He was a huge man, the secretary, deep, broad, and tall, with a slow, heavy fashion of speech which had been his main asset in his political career.

Von Bork laughed.

"They are not very hard to deceive," he remarked. "A more docile, simple folk could not be imagined."

"I don't know about that," said the other thoughtfully. "They have strange limits and one must learn to observe them. It is that surface simplicity of theirs which makes a trap for the stranger. One's first impression is that they are entirely soft. Then one comes suddenly upon something very hard, and you know that you have reached the limit, and must adapt yourself to the fact. They have, for example, their insular conventions which simply *must* be observed."

"Meaning, 'good form' and that sort of thing?" Von Bork sighed as one who had suffered much.

"Meaning British prejudice in all its queer manifestations. As an example I may quote one of my own worst blunders—I can afford to talk of my blunders, for you know my work well enough to be aware of my successes. It was on my first arrival. I was invited to a week-end gathering at the country house of a Cabinet Minister. The conversation was amazingly indiscreet."

Von Bork nodded. "I've been there," said he dryly.

"Exactly. Well, I naturally sent a resumé of the information to Berlin. Unfortunately our good Chancellor is a little heavy-handed in these matters, and he transmitted a remark which showed that he was aware of what had been said. This, of course, took the trail straight up to me. You've no idea the harm that it did me. There was nothing soft about our British hosts on that occasion, I can assure you. I was two years living it down. Now you, with this sporting pose of yours."

"No, no, don't call it a pose. A pose is an artificial thing. This is quite natural. I am a born sportsman. I enjoy it."

"Well, that makes it the more effective. You yacht against them, you hunt with them, you play polo, you match them in every game, your four-in-hand takes the prize at Olympia. I have even heard that you go the length of boxing with the young officers. What is the result? Nobody takes you seriously. You are a 'good old sport,' 'quite a decent fellow for a German,' a hard-drinking, night-club, knock-about-town, devil-may-care young fellow. And all the time this quiet country house of yours is the centre of half the mischief in England, and the sporting squire the most astute Secret Service man in Europe. Genius, my dear Von Bork—genius!"

"You flatter me, Baron. But certainly I may claim that my four years in this country have not been unproductive. I've never shown you my little store. Would you mind stepping in for a moment?"

The door of the study opened straight on to the terrace. Von Bork pushed it back, and, leading the way, he clicked the switch of the electric light. He then closed the door behind the bulky form which followed him and carefully adjusted the heavy curtain over the latticed window. Only when all these precautions had been taken and tested did he turn his sunburned aquiline face to his guest.

"Some of my papers have gone," said he; "when my wife and the household left yesterday for Flushing they took the less important with them. I must, of course, claim the protection of the Embassy for the others."

"Your name has already been filed as one of the personal suite. There will be no difficulties for you or your baggage. Of course, it is just possible that we may not have to go. England may leave France to her fate. We are sure that there is no binding treaty between them."

"And Belgium?"

"Yes, and Belgium, too."

Von Bork shook his head. "I don't see how that could be. There is a definite treaty there. She could never recover from such a humiliation."

"She would at least have peace for the moment."

"But her honour?"

"Tut, my dear sir, we live in a utilitarian age. Honour is a mediaeval conception. Besides England is not ready. It is an inconceivable thing, but even our special war tax of fifty millions, which one would think made our purpose as clear as if we had advertised it on the front page of *The Times*, has not roused these people from their slumbers. Here and there one hears a question. It is my business to find an answer. Here and there also there is an irritation. It is my business to soothe it. But I can assure you that so far as the essentials go—the storage of munitions, the preparation for submarine attack, the arrangements for making high explosives—nothing is prepared. How then can England come in, especially when we have stirred her up such a devil's brew of Irish civil war, window-breaking Furies, and God knows what to keep her thoughts at home?"

"She must think of her future."

"Ah, that is another matter. I fancy that in the future, we have our own very definite plans about England, and that your information will be very vital to us. It is to-day or to-morrow with Mr. John Bull. If he prefers to-day we are perfectly ready. If it is to-morrow we shall be more ready still. I should think they would be wiser to fight with allies than without them, but that is their own affair. This week is their week of destiny. But you were speaking of your papers." He sat in the arm-chair with the light shining upon his broad bald head, while he puffed sedately at his cigar.

The large oak-panelled, book-lined room had a curtain hung in the further corner. When this was drawn it disclosed a large brass-bound safe. Von Bork detached a small key from his watch-chain, and after some considerable manipulation of the lock he swung open the heavy door.

"Look!" said he, standing clear, with a wave of his hand.

The light shone vividly into the opened safe, and the secretary of the Embassy gazed with an absorbed interest at the rows of stuffed pigeon-holes with which it was furnished. Each pigeon-hole had its label, and his eyes as he glanced along them read a long series of such titles as "Fords," "Harbour-defences," "Aeroplanes," "Ireland," "Egypt," "Portsmouth forts," "The Channel," "Rosythe," and a score of others. Each compartment was bristling with papers and plans.

"Colossal!" said the secretary. Putting down his cigar he softly clapped his fat hands.

"And all in four years, Baron. Not such a bad show for the hard-drinking, hard-riding country squire. But the gem of my collection is coming and there is the setting all ready for it." He pointed to a space over which "Naval Signals" was printed.

"But you have a good dossier there already."

"Out of date and waste paper. The Admiralty in some

way got the alarm and every code has been changed. It was a blow, Baron—the worst set-back in my whole campaign. But thanks to my cheque-book and the good Altamont all will be well to-night."

The Baron looked at his watch and gave a guttural exclamation of disappointment.

"Well, I really can wait no longer. You can imagine that things are moving at present in Carlton Terrace and that we have all to be at our posts. I had hoped to be able to bring news of your great coup. Did Altamont name no hour?"

Von Bork pushed over a telegram.

"Will come without fail to-night and bring new sparking plugs.—ALTAMONT."

"Sparking plugs, eh?"

"You see he poses as a motor expert and I keep a full garage. In our code everything likely to come up is named after some spare part. If he talks of a radiator it is a battleship, of an oil-pump a cruiser, and so on. Sparking plugs are naval signals."

"From Portsmouth at midday," said the secretary, examining the superscription. "By the way, what do you give him?"

"Five hundred pounds for this particular job. Of course he has a salary as well."

"The greedy rogue. They are useful, these traitors, but I grudge them their blood-money."

"I grudge Altamont nothing. He is a wonderful worker. If I pay him well, at least he delivers the goods, to use his own phrase. Besides he is not a traitor. I assure you that our most pan-Germanic Junker is a sucking dove in his feelings towards England as compared with a real bitter Irish-American."

"Oh, an Irish-American?"

"If you heard him talk you would not doubt it. Sometimes I assure you I can hardly understand him. He seems to have declared war on the King's English as well as on the English King. Must you really go? He may be here any moment."

"No. I'm sorry, but I have already overstayed my time. We shall expect you early to-morrow, and when you get that signal-book through the little door on the Duke of York's steps you can put a triumphant Finis to your record in England. What! Tokay!" He indicated a heavily sealed dust-covered bottle which stood with two high glasses upon a salver.

"May I offer you a glass before your journey?"

"No, thanks. But it looks like revelry."

"Altamont has a nice taste in wines, and he took a fancy to my Tokay. He is a touchy fellow and needs humouring in small things. I have to study him, I assure you." They had strolled out on to the terrace again, and along it to the further end where at a touch from the Baron's chauffeur the great car shivered and chuckled. "Those are the lights of Harwich, I suppose," said the secretary, pulling on his dust coat. "How still and peaceful it all seems. There may be other lights within the week, and the English coast a less tranquil place! The heavens, too, may not be quite so peaceful if all that the good Zeppelin promises us comes true. By the way, who is that?"

Only one window showed a light behind them; in it there stood a lamp, and beside it, seated at a table, was a dear old ruddy-faced woman in a country cap. She was bending over her knitting and stopping occasionally to stroke a large black cat upon a stool beside her.

"That is Martha, the only servant I have left."

The secretary chuckled.

"She might almost personify Britannia," said he, "with her complete self-absorption and general air of comfortable somnolence. Well, au revoir, Von Bork!"—with a final wave of his hand he sprang into the car, and a moment later the two golden cones from the headlights shot forward through the darkness. The secretary lay back in the cushions of the luxurious limousine, with his thoughts so full of the impending European tragedy that he hardly observed that as his car swung round the village street it nearly passed over a little Ford coming in the opposite direction.

Von Bork walked slowly back to the study when the last gleams of the motor lamps had faded into the distance. As he passed he observed that his old housekeeper had put out her lamp and retired. It was a new experience to him, the silence and darkness of his widespread house, for his family and household had been a large one. It was a relief to him, however, to think that they were all in safety and that, but for that one old woman who had lingered in the kitchen, he had the whole place to himself. There was a good deal of tidying up to do inside his study and he set himself to do it until his keen, handsome face was flushed with the heat of the burning papers. A leather valise stood beside his table, and into this he began to pack very neatly and systematically the precious contents of his safe. He had hardly got started with the work, however, when his quick ears caught the sound of a distant car. Instantly he gave an exclamation of satisfaction, strapped up the valise, shut the safe, locked it, and hurried out on to the terrace. He was just in time to see the lights of a small car come to a halt at the gate. A passenger sprang out and advanced swiftly towards him, while the chauffeur, a heavily built, elderly man, with a grey moustache, settled down, like one who resigns himself to a long vigil.

"Well?" asked Von Bork eagerly, running forward to meet his visitor.

For answer the man waved a small brown-paper parcel triumphantly above his head.

"You can give me the glad hand to-night, Mister," he cried. "I'm bringing home the bacon at last."

"The signals?"

"Same as I said in my cable. Every last one of them, semaphore, lamp code, Marconi—a copy, mind you, not the original. That was too dangerous. But it's the real goods, and you can lay to that." He slapped the German upon the shoulder with a rough familiarity from which the other winced.

"Come in," he said. "I'm all alone in the house. I was only waiting for this. Of course a copy is better than the original. If an original were missing they would change the whole thing. You think it's all safe about the copy?"

The Irish-American had entered the study and stretched his long limbs from the arm-chair. He was a tall, gaunt man of sixty, with clear-cut features and a small goatee beard which gave him a general resemblance to the caricatures of Uncle Sam. A half-smoked, sodden cigar hung from the corner of his mouth, and as he sat down he struck a match and relit it. "Making ready for a move?" he remarked as he looked round him. "Say, Mister," he added, as his eyes fell upon the safe from which the curtain was now removed, "you don't tell me you keep your papers in that?"

"Why not?"

"Gosh, in a wide-open contraption like that! And they reckon you to be some spy. Why, a Yankee crook would be into that with a can-opener. If I'd known that any letter of mine was goin' to lie loose in a thing like that I'd have been a mug to write to you at all."

"It would puzzle any crook to force that safe," Von Bork answered. "You won't cut that metal with any tool."

"But the lock?"

"No, it's a double combination lock. You know what that is?"

"Search me," said the American.

"Well, you need a word as well as a set of figures before you can get the lock to work." He rose and showed a double-radiating disc round the keyhole. "This outer one is for the letters, the inner one for the figures."

"Well, well, that's fine."

"So it's not quite as simple as you thought. It was four years ago that I had it made, and what do you think I chose for the word and figures?"

"It's beyond me."

"Well, I chose August for the word, and 1914 for the figures, and here we are."

The American's face showed his surprise and admiration.

"My, but that was smart! You had it down to a fine thing."

"Yes, a few of us even then could have guessed the date. Here it is, and I'm shutting down to-morrow morning."

"Well, I guess you'll have to fix me up also. I'm not staying in this goldarned country all on my lonesome. In a week or less, from what I see, John Bull will be on his hind legs and fair ramping. I'd rather watch him from over the water."

"But you're an American citizen?"

"Well, so was Jack James an American citizen, but he's doing time in Portland all the same. It cuts no ice with a British copper to tell him you're an American citizen. 'It's British law and order over here,' says he. By the way, Mister, talking of Jack James, it seems to me you don't do much to cover your men."

"What do you mean?" Von Bork asked sharply.

"Well, you are their employer, ain't you? It's up to you to see that they don't fall down. But they do fall down, and when did you ever pick them up? There's James—"

"It was James's own fault. You know that yourself. He was too self-willed for the job."

"James was a bonehead—I give you that. Then there was Hollis."

"The man was mad."

"Well, he went a bit woozy towards the end. It's enough

to make a man bughouse when he has to play a part from morning to night with a hundred guys all ready to set the coppers wise to him. But now there is Steiner—"

Von Bork started violently, and his ruddy face turned a shade paler.

"What about Steiner?"

"Well, they've got him, that's all. They raided his store last night, and he and his papers are all in Portsmouth gaol. You'll go off and he, poor devil, will have to stand the racket, and lucky if he gets off with his life. That's why I want to get over the water as soon as you do."

Von Bork was a strong, self-contained man, but it was easy to see that the news had shaken him.

"How could they have got on to Steiner?" he muttered. "That's the worst blow yet."

"Well, you nearly had a worse one, for I believe they are not far off me."

"You don't mean that!"

"Sure thing. My landlady down Fratton way had some inquiries, and when I heard of it I guessed it was time for me to hustle. But what I want to know, Mister, is how the coppers know these things? Steiner is the fifth man you've lost since I signed on with you, and I know the name of the sixth if I don't get a move on. How do you explain it, and ain't you ashamed to see your men go down like this?"

Von Bork flushed crimson.

"How dare you speak in such a way!"

"If I didn't dare things, Mister, I wouldn't be in your service. But I'll tell you straight what is in my mind. I've heard that with you German politicians when an agent has done his work you are not sorry to see him put away."

Von Bork sprang to his feet.

"Do you dare to suggest that I have given away my own agents!"

"I don't stand for that, Mister, but there's a stool pigeon or a cross somewhere, and it's up to you to find out where it is. Anyhow I am taking no more chances. It's me for little Holland, and the sooner the better."

Von Bork had mastered his anger.

"We have been allies too long to quarrel now at the very hour of victory," he said. "You've done splendid work and taken risks, and I can't forget it. By all means go to Holland, and you can get a boat from Rotterdam to New York. No other line will be safe a week from now. I'll take that book and pack it with the rest."

The American held the small parcel in his hand, but made no motion to give it up.

"What about the dough?" he asked.

"The what?"

"The boodle. The reward. The £500. The gunner turned damned nasty at the last, and I had to square him with an extra hundred dollars or it would have been nitsky for you and me. 'Nothin' doin'!' says he, and he meant it, too, but the last hundred did it. It's cost me two hundred pound from first to last, so it isn't likely I'd give it up without gettin' my wad."

Von Bork smiled with some bitterness. "You don't seem to have a very high opinion of my honour," said he, "you want the money before you give up the book."

"Well, Mister, it is a business proposition."

"All right. Have your way." He sat down at the table and scribbled a cheque, which he tore from the book, but he refrained from handing it to his companion. "After all, since we are to be on such terms, Mr. Altamont," said he, "I don't see why I should trust you any more than you trust me. Do you understand?" he added, looking back over his shoulder at the American. "There's the cheque upon the table. I claim the right to examine that parcel before you pick the money up."

The American passed it over without a word. Von Bork undid a winding of string and two wrappers of paper. Then he sat gazing for a moment in silent amazement at a small blue book which lay before him. Across the cover was printed in golden letters *Practical Handbook of Bee Culture*. Only for one instant did the master spy glare at this strangely irrelevant inscription. The next he was gripped at the back of his neck by a grasp of iron, and a chloroformed sponge was held in front of his writhing face.

"ANOTHER GLASS, WATSON!" said Mr. Sherlock Holmes as he extended the bottle of Imperial Tokay.

The thick-set chauffeur, who had seated himself by the table, pushed forward his glass with some eagerness.

"It is a good wine, Holmes."

"A remarkable wine, Watson. Our friend upon the sofa has assured me that it is from Franz Josef's special cellar at the Schoenbrunn Palace. Might I trouble you to open the window, for chloroform vapour does not help the palate."

The safe was ajar, and Holmes standing in front of it was removing dossier after dossier, swiftly examining each, and then packing it neatly in Von Bork's valise. The German lay upon the sofa sleeping stertorously with a strap round his upper arms and another round his legs.

"We need not hurry ourselves, Watson. We are safe from interruption. Would you mind touching the bell. There is no one in the house except old Martha, who has played her part to admiration. I got her the situation here when first I took the matter up. Ah, Martha, you will be glad to hear that all is well."

The pleasant old lady had appeared in the doorway. She curtseyed with a smile to Mr. Holmes, but glanced with some apprehension at the figure upon the sofa.

"It is all right, Martha. He has not been hurt at all."

"I am glad of that, Mr. Holmes. According to his lights he has been a kind master. He wanted me to go with his wife to Germany yesterday, but that would hardly have suited your plans, would it, sir?"

"No, indeed, Martha. So long as you were here I was easy in my mind. We waited some time for your signal to-night."

"It was the secretary, sir."

"I know. His car passed ours."

"I thought he would never go. I knew that it would not suit your plans, sir, to find him here."

"No, indeed. Well, it only meant that we waited half an hour or so until I saw your lamp go out and knew that the coast was clear. You can report to me to-morrow in London, Martha, at Claridge's Hotel."

"Very good, sir."

"I suppose you have everything ready to leave."

"Yes, sir. He posted seven letters to-day. I have the addresses as usual."

"Very good, Martha. I will look into them to-morrow. Good night. These papers," he continued, as the old lady vanished, "are not of very great importance, for, of course, the information which they represent has been sent off long ago to the German Government. These are the originals which could not safely be got out of the country."

"Then they are of no use."

"I should not go so far as to say that, Watson. They will at least show our people what is known and what is not. I may say that a good many of these papers have come through me, and I need not add are thoroughly untrustworthy. It would brighten my declining years to see a German cruiser navigating the Solent according to the minefield plans which I have furnished. But you, Watson," he stopped his work and took his old friend by the shoulders; "I've hardly seen you in the light yet. How have the years used you? You look the same blithe boy as ever."

"I feel twenty years younger, Holmes. I have seldom felt so happy as when I got your wire asking me to meet you at

Harwich with the car. But you, Holmes—you have changed very little—save for that horrible goatee."

"These are the sacrifices one makes for one's country, Watson," said Holmes, pulling at his little tuft. "Tomorrow it will be but a dreadful memory. With my hair cut and a few other superficial changes I shall no doubt reappear at Claridge's to-morrow as I was before this American stunt—I beg your pardon, Watson, my well of English seems to be permanently defiled—before this American job came my way."

"But you have retired, Holmes. We heard of you as living the life of a hermit among your bees and your books in a small farm upon the South Downs."

"Exactly, Watson. Here is the fruit of my leisured ease, the *magnum opus* of my latter years!" He picked up the volume from the table and read out the whole title, *Practical Handbook of Bee Culture, with Some Observations upon the Segregation of the Queen.* "Alone I did it. Behold the fruit of pensive nights and laborious days, when I watched the little working gangs as once I watched the criminal world of London."

"But how did you get to work again?"

"Ah, I have often marvelled at it myself. The Foreign Minister alone I could have withstood, but when the Premier also deigned to visit my humble roof—! The fact is, Watson, that this gentleman upon the sofa was a bit too good for our people. He was in a class by himself. Things were going wrong, and no one could understand why they were going wrong. Agents were suspected or even caught, but there was evidence of some strong and secret central force. It was absolutely necessary to expose it. Strong pressure was brought upon me to look into the matter. It has cost me two years, Watson, but they have not been devoid of excitement. When I say that I started my pilgrimage at Chicago, graduated in an Irish secret society at Buffalo, gave serious trouble to the constabulary at Skibbareen, and so eventually caught the eye of a subordinate agent of Von Bork, who recommended me as a likely man, you will realize that the matter was complex. Since then I have been honoured by his confidence, which has not prevented most of his plans going subtly wrong and five of his best agents being in prison. I watched them, Watson, and I picked them as they ripened. Well, sir, I hope that you are none the worse!"

The last remark was addressed to Von Bork himself, who after much gasping and blinking had lain quietly listening to Holmes's statement. He broke out now into a furious stream of German invective, his face convulsed with passion. Holmes continued his swift investigation of documents while his prisoner cursed and swore.

"Though unmusical, German is the most expressive of all languages," he observed when Von Bork had stopped from pure exhaustion. "Hullo! Hullo!" he added as he looked hard at the corner of a tracing before putting it in the box. "This should put another bird in the cage. I had no idea that the paymaster was such a rascal, though I have long had an eye upon him. Mister Von Bork, you have a great deal to answer for."

The prisoner had raised himself with some difficulty upon the sofa and was staring with a strange mixture of amazement and hatred at his captor.

"I shall get level with you, Altamont," he said, speaking with slow deliberation. "If it takes me all my life I shall get level with you!"

"The old sweet song," said Holmes. "How often have I heard it in days gone by. It was a favourite ditty of the late lamented Professor Moriarty. Colonel Sebastian Moran has also been known to warble it. And yet I live and keep bees upon the South Downs."

"Curse you, you double traitor!" cried the German, straining against his bonds and glaring murder from his furious eyes.

"No, no, it is not so bad as that," said Holmes, smiling. "As my speech surely shows you, Mr. Altamont of Chicago had no existence in fact. I used him and he is gone."

"Then who are you?"

"It is really immaterial who I am, but since the matter seems to interest you, Mr. Von Bork, I may say that this is not my first acquaintance with the members of your family. I have done a good deal of business in Germany in the past and my name is probably familiar to you."

"I would wish to know it," said the Prussian grimly.

"It was I who brought about the separation between Irene Adler and the late King of Bohemia when your cousin Heinrich was the Imperial Envoy. It was I also who saved from murder, by the Nihilist Klopman, Count Von und Zu Grafenstein, who was your mother's elder brother. It was I—"

Von Bork sat up in amazement.

"There is only one man," he cried.

"Exactly," said Holmes.

Von Bork groaned and sank back on the sofa. "And most of that information came through you," he cried. "What is it worth? What have I done? It is my ruin for ever!"

"It is certainly a little untrustworthy," said Holmes. "It will require some checking and you have little time to check it. Your admiral may find the new guns rather larger than he expects, and the cruisers perhaps a trifle faster."

Von Bork clutched at his own throat in despair.

"There are a good many other points of detail which will, no doubt, come to light in good time. But you have one quality which is very rare in a German, Mr. Von Bork: you are a sportsman and you will bear me no ill-will when you realize that you, who have outwitted so many other people, have at last been outwitted yourself. After all, you have done your best for your country, and I have done my best for mine, and what could be more natural? Besides," he added, not unkindly, as he laid his hand upon the shoulder of the prostrate man, "it is better than to fall before some more ignoble foe. These papers are now ready, Watson. If you will help me with our prisoner, I think that we may get started for London at once."

It was no easy task to move Von Bork, for he was a strong and a desperate man. Finally, holding either arm, the two friends walked him very slowly down the garden walk which he had trod with such proud confidence when he received the congratulations of the famous diplomatist only a few hours before. After a short, final struggle he was hoisted, still bound hand and foot, into the spare seat of the little car. His precious valise was wedged in beside him.

"I trust that you are as comfortable as circumstances permit," said Holmes when the final arrangements were made. "Should I be guilty of a liberty if I lit a cigar and placed it between your lips?"

But all amenities were wasted upon the angry German.

"I suppose you realize, Mr. Sherlock Holmes," said he, "that if your Government bears you out in this treatment it becomes an act of war."

"What about your Government and all this treatment?" said Holmes, tapping the valise.

"You are a private individual. You have no warrant for my arrest. The whole proceeding is absolutely illegal and outrageous."

"Absolutely," said Holmes.

"Kidnapping a German subject."

"And stealing his private papers."

"Well, you realize your position, you and your accomplice here. If I were to shout for help as we pass through the village—"

"My dear sir, if you did anything so foolish you would probably enlarge the two limited titles of our village inns by giving us 'The Dangling Prussian' as a sign-post. The

Englishman is a patient creature, but at present his temper is a little inflamed, and it would be as well not to try him too far. No, Mr. Von Bork, you will go with us in a quiet, sensible fashion to Scotland Yard, whence you can send for your friend, Baron Von Herling and see if even now you may not fill that place which he has reserved for you in the ambassadorial suite. As to you, Watson, you are joining us with your old service, as I understand, so London won't be out of your way. Stand with me here upon the terrace, for it may be the last quiet talk that we shall ever have."

The two friends chatted in intimate converse for a few minutes, recalling once again the days of the past whilst their prisoner vainly wriggled to undo the bonds that held him. As they turned to the car Holmes pointed back to the moonlit sea and shook a thoughtful head.

"There's an east wind coming, Watson."

"I think not, Holmes. It is very warm."

"Good old Watson! You are the one fixed point in a changing age. There's an east wind coming all the same, such a wind as never blew on England yet. It will be cold and bitter, Watson, and a good many of us may wither before its blast. But it's God's own wind none the less, and a cleaner, better, stronger land will lie in the sunshine when the storm has cleared. Start her up, Watson, for it's time that we were on our way. I have a cheque for five hundred pounds which should be cashed early, for the drawer is quite capable of stopping it, if he can."

The Case of the Reluctant Agent

"There's an east wind coming, Watson."

"I think not, Holmes. It is very warm."

"Good old Watson! You are the one fixed point in a changing age. There's an east wind coming all the same, such a wind as never blew on England yet. It will be cold and bitter, Watson, and a good many of us may wither before its blast."

—Sherlock Holmes in
"His Last Bow—An Epilogue of Sherlock Holmes"
in *His Last Bow* by Sir Arthur Conan Doyle © 1917

Chapter One

Sussex Downs, England.
November 7th, 1917.

"Gawd, it's quiet, ain't it, guv?"

"Too quiet," Gregson said from the Bentley's back seat. He drew a calming breath, curled his gloved hand over the lowered window and peered into the gloaming.

The November evening was bitterly cold and drab, matching Gregson's mood. He stared at the dim glow of whitewashed walls glimpsed through a copse of alders and poplars beginning just ahead of the elegant nose of the Bentley. Digby had extinguished the lamps, leaving only the gibbous moon aloft to light the scene.

"I'd say 'e's not 'ome," Digby murmured. "But even if 'e is, can't we just go up an' knock?"

"For any other night, for any other person, perhaps." He saw the whites of Digby's eyes roll, and added, "Why don't you go ahead and knock, then?"

"Right, sir." The bobby reached for the car's door handle with alacrity, and Gregson, not for the first time, envied him his innocence.

Digby put only one foot on the gravel, his hands swinging the door wide, when a single shot, loud in its unexpectedness, volleyed across the clearing. The bullet kissed the frame of the windscreen and careened away with a sour note, sliding neatly between the Bentley and Digby's remarkable ear.

"Strewth!" It was a high, breathless hiss. Digby froze.

Gregson remained silent.

"I aimed to miss," came a low, guarded call from a patch of total darkness beneath the trees.

"I appreciate that," Gregson remarked through the open window.

"Your contraption has been sitting staring at my abode for ten minutes now. If you were innocent in purpose you would have at least come and knocked on the door."

"Told you we should've," Digby muttered under his breath.

Gregson shifted closer to the window and wound it down fully. He addressed the patch of black shadows. "Forgive me, Holmes. I would have knocked, but I had been warned your mood today would be . . . less than jovial."

Again, there was a thoughtful silence, while the tops of the poplars rubbed in the little wind.

A long, thin shadow detached itself from the main and moved out onto the roadway, a pace or two from the car. A wide-brimmed hat, a greatcoat, the collar standing up, leaving the face in complete darkness. Only the flesh on the hand that held the revolver showed white.

"Bloody 'ell . . ." Digby muttered, startled again.

From beneath the brim issued the familiar voice. "Gregson. Chief of Police, Tobias Gregson. And young Digby, I assume. Get back in, lad. You'll freeze without your coat."

Digby scrambled back into the Bentley and slammed the door, rocking the vehicle.

Holmes pocketed the revolver. "You've obviously been sent, Gregson. Only two people could have warned you of my mood, and I wouldn't put it above either of them to send a message boy. I'm surprised it's you they ferreted out. All the way from Scotland Yard on a night like this—should I be flattered?"

"You've already guessed otherwise, I'm sure," Gregson said mildly.

"As soon as I heard your voice and realized who it was sitting staring at my cottage," Holmes agreed. "Come, Gregson, you've had courage enough in the past to bait me in my den regardless of my mood. Why baulk now?"

Gregson gripped the window again, feeling the chill creep further into his flesh.

"It's your brother, Holmes."

Again, there was a small, telling silence. Holmes would be reaching for those logical connections that to a layman appeared to be plucked from thin air.

"Mycroft wasn't the one who sent you," Holmes said.

"No, Holmes."

"Is he dead?"

"He's at Saint Thomas's Hospital. It was a messy affair ... they don't expect him to live. I'm sorry."

Gregson heard him draw a deep breath, and let it out. A sigh. Holmes' voice came again, lower. "Someone attempted to murder him. That's why you're here."

THE BENTLEY MOTORED across the Downs, a now-calm Digby at the wheel, while the two older men conversed with truncated phrases, pooling information with swift professionalism.

"They found him in his office this afternoon. Three o'clock, when the clerk brought tea."

"The weapon?"

"His own revolver. Lord Stainsbury assures me it is Mycroft's. He kept it in his desk, locked in the middle drawer."

"Then the murderer was someone he trusted. He would not have allowed anyone else to reach that gun. It is still there?"

"Oh, yes. I ordered nothing be touched. I have two of my best officers guarding the room. I knew you would want to see it."

"No-one heard a shot?"

"Muffled."

"The silk cushion on the sofa?"

"Yes. Of course, you've been to his office on a number of occasions, haven't you?"

"Where was Mycroft, in the room?"

"Slumped over his desk."

"Where did the shot hit him?"

"High in the back, just to the right of the spine. It was from behind. I'm sorry, Holmes."

Holmes' sharp chin turned away, and he stared at the ghostly, rolling dales a moment. "He was always keen on physical inertia. He may have found the perfect solution." He pulled back into the corner of the cab, his hat brim lowering over the glittering eyes. "I must think," he said briefly, and fell into silence.

Gregson settled into his own corner, his heart heavy, and listened to the chatter of the engine, resting his mind and body. It would be a long trip back to London, and Holmes would ensure there was no opportunity for rest when they arrived.

DAYLIGHT WAS CREEPING in past the drawn curtains, illuminating Gregson's spot on the wide, comfortable sofa where he sprawled, exhausted, when there was a murmur of footsteps and voices in the corridor outside the office.

Holmes looked up from his study of the bloody desk top. "That would be Lord Stainsbury, I'd say, pulling rank on your men."

The door opened, and a man taller than Holmes stepped in. His excellent suit, with an immaculate pocket kerchief, and his shining tailored shoes set him well above the average clerk. His refined features—the sharp, sloping chin, sharper blue eyes, and the shining high forehead surrounded by carefully groomed hair spoke of intellect. The erect bearing and squared shoulders spoke of power.

"Good morning, gentlemen," Lord Stainsbury intoned.

"My lord," Gregson acknowledged.

"You are early, my lord," Holmes observed. "It is not yet fully daylight."

"I wanted to speak to you before you finished your investigation here."

"I consider such an exchange an entirely necessary part of the investigation," Holmes returned. "Your foresight is appreciated." He stepped away from the desk, his hands on his hips, his forearms bare. His coat and jacket had long since been discarded—they lay next to Gregson on the sofa. It had not been particularly arduous work Holmes had been doing, but rather bloody and delicate.

"You have my condolences, Sherlock. God knows this business with your brother would be difficult enough under any circumstances, but your last meeting was less than amicable. That's an added load I don't envy you."

Holmes smiled—one of the predatory expressions that Gregson remembered of old—and looked over at him. "Gregson, this is one of the two men who knew of my disposition tonight and might have warned you."

"The other was Mycroft, then," Gregson concluded.

Stainsbury cleared his throat. "I hope you didn't mind

my sending Gregson, here. I thought it best he break the news . . ."

"Your thoughtfulness was not wasted. Gregson and I put the time to good use, after all." Holmes turned and strolled around the perimeter of the well-appointed chamber. It was a high-ceilinged room, and with the coming morning, it appeared light, airy, and gracious. A pair of tall sash windows on the west wall was bracketed by white bookcases that reached up to the ceiling. The north wall was a bank of the shelves. All of them carried their share of the paper, books and paraphernalia of a mentally active man's work.

It was here that the first signs of violence appeared. Not far away from the shelves, a revolver lay on the carpet.

Holmes moved past the door on the east wall, around Stainsbury, stepping over Gregson's splayed foot, back to the windows on the west wall, to turn and face the majestic French Empire desk that dominated the room. It commanded attention for both its size and beauty. And at this moment, it drew the eye in its role as the centre stage of the tragedy. A pool of blood spread across the inlay, and the two ends of the desk—as well as the floor behind it. They were liberally covered in a gruesome confetti. Feathers and down stirred even in the small disturbances of current that Holmes created as he moved thoughtfully around the desk once more.

The torn silk casing from which the feathers had been ripped lay three feet behind the gilt chair, presumably dropped there by the murderer once its use as a muffler had expired. Gregson shifted his hips against the remaining trio of cushions.

Stainsbury cleared his throat again. "I have cleaners waiting. Perhaps . . . if you're finished, Holmes . . ."

Holmes held up his hand imperiously, staring at the desk top.

"Whom was Mycroft meeting?" he demanded.

Stainsbury did not seem to object to the tone. "Given the subject under discussion between us at the meeting this morning . . . yesterday morning, rather, I would have thought that was obvious."

Holmes nodded, satisfied.

Gregson shifted, tired bones protesting, and leaned forward. "Obvious to you two, perhaps. You'll have to spell it out for me."

Stainsbury, for the first time since he had entered the room, showed a sign of genuine discomfort. "I'm afraid it falls under the domain of the King's official secrets, my good fellow."

"Nonsense!" Holmes barked. "You involved Gregson in this when you sent him to collect one irritable old agent tonight. You can't extend the privilege only when it suits you. Poor Gregson might have had his nose shot off and never known he was mixed up in the affairs of the empire. You owe him an explanation at the very least."

Gregson blinked at the unexpected support. "Really, that's not necessary at all. I do understand why some operations must remain covert. And I hardly need to know all the facts when Holmes is on the case."

Holmes strode to the armchair that sat angled beside the sofa, and pulled it further into the room. He sat, and spread his hands on his knees. It brought him close to Gregson's side.

"You would do me a service if you took the time to hear all those facts, Gregson, in much the same way as Watson would listen, and allow me to order my thoughts as I went. Do you mind?"

Gregson thought of the valiant doctor, who he happened to know was occupied on the Western front, right now facing the Huns.

"Why, certainly, Holmes," he replied warmly.

Holmes nodded. He looked up at Stainsbury. "You might assist me, my lord?"

"An airing of the facts?" Stainsbury pulled up the chair that sat in front of the desk, and sat, crossing his legs. "Shall I start?"

Holmes steepled his fingers together, close to his face, and his eyes narrowed. "Please," he murmured.

"Mycroft asked Sherlock to call yesterday morning, as early as the trains would allow, as he had some business to discuss. Sherlock arrived a little past eight o'clock, and I was at that meeting . . ."

THE TWO BROTHERS shook hands cordially, and Stainsbury was introduced to the younger.

"I was never a reader of *The Strand*, where all your adventures were reported by Doctor Watson," Stainsbury confessed airily, "but your achievements are great enough to have reached ears as insulated as mine. It is an honour to meet you, Mr. Holmes."

Sherlock smiled a little. "Insulated? I think you disparage your own position, Lord Stainsbury. You stand here in this office, introduced to me by Mycroft, who carefully avoided giving you a title beyond your peerage. As Mycroft would rather rot in this edifice than voluntarily move, and as he does not hold ultimate power in Whitehall, he must have a liaison there. And here you stand. You make a most unsuitable underling, my lord. Therefore, it would be safe to assume you are Mycroft's superior. Such influence precludes isolation of any sort."

Stainsbury glanced at Mycroft, who shrugged.

"You are as perceptive as promised, I see," Stainsbury said. "But, please, listen to Mycroft. I am here merely to observe."

Holmes frowned. "Another understatement, my lord. I believe you are here to add weight to my brother's . . . what is it to be, Mycroft? A request? A proposal?"

"Both, actually."

"To neither of which you expect me to agree easily. Hence, Lord Stainsbury. A personage designed to impress me with the gravity of the situation."

Mycroft *hhhrmmp*ed. "And now that you have shown off sufficiently, perhaps you could seat yourself and we could begin?"

"By all means," Sherlock agreed.

Mycroft offered tea, and the humidor, both of which were refused. The chair, however, was accepted. Sherlock perched restlessly while Mycroft worked at the end of his cigar. Stainsbury settled quietly on the sofa, well away from the brothers.

Once Mycroft had his cigar going to his satisfaction, he sat back.

"You must know, Sherlock, that my job is a matter of dealing in redundancies."

"In information, or in people? You deal in both."

"I'd rather the redundancies occur with data only, but . . ." Mycroft shrugged. "I have had a stable of agents in and around the Ottoman Empire since before the first bullets were fired across the Dardanelles. Their information has flowed across this desk. Mountains of it. Most of it repetitious. Each agent hears the same rumours, each agent picks up the same facts, each agent—from his different position and location—will see events and people and report them to me."

"Hence, redundancies," Sherlock said.

"Ah, yes, but very specific redundancies. Take that repetition away, and it is from within the *differences* that tales are told."

"And how do you know those differences can be relied upon?"

"Because of their associated repetitions. The very redundancies that give this desk its bowed back are the provenances that let me sleep at night."

"So, you relax when the information you get from your agents is very nearly the same."

"Precisely."

"And . . . ?"

"For the last few months it has been too much the same."

Sherlock rubbed his temple. "I don't see a benchmark on that desk that says 'this close, but no closer.' You cannot quantify 'very nearly' and 'too much.' Do you have anything more than an uneasy feeling?"

Stainsbury spoke from behind them. "Actually, I was the one with the uneasy feeling. Mycroft felt much as you do—that one cannot act on a change in conditions when the entire playing field is constantly shifting to begin with."

"*Felt.* Past tense." Sherlock turned back to Mycroft. "What has happened to change your mind?"

"I will deal with that matter in a moment. There is another small issue, too, one of odd rumours. None of my usual sources can track the origins of the rumours down. Neither can they find any direct proof . . . but despite superior intelligence, the Turkish army is having severe problems dealing with guerrillas north of Iskenderun." Mycroft shrugged. "We have no *agents provocateurs* out there."

Sherlock shrugged. "Send in an infiltrator."

"I did. One of my best. No word." He didn't expand on the failure. Sherlock did not press the matter.

"What about your agents in Berlin? Or someone in the German Imperial Army?"

Mycroft raised one eyebrow and Sherlock smiled. "Come, Mycroft, I'm not a complete fool. If you have agents in the German and Ottoman Empires, you must have them in their standing armies out there."

"Granted. I have no need to explain the limitations an agent must work with to you. And mine are all working under considerable restriction of freedom, quite apart from the German High Command's paranoid security precautions at this point in time."

"Paranoid? Don't tell me . . . they are afraid they have a spy amongst their number?"

Mycroft merely smiled. He tapped his cigar on the ashtray at his elbow, concentrating on the task, then glanced at Holmes. "You know your way about out there," he added casually.

Sherlock rose to his feet, his face thoughtful. He turned to look out the window. "I'd planned to return to Sussex," he said quietly.

"You spent years in the Middle and Far East, Sherlock. You know the people and the language, and some of your contacts probably still exist . . ."

"Hardly. That was a long time ago. And much has changed since then. Not least of all is that since the disastrous Gallipoli campaign, the Germans have been swarming all over the Turkish Empire. I know the Turks are their allies, but the German army has never felt completely happy unless it held direct control of everything under its power."

"So you have been watching that part of the world. I suspected as much. That only goes to prove my point—I don't have another person on hand with your experience and proven ability to . . . cope. And I refuse to send just any green recruit. I will not allow my people to be unjustifiably put in danger simply because of careless selection."

Sherlock raised his brow. "You have been accused of that?"

Mycroft shook his head irritably. "I lost a man yesterday. A boy. He was barely eighteen, but so terribly eager to deal his blow to the Hun . . ." He stabbed out his cigar. "Besides, if you go, it saves me the bother of officially informing Whitehall."

Sherlock sat back in his chair, his eyes narrowed. "I

don't believe the German High Command are alone in their paranoia."

"Perhaps we are all justified."

"Perhaps?"

Mycroft shrugged. "I'm pandering to my uneasy feeling."

"Your redundancies?" Sherlock placed his fingertips together. "What makes you think one old man could do any more than a young boy?"

"I'm not asking you to penetrate the German High Command again, little brother. Hardly that . . . you would be summarily executed if you were caught and recognized. Your *von Karnch* persona has died an honourable and timely death, and he should not be resurrected. The Germans hold a justifiable grudge against you. No. I just want someone out there who can blend into the countryside without depending on allied armies for support or information. I want someone to sniff around and find out exactly what is going on there."

"Then recruit a Bedouin. That Lawrence chap—one of his should be able to blend in nicely."

"They've only just taken Gaza. I need you farther north. Damascus. Then west—into Constantinople."

"No." Sherlock stood abruptly and picked up his hat. "Thank you all the same. But I have better things to do."

"Skulking around at home?"

"Why not?" Sherlock nodded to Stainsbury. "Good day, my lord." He strode to the door.

"A moment, Sherlock," Stainsbury called.

He halted with his hand on the door.

"This isn't exactly a frivolous assignment. And it's not entirely a request from one brother to another. I, as His Majesty's representative, am making this demand through Mycroft. And I deserve more than a curt refusal. An explanation is in order."

Sherlock turned. "Not a frivolous assignment? My lord, I think you greatly underestimate my abilities. What you have proposed here is nothing more than . . . a messenger-boy's task. Sniff out the lay of the land? Investigate rumours?" He drew himself erect, which put him barely an inch higher than Stainsbury. "I am Sherlock Holmes. I have grappled with men who make your finest Prussian opponents look like third-rate thugs. I have an intellect that has been challenged by the shrewdest and keenest minds of this and the last century combined. In 1915 I spent four months posing as an Austrian, working in the German High Command, in Berlin. Last year I spent six months in St. Petersburg, and the remainder of the year on the Russian front, analyzing their command. I predicted the actions of the Bolsheviks." He spread his hands. "I am a willing tool for His Majesty, but a sharp one. And I refuse to be sent on . . . an errand!"

Mycroft gave a series of light claps with his hands. "Bravo!" he intoned. "And may I point out, little brother, that we sent you to British East Africa last Christmas to observe German activities, and hand over certain papers to English irregular cavalry there? That was the sum total of your brief. Does that not fall under the definition of 'errand boy'?"

"I uncovered a pocket of pro-German sympathizers who were planning to blow up the harbour at Mombasa."

"Irrelevant. You were asked to deliver messages, and that was all. A task even more puny than this one."

"I've done enough for King and country!" Sherlock cried, opening the door.

"Then you will not go to Constantinople?" Stainsbury asked.

"I would sooner inhale mustard gas!"

The door slamming was Sherlock Holmes' final punctuation.

Stainsbury turned back to Mycroft. "I believe you just won your ten guineas. How did you know he would refuse? And so vehemently, at that?"

Mycroft smiled grimly. “Family history,” he said succinctly.

“Will nothing move him?”

“Stubbornness is one of the few inherent gifts my brother has in greater abundance than I.”

“I see. Damn!” Stainsbury clenched his fists. “We need him out there, Mycroft. Think of a way!”

Chapter Two

"THAT WAS THE LAST TIME I SAW YOUR BROTHER," STAINSBURY added. "I left shortly afterwards to tend to other matters, expecting Mycroft to deal with . . ."

"Coaxing me?" Holmes suggested.

Stainsbury nodded.

Gregson rubbed weariness from his eyes. "Then who was it Mycroft was meeting, if it wasn't you, my lord?"

Holmes answered. "An agent or courier from the Ottoman Empire."

"A courier," Stainsbury confirmed.

"Then that's the blighter you're after?" Gregson asked.

"Unfortunately, that particular blighter is dead," Stainsbury responded with a sigh. "It was the first lead I pursued, even before I brought you in on it, Chief Inspector. I had some of my chaps hunt him up. He arrived on a steamer last night. My fellows found him in a dockside hostel around three o'clock this morning. He'd been strangled."

"There is someone else in on this play whom we don't know and can't predict as yet," Holmes murmured.

"Actually, I think I *can* give you a prediction," Stainsbury said.

"Yes?"

"The information that has been worrying us—Mycroft's redundancies. If you were to compare the various sets, you would find that all of them bear a remarkable resemblance to each other. Except for one."

Holmes leaned forward. "Go on."

"Mycroft has a loose cannon. A rogue agent he has doubts about. The information he has been receiving from this agent is almost completely different from that of the others. That is alarming enough in itself, but now with his other agents all disappearing—"

"The lad yesterday, the one of whom Mycroft spoke—he was not the first?"

"No. He is the third, this year."

"Very alarming, indeed!" Holmes stood, rolling down his sleeves. "You think this rogue agent of Mycroft's is behind the disappearances?"

"Almost certainly. He was never part of the recruiting chain like the others. He did not report to Mycroft's coordinator out there. And his information is different. Therefore it is unsubstantiated, and must be treated as suspect."

"Mycroft shared these suspicions with you?"

"Yes. Which is why we approached you. If this rogue agent is indeed working his way back through our agent network, then we can't use that network. We have to send in an independent. You, Holmes."

Holmes lifted his attention from his cuffs. "You don't know what you are asking of me."

"No, I don't. But Mycroft did, and he asked you regardless of that knowledge. And now he's been shot, and left for dead. We don't know why he was assaulted in this cowardly way, and that leaves you no choice."

Holmes continued to button his cuffs silently.

"Why does it leave him with no choice?" Gregson asked, puzzled.

Holmes grimaced. "Until we know who shot Mycroft, and why, we have to operate on the assumption that only Mycroft's death will satisfy the assailant. They may return to finish the deed." He glanced at Stainsbury. "I have to find out who, and why, before they do return."

"If it's of any consolation, Holmes," Stainsbury continued, "it looks as though our own agent network is being turned against us. There are some formidable minds at work in Constantinople, and they aren't Turk. You'll be scrapping with some of the best of your third-rate Prussian thugs."

ALEXANDER VON STEIN, officer of the German Army and scion of a venerable Prussian family, was in exquisite pain. He ignored it.

Ten years before, he had crushed his ankle in a mountain climbing accident, and the bones had healed awkwardly. Whenever he spent too long on his feet or asked too much of the fused joint, it would begin to protest. If he refused to accept the warning, the ankle would gradually grow more painful, to the point where each step he took would generate a wave of agony that could sink him to his knees, and even when he was at rest, the pain would radiate throughout his body.

He had been on his feet for precisely twenty hours this day already, and the evening's gala ball held in honour of the German officers stationed in Constantinople had only just begun. Von Stein's work day was not yet over, even here.

So despite the residual ache and the rhythmic bite of each step, he gave away nothing but sharp attention to his junior officers.

They grouped around him in the corner created by the sweeping curve of the stone stairs that dominated this end of the ballroom. The officers behaved as if they were chatting idly, yet the topics were anything but frivolous.

They were good men, Von Stein reflected. Despite the grim realities facing them, the setbacks and disappointments they had borne, they still stood proud and courageous in the face of their numerous enemies. Even though their final reports for the day were less than positive, they managed to project an attitude that declared their frustrations were mild and temporary, soon to be washed away in the glow of victory.

As each officer completed his report, he moved away, free to turn to purely social matters.

Finally Von Stein was left with his second in command, Heinz Aldrich, a capable lieutenant with a sharp mind and no imagination.

"It could be better, hey, Heinz?" Von Stein prompted with a smile. "The British north of Gaza. Still, they are not at Damascus yet."

Heinz frowned. "But it is appalling!" he protested. "Another cavalry unit lost . . . gone into thin air! On a routine patrol! It's making the men uneasy. Troops are becoming reluctant to march east for fear the same fate will befall them."

"Fate! A man, Heinz. A man. That is no fate to fear."

"The Divine Wind, sir?" Heinz's glasses reflected the yellow light from the old-fashioned electric sconces on the walls as he lifted his chin, his attention caught. "There is still nothing to indicate that he is the cause for all these strange disappearances, or the raiding."

"Who else would it be?"

"But you are always quick to dismiss the notion when your men suggested it."

"Naturally. They're already edgy—you're quite correct there, Heinz. And I've heard what they say about this

Divine Wind. If I have heard it, so have they, and probably more often than I. If I were to confirm their suspicions that the mad Arab is the culprit they'll become more skittish than a colt at the sight of the bit."

"But without evidence, we have nothing to confirm."

Von Stein stared at Heinz, feeling the throb of dull anger in his temples. "No evidence?" he asked quietly. "You call the disappearance of an entire cavalry brigade nothing?"

Heinz's eyes behind the lenses widened. "I meant no disrespect to the memory of—" he began.

"Yes, yes, you are contrite and suitably aghast at your lack of tact. Continue, Heinz."

The small man took a moment to re-gather his concentration.

"They say the Divine Wind is not a man at all. A will-o'-the-wisp. Hell's fury given righteous life, to bring justice on us all. And maybe they're right. Despite three years of careful investigation, we've yet to even prove there is a man at the root of all these fairy stories."

Von Stein felt his anger stir once again. "Justice delivered only upon Germans and Turks? Upon William, who was so innocent he had not yet fired his shiny new rifle? Since when does he take sides? No, my good Heinz, you can relax your grip on your psalter. This Divine Wind is a man just like the rest of us. If he's a man, he can be caught. He *will* be caught!"

Heinz squared his shoulders. "Of course he will!" he declared stoutly.

"His execution is already a certainty! You can draw names for the firing squad upon the morrow."

"But of course! He has Von Stein on his trail!" Heinz smiled a little.

Von Stein clapped his arm. "We'll have him shaking in his carpet slippers yet, Heinz. I have been thinking about your will-o'-the-wisp and his mysterious ways, and I believe I have discovered his weakness."

"The men seem to think he has no weakness."

Von Stein pushed away their concerns with a back flick of his fingers. "They see only what is in front of them. They don't lift their noses to look beyond that. But I have, and what worries me more than this Divine Wind's functional attack and fadeaway tactics is how uncannily effective he is at being in the right place at the right time."

Heinz's eyes behind the lenses grew smaller and unfocussed. "His information must be good."

"Exceptional, I'd say. Anatolia is not a small place, Heinz. What is it they say of him? He is here, he is there, always just where he will prick the deepest. A cavalry troop, a patrol, a garrison blown up just after the arrival of six months' supply of arms and munitions . . ."

Heinz cocked his head to one side. "You suspect he is getting his information from here? From Constantinople itself?"

"I *know* he is getting his information from here. I just can't prove it yet. But I will, Heinz. I will. And then we'll see how righteous this mighty Arab really is!"

Heinz chuckled. "I look forward to the day, sir."

Von Stein caught site of a refined, striking brunette woman across the room, on the arm of one of his officers. Her beaded dress shimmered—it was by far the most attractive gown in the room, to Von Stein's mind. "I see Madame Häfner has arrived, Heinz. I'll bid you goodnight." He pulled at his gloves, straightening them. "I was promised at least three waltzes."

Heinz gave a little flip of his hand, an informal salute, and strode away.

Von Stein crossed the room, feeling the grind of dull, thick pain climb his leg. But he did not allow himself to limp. He had at least three waltzes to complete. Limping was not permissible.

THE HOSTEL WAS a poor place, rank with the stench of unwashed bodies and inadequate plumbing.

In a small room at the end of the first-floor corridor, Gregson and Lord Stainsbury stood waiting. Inside, Sherlock Holmes quartered the room with swift efficiency. When he was finished, he joined the men in the corridor.

"They did not touch anything," Gregson told him. "You have the room in the condition Lord Stainsbury's men found it. I assume that as usual you discovered what none of my men saw?"

"You flatter me, Gregson. Even I cannot pluck information from a vacuum. I must have material to work with. The Ottoman courier did not occupy the room long enough to stamp any impression of himself upon it. A moment or two only before he met his unfortunate end. Your men established that fact for themselves."

"Yet you insisted on inspecting the room?"

"Naturally. One does not fail to investigate every source of information available, even if it is only to confirm that the source provides no data at all."

"Then you're satisfied the answers you seek can only be found in the Near East?"

"Is a donkey ever satisfied when the whip cracks behind him?" Holmes' lips curved down at the corners.

Stainsbury pulled out an antique pocket watch and consulted it. "You insist on exhausting all the possibilities at the risk of missing the Plymouth train. It leaves Victoria Station in twenty-three minutes."

"Then we have time to spare," Holmes responded. "In that well-appointed motor car of yours, we can reach the station from here in fourteen minutes. Rest easy, my lord—you will see me securely on my way to the ship to Alexandria."

He nodded at Gregson, and strode down the corridor, leaving the two to follow in his wake.

The trip to Victoria Station took the advertised fourteen

minutes, and as the driver pulled the vehicle up to the front of the station, Holmes gripped the handle of his single piece of luggage and prepared to exit.

Stainsbury, sitting on the rear-facing seat behind the driver, held out his hand. "God speed and good luck, Holmes."

Holmes shook the offered hand briefly. "Speed is guaranteed, and luck is not necessary. I'll send word when I reach Damascus."

Stainsbury pulled an envelope from his inside breast pocket. "Take this. These are the best of my irregular contacts within the British Expeditionary Force. None of them have anything to do with my department and can be considered untainted."

"In that part of the world, my lord, no-one can be considered above suspicion. To do ought else can be quite fatal."

Sherlock Holmes nodded to the two men, then stepped out of the motor car into the swirling throng of pedestrians, was swallowed up by it, and was gone.

The driver emerged from behind his controls, and shut the door once more, while Gregson and Stainsbury sat silently.

"I'll get you back to Scotland Yard," Stainsbury said at last. He leaned closer to the small window that gave access to the driver and conveyed the new destination to him. The vehicle slid back into the traffic.

Stainsbury settled back onto the seat, and looked at Gregson.

"You have known Holmes for many years," he said.

"Many, indeed."

"You were not surprised when I told you of Holmes' refusal to go to Constantinople."

"No, I was not surprised."

"I wish to understand Holmes' refusal."

"It is not my story to tell, my lord."

"I am concerned that whatever prompted his reluctance will grow more persuasive the closer he gets to Constantinople."

Gregson gave a gusty, silent wheeze of laughter. "My lord, you have secured Holmes' agreement to solve a mystery. There is nothing that will distract him from that task now."

"Ah, yes, his renowned relentlessness."

"It is true that when his passions are engaged, very little will pull him from his selected path. But that is not what I speak of."

"No? Then I remain concerned, Chief Inspector."

"Was it not Archimedes who said, 'give me a long enough lever, a fulcrum and a place to stand, and I can move the world'?"

"I believe so."

"You found the long lever, my lord—the one lever that would overcome Holmes' aversion to returning to Constantinople: his brother's well-being."

"It was not intentional."

Gregson lifted his hand. "I know."

"If the life of his brother is the only pressure that would overcome Holmes' abhorrence, then I am even more greatly concerned. Such repugnance can be prompted only by the most terrible power."

Gregson nodded. "A most terrible power indeed, my lord. One of the most powerful forces in the world today—a force that underlies many of the crimes my men investigate."

"You have my complete attention, Gregson."

"*Amour*, my lord."

Stainsbury drew a deep breath, his nostrils flaring. His face turned dark red. "Really, Chief Inspector—"

"I do not ask you to subscribe to the theory, my lord. You wished to know why Holmes avoids Constantinople. I have given you your answer."

"I know Holmes travelled out there in the nineties . . . are you telling me he had some sort of *affaire de coeur* in Constantinople? *That* is the terrible power that only the near-death of his brother is sufficient to overcome?"

"You see only part of the story. I see I must give you the whole picture now." Gregson looked out the window and noticed the Embankment sliding by. "Perhaps your driver would care to pull to one side of the road for a moment or two?"

Without turning his gaze away from Gregson, Stainsbury rapped on the dividing glass. "Pull aside," he said quietly.

The car instantly eased over to the side of the road, bumping up against the curb.

Stainsbury spread his hand. "I am listening."

"I don't confess to know the entire story, but I will tell you what I do know. It might be enough. In 1891, a young woman called Elizabeth Sigerson became entangled in Holmes' struggles to bring the late Professor Moriarty to justice. Holmes was forced to flee to France to avoid Moriarty's retribution, and he took Doctor Watson and Elizabeth—Miss Sigerson—with him. In Switzerland, Moriarty caught up with them. At Reichenbach Falls, he contrived to have Watson coaxed away from Holmes' side. With Watson out of the way he confronted Holmes."

"I remember this report from the papers. But there was no woman involved."

"Elizabeth's presence was carefully edited by Watson, who returned from Switzerland alone. Watson believed Holmes dead, but in fact, Holmes was running for his life—trying to avoid Moriarty's deadly lieutenant, Moran. And Holmes had Elizabeth with him. They travelled together, crossing the Alps on foot. They dodged their pursuers all the way to Constantinople, and it was there they met a Persian called Sullah. Sullah took them to his home in the north-east corner of Persia. Later, Holmes and Elizabeth travelled to Tibet, and they stayed there for nearly two years. Three years after leaving London, Holmes and Elizabeth returned home."

Stainsbury's eyes were growing larger and larger as Gregson related the tale in a matter-of-fact monotone.

"Gregson, this is incredible! No woman would submit to being dragged hither and yon across half the globe . . . and to Tibet? For two years?"

"Not every woman, certainly. A small handful, perhaps. Elizabeth was one of that small handful. Elizabeth was . . . different."

"You met her?"

"Certainly. After their return to London, Elizabeth remained with Holmes at Baker Street."

"You mean they . . . ?" Stainsbury spread his hand delicately.

"Yes," Gregson confirmed in a flat voice. "They stayed in the rooms at Baker Street for another nine years. Until 1903, when Moran escaped from Dartmoor Prison and abducted Elizabeth."

Stainsbury leaned forward eagerly. "And Holmes rescued her," he guessed.

"No."

"I beg your pardon?"

"Oh, he tried. And in the process, he caught Moran just as he was about to leave London on a freighter that was smuggling arms back to India for political rebels. The ship was blown apart when the ammunition in the cargo holds was ignited and exploded. Moran was killed—either by the explosion, or by drowning, or . . ."

"Or what?"

Gregson frowned. "There was no evidence, but I've always fancied Holmes had something to do with Moran's death."

"You mean he killed him?"

"Why not? Moran had taken away the one thing in Holmes' life that gave it meaning, stability, and purpose."

"But this is . . . preposterous! You want me to accept that a public figure of Holmes' stature kept an integral part of his life completely and utterly secret from the public for nearly a decade?"

"I do not ask you to accept or believe. I am telling you the facts as I know them. I was one of a privileged few who knew Miss Elizabeth. I willingly assisted Holmes' and Watson's effort to keep her from the public gaze."

"But why?"

"To keep her from harm that might befall her if her importance to Holmes was known."

Stainsbury sat back again. "You failed, then, didn't you? For did not this Moran fellow abduct her to manipulate Holmes?"

"You are absolutely correct, my lord. We all failed. Holmes felt his failure more keenly than any of us. Shortly after Moran's death, when it was clear that Miss Elizabeth would never be found, or her fate known, Holmes retired to his cottage on the Sussex Downs—the same cottage from where I retrieved him yesterday evening. Miss Elizabeth has never been seen since."

Stainsbury absorbed the story in silence for a moment.

"It is an astonishing story, Gregson, but it does not explain Holmes' particular abhorrence for Constantinople."

"That, my lord, is where I must begin to speculate."

"Given your knowledge of these events, your speculations would be more reliable than mine. Clearly, something happened in Constantinople that marked the city unpleasantly in Holmes' mind and sentiments."

"I don't believe it is an unpleasant experience. Quite the opposite," Gregson replied quietly. "Are you married, my lord?"

"Why, yes, but I fail to see what that has to do with . . .

ah! . . . I understand. Then you are proposing that he has a sentimental remembrance of the city?"

"No, my lord. I believe any sentiment he held for the city has long since shrivelled beneath the burden of another, far stronger emotion."

"And that is?"

"Grief, Lord Stainsbury."

The noble lord sat for another long moment, his lips pursed, as he considered.

"And I forced him to return," he said at last, quietly.

"That you did, my lord."

Chapter Three

THE NEW CITY OF JERUSALEM SHARED THE HORIZON WITH bare, jagged hills, its modern attitude declared by the pockets of decadent water-hungry trees and exotic gardens. Yet it was not the destination of the many, many travellers on the east road.

They were bound for the Old City, with its narrow, dark streets and cramped buildings.

A tall European was among them, approaching Herod's Gate along the hard sun-baked strip of road just as millions of pilgrims and visitors had before him: on foot. There had been many Europeans to walk this road of late. Yet the alert observer might have noticed the small signs and odd reactions that made this man unique among their number.

He did not wear a uniform as so many of his fellow men did. Rather, he wore a good dark suit, the tie still neatly tied, and the collar and pins still firmly in place, the waistcoat still buttoned despite the lingering heat of the day. He carried an old, well-cared-for Gladstone bag in one hand but was otherwise unburdened. His hat shaded his eyes, but it was more suitable for the untaxing sun of London than for the Holy Land.

Despite his unsuitable garb, he appeared quite comfortable and at ease with his situation.

More curiously, as he bypassed slower pedestrians, they sometimes uttered a comment, often about his appearance, or his speed—which was uncommon and considered unhealthy in such a dry heat. He would answer them easily, often in their own language, employing French, English, Arabic, and even Persian. A few words, a nod, and he would move on, heading for the city.

He travelled over rocky and desolate land, pocked with little patches of stunted grasses and weeds that gasped for life during this cooler season. The earth glowed red in the dying sun's light.

The first of the houses at the edge of the old city were poor, mud-daubed shelters that blended with the landscape, deceiving the eye into believing they had sprung from the earth itself. The city walls rose from those roots, venerable and enduring, and beyond them lay the mosques, synagogues, churches and buildings of Jerusalem itself.

The man passed under the gate and into the cool streets of the city. He had arrived in the Muslim section, although this was not his final destination. He stopped a few times to speak to merchants, asking for directions, invariably employing Arabic. He concluded each transaction with a gracious bow, and a quiet "May Allah be with you."

Eventually he made his way across the city to the northwestern section—the Christian quarter. Here, the streets were filled with armed men in khaki, busily going about their business.

The man stepped aside for those who were in a greater hurry than he, and he asked no-one for directions. Eventually he came to a building that seemed larger than most, and far busier than any he'd seen so far. Only men in uniform were allowed in or out of the building, and the entrance was guarded by two useful-looking privates in British army uniform.

The man walked up to them and put down his bag. "I'm looking for Major Reginald Porter."

"SIR, THERE'S A chap here to see you."

Porter looked up from his paperwork, trying to contain his frustration, for this was the eighteenth such interruption since lunch.

He scowled at Jenkins. "How am I to finish this if every Tom, Dick and Harry comes calling?"

"Sir?"

"Never mind, Private. I was bewailing the lot of a major—he's just high enough to bear the responsibility and too low on ladder to hand it any further down. How I'm supposed to find an icebox for the officers' barracks by tonight, when I can't fill in a simple form for all the interruptions . . ." He threw his pen down.

Jenkins stood firmly at attention, not even a quiver giving away his reaction. Good. Porter appreciated the discipline he had finally managed to instill in the man after months of conditioning.

"Rank and name would be useful, Private."

"That's just it, sir. He don't have one. Rank, that is."

A civilian. Porter sighed. "Name, Private?"

"Sigerson, he says, sir."

Porter frowned. Where had he heard the name before? It sat at the edges of his memory, tickling and irritating.

"He wants to see me?"

"Asked for you by name, sir."

"You'd better show him in then."

The man who stepped through the door into his office sent Porter's thoughts tumbling back home, to the busy thoroughfares of Clapham and the bustle of a civilized city. It might be snowing there, by now. Christmas was just around the corner. This man looked like a banker or clerk, just stepped off the city streets.

"Good lord!" Porter breathed. He looked at the face. Late fifties, perhaps. Maybe older, but blessed with vigour and good health. "You look as if you've just stepped off the boat!"

"As of three days ago, yes. I landed at Gaza, and caught a troop transport to the army camp outside the city." His eyes, Porter realized, belonged to a much younger man. And they were busy sizing him up, which made him feel like a schoolboy, caught red-handed and with no excuses to hide behind.

Sigerson, Sigerson . . .

"Damn it! That's where I've seen the name!" Porter cried. He dived into the deep drawer that lay open next to him, pushing through the pile of papers there. Somewhere near the bottom, he suspected.

"Yes, here it is." He pulled the sheet out and smoothed it on the desk top, glancing at the contents. "Now I remember! I knew your name was familiar to me."

Sigerson nodded. "You may have heard of me some years ago."

Porter tapped the sheet. "Last month, actually. I got a wire from some Whitehall lackey laying orders about the place, as if I haven't enough to do. Telling me to expect you and extend every courtesy . . ."

The intense eyes focussed on Porter, narrowing. "You're busy, naturally. One can appreciate your immense responsibilities."

Porter studied him, wondering if he'd imagined the tiny inflection in Sigerson's voice.

The possibility that he hadn't stirred the embers of his frustration back into flaming life. "Of course I'm damn well busy. We took Jerusalem on the tenth, a massive victory for the BEF. Now we must administer the city, keep essential services running—we can't have the hospitals and power stations grinding to a halt. It wouldn't do. Only the army that suffers defeat isn't busy. Victory makes for an overwhelming load."

"I'm sure the residents of Jerusalem don't see it that way," Sigerson said quietly.

"I beg your pardon?" Porter could feel his eyes widening.

"Victory or defeat . . . it's immaterial to them who wins. They've merely swapped one master for another."

Porter took a breath. Then another. "Are you being deliberately rude, sir?"

Sigerson smiled a little. "I have no need to descend to rudeness." He seemed about to say more, then paused. "I *was*, however, attempting to point out that it's a matter of perspective. If you were to look at it differently you might find it a little less overwhelming."

Porter blinked. "I have no bloody idea what you're talking about."

Sigerson's brow lifted a little. "I see." He put the bag down, straightened up, and held out his hand. "I was requested to report in before I go north. My name—my real name—is Sherlock Holmes."

Porter paused in the act of reaching for his hand.

"Sherlock Holmes?"

"Yes."

"*The* Sherlock Holmes?"

"Yes, which is why I'm traveling as Sigerson, among other reasons." He let his hand drop.

Porter rubbed his temple. "*That's* where the wire came from. You're mixed up in all that hush-hush stuff."

"That's accurate enough," Holmes agreed.

"And what is it you expect me to do?"

"I would appreciate your getting word back to the same person who sent that wire. Report my arrival here."

"That's a small enough matter. Consider it done. Anything else?"

"I wouldn't dream of imposing on you," Holmes

returned. "I've been travelling for a month, and need to learn the lay of the land out here before I head into Anatolia. The BEF took Junction Station while I was aboard, I've learned. And Jerusalem, of course," he added with small smile. "The precise location of the front at the moment—"

"You're going *into* Anatolia?"

"I believe that is what I said."

"For god's sake, why?"

"That's hardly your concern."

"I only mean . . . why try to penetrate the front? It's moving back every day—victory is assured. If you wait, the very thing you are trying to reach will be uncovered and it will be yours for the asking."

"I don't have time to wait."

Porter shook his head. "They send a man like you to penetrate behind the front. It's laughable."

"I fail to see the humour."

"Look at you. Do you have any idea what the country is like up there? How to get about? The place is crawling with Turks. Very angry Turks who will become even more angry as we push them farther north. They're arresting anyone who looks even vaguely threatening. And you don't blend into the landscape, Mr. Holmes. They'll take one look at you and shoot you on sight. I can't see you surviving more than five minutes!"

"If I were looking from your perspective, I'd agree with you," Holmes said. He picked up his bag. "Thank you for your time, Major Porter."

"That's it? You're leaving?"

"I have no reason to stay and add to your burdens."

"It'd be irresponsible of me to let you wander out into the desert unaided."

"I'll just have to be resourceful, then, won't I?"

Porter watched the man leave, shutting the door quietly behind him.

What on earth did they think they were doing, sending out an old English gent like that one into the boiling cauldron of the Middle East?

"Ridiculous!" he muttered, returning to his form.

THE CROWDS ON the streets were beginning to thin with the coming of the evening. The smell of cooking meals, hot, rich and savoury, wound through the narrow aisles.

Holmes strolled the streets, heading back towards the Muslim sector. The number of uniformed men began to diminish, although even when he was in the heart of the Muslim domain, there were still soldiers to be seen, for they were exploring their newly conquered city.

From his conversations earlier in the evening, Holmes knew the major points of interest in the area, and he made his way through narrow side streets to a wider road. Here, a small, informal market hugged the walls along one side of the street. There were a number of vendors selling and bartering food. All of the vendors were turbaned or wore *shumags*, the red-and-white checked head cloths the Arabs used in winter. There were very few women to be seen, but many children ran between the legs of pedestrians. There were quite a few soldiers, too, but they were busy looking for a bargain, not trouble.

Holmes slowed, moving from vendor to vendor, examining their offerings. He appeared to be concentrating on the bubbling pot of one bent old Arab, but when two children brushed past him, and a third collided with him from behind, he turned with lightning speed, and grasped the thin wrist of one of the pair moving away.

"A moment, boy."

The dark-eyed boy began to scream, and jabbered in Arabic. "Let me go. Help. He's hurting me! Help!"

"I'll have that wallet back," Holmes said, also in Arabic.

"He's trying to take it from me!" the boy said, lifting his voice.

"Hey, *Englisher*! Let him go!" The call came from within the gathering crowd.

"I will release the boy when he returns my wallet," Holmes replied. Despite the boy's rapid spinning and tugging, Holmes' grip on the bony wrist remained steadfast, and he remained quite still, unmoved by the boy's struggles.

"He says it's his!"

"A boy running in the street at this time of night, with no family who cares enough to see him home and fed—a boy like this does not have a wallet of his own."

"He does not speak like an *Englisher*!" came a dry hiss from behind.

"He looks like one! He smells like one!"

Holmes shook the boy's wrist, and the boy howled as if he was in pain.

"Give it up, lad," Holmes said quietly.

The boy turned and spat in his face.

Calmly, Holmes dropped his Gladstone and wiped the offending matter away. Then he reached beneath the boy's dirty grey outer robe, searching for pockets in the *dishdashah* beneath, provoking a protest from the boy.

There was a great outcry from the gathered Arabs, who moved in towards Holmes.

"What the blue blazes is going on here?" came a thunderous bellow, in English.

Holmes glanced up long enough to notice the bent side brims of several soldiers' hats pushing through the crowd towards him.

Then a sharp, unexpected blow to the back of his head took his consciousness away.

HOLMES OPENED HIS eyes to gloom and shadows leavened by light that seemed to suffuse the walls themselves.

He was lying on a narrow cot, and there was a scratchy blanket beneath him. He studied the walls, noticing sharp shadows moving across them. The light was flickering like one a lamp or open fire would make.

The shadow of a man walked across the wall.

And then he recognized his location. He was inside a tent, and somewhere outside a camp fire raged, casting shadows across the canvas that he could see inside.

By his head, a flap of the tent was pulled aside.

"So you're awake at last. You've had a long sleep there, mate."

Holmes pushed himself up a little, and quickly lay down again. "It was quite a blow, apparently," he observed, his voice emerging thickly.

The speaker stepped around so Holmes could see him. He was a thick, ruddy fellow, his light-coloured eyes twinkling with good cheer, and a luxuriant moustache twitching.

"Don't you worry about it. We're not about to throw you out on your ear. Not just yet. Sleep it out. Get some grub. And then we'll see what's what. Okay?"

The accent was thick, and the idiom unmistakable. Australian. Holmes recalled the peculiar angle on the side brims of the hats he'd seen during the last moments in Jerusalem.

"You and your men retrieved me from the market?"

"That's right. Just as bloody well, mate. They were about to make mincemeat of you. But my blokes soon sorted them out. We brought you back to camp, coz we couldn't figure out what else to do with you. Not with you out cold like that. So you rest up, right?"

"Yes. I will," Holmes agreed, his eyes closing entirely without prompting. The man's manner and speech were rough and barely educated, but there was a strong air of competency about him that was reassuring.

Holmes slept.

THE AUSTRALIAN CAVALRY captain was shaving with the assistance of a three-inch square mirror mounted on his tent's pole between a couple of horseshoe nails and a tin mug of warm water stolen from the kettle hanging over the cooking fire.

He shaved at his tent like this every morning, for the position afforded him a view that overlooked almost the entire camp. From here he could observe his men moving about the camp, preparing for the day ahead. He could count noses, assess how easily those newly recovered from wounds were moving, tally the mood of the camp, decide on positions, assignments, and weigh up the overall strength of his unit.

But this morning almost all his attention was taken up by the tall, solitary Englishman his sergeant had fished out of trouble in the city the previous evening.

Hughes came up from behind and dropped a freshly laundered towel over the tent ropes. "There ya go, Captain."

"Thank you. Sergeant?"

"Yes, sir?"

"What do you make of your stray? Have you spoken to him this morning?"

Hughes turned to look at the Englishman, who was crouched on the ground opposite one of the doe-eyed Arab children who seemed always to appear at the camp no matter where they went. The child squatted, too, and their conversation was intense enough to hold the child's complete attention.

"He's a rum customer, ain't he?" Hughes ventured, fingering his moustache.

"He really was speaking in Arabic when you saw him in the street?"

"He really was," Hughes confirmed. "It's hard not to mistake that stuff with anything else." He nodded towards the man and child crouched in the dirt, talking intently. "Probably what they're talking in now."

The Englishman unstrapped his wristwatch as they considered the pair and gave it to the boy.

"Hello," Hughes murmured.

The boy's face widened with a large smile, and he leapt to his feet and raced away, back through the camp, with the speed of a startled rabbit.

"Very rum," Hughes muttered.

"And no uniform . . ."

"Odd, heh?"

"Very rum, as you say, Hughes. I think I might have a word with him before we turn him loose again. Perhaps you could arrange it?"

"Right, sir."

HUGHES BROUGHT THE Englishman to him after breakfast.

"I'm Captain Cameron Rowe, Australian First Cavalry Division under Chauvel."

The man shifted a tight bundle of cloth from under his right arm to the other, and accepted his offered hand with a brief, strong shake. "Sigerson. My thanks to your men, Rowe. They plucked me from trouble last night." A small shadow crossed the bright, keen eyes, and a tiny furrow appeared between his brows.

Captain Rowe noted the odd reaction, and waved to the pair of canvas chairs and the small folding table set up in front of his tent. "Did Sergeant Hughes see you got a meal?"

"I've had a most excellent breakfast, thank you. You've been far more generous than I deserve," Sigerson said as he sat. He placed the bundle of cloth on the table, a little to one side.

"Hughes deserves that credit," Rowe said. "Not knowing the way things work out here can get you into serious trouble rather quickly, and Hughes has got into the habit of rescuing westerners who don't know their way about. I indulge him, as he's the best damned sergeant a man could ask for."

"Yes, I am rusty," Sigerson said, and his glance slid to the bundle.

"By the way, your bag and wallet are in my tent. Hughes managed to retrieve both of them, with the contents pretty much intact. If you've lost anything at all, you should consider it a small price to pay. You won't get it back now."

Sigerson smiled. "That they were retrieved at all is astonishing, and I am doubly grateful. Is there an appropriate way to thank your sergeant?"

"You could begin by satisfying my curiosity. British civilians aren't too thick on the ground around here. I'm guessing you've got your own agenda. Does it have any military connection?"

Sigerson considered Rowe for a moment, then nodded, as if he had made a decision. "It has a loose connection," he answered. "I've been assigned to travel north of the front and carry out a small investigation."

"Then you've not got far to go. The front is barely a day's ride from here."

Sigerson's brow rose. "Is that so? I was informed by another that the front was much farther north."

Rowe snorted at the ridiculousness of the idea. "We may have kicked the Turks out of Jerusalem, but they didn't fall back very far at all. Who told you it was farther north?"

"An officer I was reporting to, in Jerusalem. He was less than helpful in other respects. I did suspect this information, too."

"You sound as if you've had a rough time of it, Sigerson." Rowe leaned back in his chair. "Problem is, you're not in uniform. It draws attention to you. The wrong attention, last night."

"Yes, I am aware of that." And again, Sigerson's gaze fell on the bundle of cloth.

Rowe pointed to it. "Where did you get that?"

"From a boy."

"The one you gave your watch to?"

"Yes, that's the one."

"What is it?"

"Clothing." Sigerson touched it gently. "To help me blend in, as you suggest."

"You've been in this country before, haven't you?"

"I've never been to Jerusalem."

"But you speak Arabic, Hughes says."

"That is correct."

Rowe made the connection. "Further north. That's where you've been before. That's where you learned Arabic. That's why they're sending you in."

"You're very quick, Captain."

"It's an obvious inference." Rowe tapped the chair arm thoughtfully. "I've had a lot to do with the BEF since we landed here. I've learned to look past the appearance of any Englishman. I'm assuming, Sigerson, that there's more to you than first glance tells."

"I think that's a wise assumption," Sigerson said, and the corner of his mouth lifted.

"If you are to penetrate behind the front, then I should warn you that the military has Amman in their sights. You should avoid that area altogether. The Turks are strong there."

Sigerson frowned. "Is this information not restricted? I

can't see the BEF openly announcing its next target in this fashion."

"You're right. I just gave you a military secret. You're entitled to shoot me now." Rowe smiled a little. "Just as you have been less than discreet. You've all but declared you are an agent."

Sigerson gazed steadily at him, then relaxed back into his chair. "We understand each other."

"We do."

"Then would you be willing to assist me? I have some information to gather before I can go north, and my last source was less than helpful."

"What do you want to know?"

Sigerson proceeded to ask him half-a-dozen pointed questions designed to establish a precise overview of the battle ground and military dispositions. Rowe recognized the pattern from countless other debriefings, and shaped his answers accordingly.

"Thank you," Sigerson said finally. "I can see, now, what I must do." He steepled his fingers together thoughtfully. "There's something else. The boy I spoke to this morning spoke of an Arab leader behind the lines, who is fighting his own little war—a very successful one, if I can believe the boy. He called this Arab *the Divine Wind*. Have you heard of him?"

"In passing. I think he's a myth created to cheer up the Arabs. His exploits are certainly the stuff of myth. He is credited with feats that a mere mortal would be hard pressed to follow."

"Not according to the boy. He recited a list of the man's victories. There was no embroidery there I could detect. News passes amongst these people in the most mysterious fashion, but I've learned it can be relied upon."

"Then you must have heard different tales than those I have heard. Even the name is a joke: *the Divine Wind*, nurturer of justice."

"You have to sift for the seeds of truth," Sigerson replied.

Rowe cocked his head to one side. "You believe this Divine Wind exists?"

"Yes."

"Is that what you are here for? To find him?"

"No. But if there is a band of Arab guerrillas moving about Anatolia, I may find them a valuable ally if I need assistance. Friendly faces will be few indeed, there."

"I wish you luck, then. The tales about the Divine Wind talk about him being seen only by the chaos he leaves behind—like the wind. No-one has ever reported meeting him face to face. If you do want assistance out there, you'll have to find it first."

"I'm very good at uncovering secrets," Sigerson responded, with another small smile.

"I believe you," Rowe said quietly. Then, almost as if he were changing subjects, he continued: "I grew up on a farm in Western Australia. The house I lived in is very old, very big. It's one of the few houses in the area to have a cellar, although the cellar is mostly used for storage. I used to spend hours there as a boy, and one of the treasures I found was a box of old copies of a magazine that must have been mailed out from London one at a time. I read every single one of them. More than once."

Sigerson nodded. "And the name of the magazine?"

"*The Strand.*"

"I see."

"That is why I know I can trust you. And I know you will find the Divine Wind if that is your intention." Rowe sat up and straightened his jacket. "So . . . what are your plans, Sigerson?"

"I will take your advice, Captain. I will swing around Amman by a good margin and head north. I need a horse. Do you know where I can get one? I have funds."

"You can take one of mine."

"I would not deprive your men, nor weaken your troop's strength."

"The Turks are already eating into my strength. The animal I offer you belonged to a man who died in the offense upon Gaza. We have had to feed and care for the horse since then. In truth you would be assisting me if you were to take it."

"Then I accept with deep gratitude. My destination is Constantinople, and I will go there as quickly and directly as I can manage. A horse will aid my speed."

"You're not going to get too far, looking like you do. I'm not a great believer in all that theatrical nonsense, but it strikes me that, as you already speak Arabic, you'd be far better off dressed as a Bedouin—"

Sigerson rested his hand on the bundle of cloth, smiling.

"I see," Rowe said simply. "I'm surprised you haven't made this arrangement long before now."

"I should have," Sigerson agreed candidly. "But I have been fighting with old memories, and it makes me reluctant to take this step."

Rowe nodded. "You spent a long time out here, before, didn't you?"

"Years. But many years have passed since then."

"Not enough years for you to have forgotten everything."

Rowe heard the tiny sigh. "No."

Chapter Four

EVENING PRAYER WAS ZEKI'S FAVOURITE TIME OF THE DAY. A day could be fraught with difficulties and tension, but the simple act of entering the mosque for *rak'ah* would free his shoulders of their tightness. By the time he emerged from the mosque he would feel relaxed and at peace.

Tonight after prayer, he would go home to his simple room and prepare a special meal for himself. Just yesterday he had found an eel for sale in the Grand Bazaar, and the price had been a bargain, given the general trend of prices these days. He had some spices tucked away that he had been saving for a meal such as this. The pleasant dilemma that occupied him as he moved onto the streets of Stamboul, Constantinople's oldest and grandest sector, was what side dish he could prepare to accompany the spiced eel.

A man stepped up beside Zeki, matching him pace for pace.

"Good health to you, young Zeki," he murmured in Arabic, and all Zeki's daydreams about his evening meal disappeared.

"Who are you?" Zeki demanded in an undertone, but in his bones, he already knew.

"Good, good. You're a cautious one, at least. You can call me Sigerson."

Zeki stole a sideways glance at his uninvited companion. He was older than Zeki and a little taller. He looked just like any other prosperous Turk, with a good dark suit, clean, crisp collar, and carefully groomed hair. He wore no fez. And he seemed a little taller than most.

"You're not a Turk," Zeki ventured softly. "Sigerson is not a good Turk name."

"It is of little matter. I only pass as Turk at first glance, which is enough to get me beyond strolling Germans. One has only to look at my eyes to know I am not. Or listen to my less than adequate grasp of the Turkish tongue."

Zeki looked, and Sigerson turned his head obligingly. The brow over the clear, bright eyes lifted a little before he turned back to watch his step along the uneven cobblestones.

"So, you are not Turk. It does not tell me who you are, and why you walk beside me."

"You were expecting me."

"I was?"

"You received your orders ten days ago, now."

"Orders from whom? I am a simple secretary. I work for the assistant to the Grand Vizier. My orders come from him, and I recall none that used the name Sigerson."

Sigerson was silent for a pace or two. "Was any name mentioned?"

"To confirm that would be to show my hand, yes?"

"Mycroft."

"Another odd name."

"Your caution is excellent, Zeki. Listen to me." His voice dropped lower. "Your courier to Mycroft was murdered. Mycroft lies dying or dead as we speak. Your entire network here is being systematically compromised and is in danger of being ground whole under the heel of the Germans."

Zeki felt the sweat suddenly break out on his temples and armpits, hot, prickly and uncomfortable. His heart picked up pace.

"If I knew what you were talking about, I suppose I would ask you why you are the one telling me that."

"I'm here to help you."

"I am in need of help?" Zeki asked innocently.

Sigerson laid a hand on his shoulder and steered him around a square fountain trough to stand behind the curtain of falling water. It shielded them from casual passersby. Zeki faced Sigerson and watched an amazing thing happen.

The man seemed to grow taller. He flexed his shoulders as if he had been holding them in an unaccustomed position for too long, and his frame seemed to straighten and fill out. Even his face moved and grew sharper and better defined. The eyes widened, so that the very un-Turkish, startling colours were undisguised.

"You met my brother, once, when you ventured to England at the start of the war. He is larger than I am, but I'm told the resemblance is there."

Zeki studied the face, recalling the men he had met in London. Then he saw it. "You mean Mr. Holmes? Mr. Mycroft Holmes?"

"Yes."

"But you said your name was Sigerson."

"For now, Sigerson will do. With Mycroft unable to communicate, I could not organize signals and recognition codes, and have revealed myself to you instead. But you should forget that name, now."

"Mr. Mycroft is dead?" Zeki exclaimed, automatically switching to English.

Sigerson lifted his finger in warning. "Arabic, Zeki. English is too foreign a sound here."

"I apologize most humbly," Zeki responded, in Arabic.

"But the news of Mr. Mycroft is most shocking. Is he . . . did he . . . ?"

"He was not dead when I left London, but I have had no word for weeks. Did you receive your orders from London last week?"

Zeki felt no need for reservation now. "Yes. But they said Holmes, not Sigerson, and I assumed Mycroft . . ."

Sigerson's expression was one of infinite, somewhat strained patience.

Zeki bit his lip. "I understand now."

"Who signed the orders?"

"Mycroft. But you said he was dying, so he could not have."

Sigerson nodded. "It was a pre-arranged signal. The use of Mycroft's name as signature means he's still alive."

Zeki frowned. "I see. But it does not explain why you are here."

"What were you told?"

"To follow Holmes' instructions." Zeki paused. "I see. But I still do not understand."

"You will, Zeki. You will." Sigerson indicated they should move on, and fell back into his role as a Turk. The shoulders, his whole carriage, fell into a stoop. Watching him, Zeki could see how his slouch took several inches off his height. Sigerson was a very tall man, and even stooped he was tall for a Turk. The eyes were hooded, their intense gleam hidden behind lowered lids. The sharp chin was pushed into his chest.

"Where are we bound?" Sigerson asked.

"I was heading for home."

"That will do."

Zeki hesitated.

"What is it?"

"My room is small. Not that I don't wish to offer what hospitality I can . . . but the cramped quarters may strain your patience."

"Is it warm?"

"Certainly."

"Private?"

"I have worked to ensure that."

"That is all I ask. Thank you, Zeki. I accept your offer."

Zeki sighed and continued on his way, Sigerson dogging his heels.

ZEKI'S ROOM FEATURED an iron bed in one corner. An old battered armchair covered in faded paisley served as dining chair and comforter both, and was pulled up at the end of a scratched table that took up the space at the foot of the bed save for a narrow passage between table and wall. The table was used for both preparing and eating food, and a small gas hotplate and bottle took up one corner.

A washstand stood in the corner across the room from the bed, separated by the door into the room. The room's single window was beside it.

The entire room was lit by a single naked bulb hanging from flex that was secured across the ceiling by a series of nails driven into the plaster and bent over the wire. There was no switch, and the light remained permanently on. At night, to sleep, Zeki would climb on his bed, and loosen the globe in its socket until the electricity failed to reach the globe. The house Zeki's room was in was once the summer quarters of a rich merchant, and it pre-dated electricity by many years. Light fixtures were a hastily added afterthought.

Sigerson was sitting in the armchair, while Zeki washed the single cooking pot with a little water and soap. He had eaten the meal with genuine appreciation even though Zeki had deliberately added more spice than he would normally use. The heat of the spice had not appeared to bother the older man in the slightest.

While Zeki had been cooking the meal, he had walked about the small space of the room, stretching his lean length and examining the lock on the door, the catch on the window—pushing aside the photograph of Zeki's sister and mother to do so—before pronouncing the security satisfactory.

Now he sat studying the list of agents, which Zeki had hastily written using Sigerson's handsome fountain pen. For a moment he had been tempted to use Arabic script, to force the man to ask for a translation, but relented and wrote the list in Latin script instead.

Sigerson pulled out a packet of cigarettes, which he offered Zeki. They were strong black Russians, not the rough Turkish tobacco brand that a patriotic Turk would use. Zeki knew Sigerson had such a packet in another pocket, for he had used it that evening when they had been out in public.

Zeki refused the offered cigarette with a shake of his head. It was not wise to develop a taste for such luxuries.

Sigerson smoked in silence, studying the list. "Seven agents . . . and five of them gone."

"I have expressed my concerns to Mr. Holmes on any occasion where I could add freely to my report."

"He heard you," Sigerson responded. "That is why I'm here."

"To help them? They are beyond help now, Mr. Sigerson. They were taken to the Harbiye barracks."

"The significance of the name you must share, Zeki. When I was last in this city, it was simply a barracks."

"Some Germans are posted there. Including the officer they call Von Stein. I think he is in charge of many men."

"It is this Von Stein who would have dealt with them?"

"I am sure it is he who saw to their arrest and execution."

"Tell me about him."

"He is a hard man. Very hard. He is twice as German as the rest."

Sigerson smiled. "An odd, but expressive, description. Go on."

"That is all I know. I have met Colonel Von Stein once or twice. He spends a lot of time at the Topkapi, and the Palace—"

"The Dolmabahche? The Sultan's palace?"

"Yes. I have never spoken to him. I am just a secretary, you understand?"

"Perfectly."

"If ever I were to recruit new agents from among the Germans, there are many I would test, and some I would recruit. Von Stein . . . never would I even dare test. He would tear my heart from my chest before I had finished the first sentence."

"He is loyal to his country, then."

"Yes! He would make a very good Turk, in that respect."

"So once your agents were in his hands, there would be no mercy?"

"None at all." Zeki shivered, and was surprised at himself.

"Then it is as well my task is not to retrieve them. Tomorrow, Zeki, I must meet with the last two agents. Can you arrange that?"

"There is a way. But why do you wish to speak to them?"

"I'm eliminating possibilities. Someone has betrayed your agents, Zeki. It's my task to find out who, and one of these two agents who remain yet undetected might be the traitor."

ALEX VON STEIN strode back into the solarium, slapping the wire report against his thigh.

Major Häfner stood at the big windows, staring out at the last of the sunlight filtering through the canopies of the trees that lined the street. He was still in uniform. But Madeline was stretched out across the divan opposite to the one Von Stein had vacated to go and collect his coded wire. She wore a shimmering satin and lace evening dress in a deep purple that played against her dark hair and pale skin.

The glass room was luxurious by Turkish standards, decadently European in influence, with potted plants and birds in cages, and the soothing trickle of water from a central fountain. The marbled floor shone with care. The room was connected by an arch to a dining room glimpsed beyond. The dining room had the same gleaming floor, a long wooden table with multiple ladder-backed chairs in regimented rows on either side.

Both rooms were reached by stepping down two broad steps from a large, vaulted foyer. Opposite the wide, double-doored entrance the foyer serviced, a stone staircase climbed to a landing, then turned and split to climb to the next floor. The pale stone stairs were softened by a wide oriental carpet that ran the length of the staircase.

The quietly opulent house was tucked away in a residential street a good twenty-minute automobile travel north of the Harbiye barracks. Captain Häfner and his wife were model tenants, drawing no attention to themselves or to the luxury of their accommodations.

Nor did Von Stein pause to appreciate his surroundings now, for he was a regular visitor. He picked up Madeline's hand and kissed the soft skin on the back of it with a hearty, well-meant kiss, then threw himself on the other divan with a satisfied sigh.

Madeline gave him a quizzical smile. "You will, of course, share with me the reason for that smug expression you now wear."

"I am happy. That is enough, yes?"

"Not nearly enough. You were a bear with a headache when you arrived, earlier. Whatever produced this sunny disposition is a power I must cultivate. I was failing miserably in the task before you left to speak to the messenger."

"You are a constant pleasure in my life, Madame Häfner, and only you could have lifted my mood, had I been even a fraction less preoccupied. It was a noble and gallant effort against overwhelming odds. Do not feel you failed."

She gave a small smile. "You console me, Alex. But I would still know who succeeded where I did not."

"No-one, Madame."

"Ah! Then it must be the cable you hold in your hand—I recognize that disgusting grey colour they use for them."

Von Stein allowed himself a wolfish grin. "It is news that I had not expected, and its timing is immaculate." He waved the cable. "I have here the name—"

"No, Alex. No more. I do not want to share those dreadful secrets of yours. They are gruesome, I am sure!" She shivered delicately, her mouth turning down, and turned to the officer standing by the window. "William, I believe Alex is about to take you away for one of those strategic sessions of yours."

Häfner moved across the room to stand by his wife's side.

"I'm afraid Madeline is correct, Major," Von Stein said.

"I was listening, Herr Oberst. It is good news, then?"

"Very good news, and from a most unexpected source." Von Stein stood up and straightened his tunic, then turned to bow over Madeline Häfner's hand once more. "I regret, Madame."

"You do not," she said, with a smile. "But I will pretend to believe you."

Von Stein felt another smile pull at his mouth and allowed it expression. Madeline Häfner was a package of unexpected reactions. Her unpredictable, sharp intelligence was as much of a joy to behold as her still-striking beauty.

But he had work to do.

He turned to the major. "Come, Häfner. Let us catch a rat and give the men something to be truly cheerful about."

Häfner touched his wife briefly on the shoulder and walked beside Von Stein as they moved through the house to the front foyer.

"And the rat we are to catch?" Häfner asked quietly.

"A turncoat. Possibly the source of that mad Arab's information these last few years."

"The Divine Wind?" Häfner asked, opening the door. "Heinz told me your theory. It is a sound one, Herr Oberst. But what is the unexpected source of your information?"

Von Stein laughed aloud. "Berlin!" he said, and was delighted by the truly astonished expression on Häfner's face. "For once, Berlin knows more about this forgotten part of the war than we do." He strode over to the motor car sitting on the gravel drive. "We'll collect Heinz on the way to the barracks. Hurry up, Major!"

ZEKI HAD MADE contact with Fairuza without prior arrangement on three occasions in the past, and all of them had gone smoothly.

On this occasion, however, Sigerson insisted Zeki change his route of approach and come upon Fairuza's abode via side streets he had never used before. Zeki hid his impatience and led the man, tracing his way through odd alleys and paths, following his nose. He had an excellent sense of direction and rarely found himself lost.

Sigerson questioned every decision Zeki made. Every time he turned a corner, the older man would demand to know why that way, why this path, where were they now?

Zeki masterfully contained his irritation and answered. *Obey Holmes*, London had told him, and this he would do.

Finally, cautiously pleased, Zeki recognized the side fascia of Fairuza's building ahead of them. "There it is," he told Sigerson. "As usual," he could not resist adding.

The man's long, thin fingers clamped onto Zeki's arm with a power that bit into his muscles and made his arm go numb almost instantly. He was jerked backwards, almost off his feet.

Zeki felt his eyes widen as shock pumped through him. "What . . . ?"

Sigerson jerked his chin towards the road that ran past the flank of the building. "Look," he said.

Something in the man's quiet tone evaporated Zeki's protest. He turned and looked, as instructed, puzzled.

Then he saw the car. It was a black, shiny new vehicle, parked by the fencing that began at the back of the building. It was pulled up well off the road and hugging the building. From the road at the front of the building the car would not be noticed until one was directly in front of it.

Before the war there had not been too many motor cars on the streets of Constantinople. Since 1914, however, their numbers had increased, and nearly all of them were owned by the Imperial German Army.

There was no insignia on this one—its black doors were dusty and unadorned. But Zeki sensed danger, anyway. It was an instinct, developed from leading a double life for three years. The same instinct must have made Sigerson pull him backwards, off the street and out of sight of any occupants of the car.

If Zeki had not been so busy being annoyed with the man, he might have noticed the car as quickly as Sigerson had. He vowed he would not be so distracted again.

"What do we do now? They are in the building, yes?" he said.

"It cannot be a coincidence. They must be here for Fairuza."

Neither of them had questioned whether the car belonged to Germans or not, Zeki realized. Was Sigerson listening to his own instincts, as Zeki was?

"We should go. We must warn Jamal," Sigerson said.

"Yes, we must," Zeki agreed.

Neither of them moved from their position behind the protective corner of the fencing.

Already, voices and noise were issuing from inside the building. People were emerging from the narrow dark door that served the rear of the building. They staggered out into the small yard separated from the side road by the fence, and through the cracks between the paling, Zeki could see everything.

The instant they stepped outside, the volume of the voices leapt. Then Zeki realized the volume was attributable to one voice. Fairuza was held firmly between two of the German officers, all the while screaming insults, haranguing the guards and struggling valiantly to be freed. A third officer walked ahead towards the car.

Zeki tapped Sigerson's shoulder and pointed towards the officer leading the way. "Von Stein," he murmured, and Sigerson bent quickly to a gap of his own to examine the man.

Zeki watched as Fairuza was dragged across the road. The screaming was drawing attention. Heads appeared at windows and people stood in doorways, watching. But none would challenge a German in uniform.

Finally, at the car, Von Stein glanced around at the audience they were gathering, as the two officers struggled to get Fairuza into the car.

Moving almost leisurely, Von Stein removed his revolver from its holster, stepped around the wrestling trio, and brought the butt of the gun down in a short, hard blow to the back of Fairuza's head.

Zeki sighed as Fairuza's beautiful eyes closed, and she sagged between her captors.

"Get her inside," they heard Von Stein say, as he put his revolver away. His voice was dispassionate. Calm.

The two junior officers pushed the dark-haired woman into the back seat of the motorcar, and the major climbed in after her. The other hurried around to the driver's side of the vehicle.

Von Stein turned a slow full circle, checking his surroundings with careful deliberation, while Zeki and Sigerson pushed themselves further back behind the fence. Then he settled himself in the passenger seat, and the car bumped its way back onto the paving of the road and rolled to the corner, before pulling out into the small amount of traffic on the main street.

Zeki leaned back against the fence. He was trembling.

Sigerson's hand rested briefly on his shoulder. It was a dry silent gesture, but Zeki felt a moment of comfort. Then he moved out into the narrow side street, his hands on his hips, staring towards the main road where the car had gone.

After a moment, Zeki moved out to stand beside him.

"You won't be going home tonight," Sigerson said.

He nodded. Then: "Jamal," he said, remembering. "We must hurry! They might be going to him next. . . ."

"They're going back to the barracks," Sigerson said calmly.

"How do you know that?"

"There wasn't room in that car for another passenger. They'll take Fairuza to the barracks first."

"But that gives us only a little time."

"It will be enough. Come!" Sigerson rushed back down the side street toward the jumble of alleys and byways they had emerged from.

Zeki scrambled to follow him. "Where are you going?"

"To find Jamal before they do."

"But it's more direct if you follow the road."

"This way is quicker."

"I am to follow you? You haven't been in Constantinople for more than a day!"

"Hurry, boy. I haven't time or breath to spare to explain myself." And Sigerson jumped a rivulet of water wending its way into a gutter and strode away.

Chapter Five

FROM ACROSS THE STREET, SIGERSON OBSERVED THE FRONT OF Jamal's house. Forty-five minutes had passed since they had left Fairuza's house. They had hurried to the government building where Jamal was employed, and while Sigerson had waited in the shadowed alley opposite, Zeki had called upon Jamal.

He had re-emerged, troubled and alone, for a quick conversation with the clerk manning the front desk had revealed that Jamal had already left the building.

They had immediately worked their way through the back streets to Jamal's residence and carefully quartered the surrounding roads for signs of the black Imperial vehicles that would tell them the Germans had arrived before them. The roads were empty and innocent, and Zeki's knock on Jamal's front door had elicited no response.

So they had found a discreet place across the way to observe the front door and wait for Jamal's return.

"The clerk said he left the office immediately after receiving a telephone call," Zeki ventured now, still puzzling over the events.

"But he did not know who it was that telephoned Jamal," Holmes reiterated.

"No." Zeki licked his lips. "I cannot think who it might be that could call him and cause him to abandon his post without word or notice."

"Given Fairuza's abrupt and unexpected detainment, Zeki, I fear you are right to worry. The telephone call Jamal received must have a connection to that event."

"He should have reached home long before now."

"Yet there is no sign of his arrival."

"His wife—"

"He is married?" Sigerson asked abruptly.

"Yes."

"Children?"

"Three, I believe."

Sigerson was silent for a moment. "You choose your recruits in a cavalier fashion." The criticism in his tone was clear and unmistakeable.

The reproach stung. "He volunteered. He insisted, despite my refusal."

"That did not raise a question in your mind?"

"Of course. But I knew him, once. Long before."

"Ah. Then he must be one of those relentless Young Turks. You would have found many sympathetic ears among them."

"That is true, but I was careful. Their ranks were penetrated by the old guard long before the war broke out. The old ones . . . their sympathies run a different path."

Sigerson took three steps across the rough pavement, turned, and walked back. He appeared to be thinking, for his head was lowered, and his hands were behind his back.

"The timing of the telephone call, Zeki . . . it worries me. I fear—"

At that moment a muffled revolver shot sounded from the house across the street.

Sigerson whirled to face the building.

"Did Fairuza have a telephone in her building, Zeki? Quickly!"

Zeki frowned, trying to recall the three occasions he had been to Fairuza's home. "Yes, I think . . . in the hall."

At that moment, the breathless, still afternoon air was punctuated by a scream, so laden with despair and pain that the skin at the back of Zeki's neck rippled and tightened.

Sigerson swore. "We are too late," he said. He dashed across the deserted street and shouldered his way through the door and into the house.

Zeki was only paces behind, and when he entered the house he saw Sigerson stepping into one of the front rooms, from where the sound of intense sobbing could be heard.

Zeki approached the doorway reluctantly, for the scream he had heard, and the gasping, pitiful cries he listened to now told him a tragedy had occurred—one he was reluctant to observe. The helpless sobs tightened his stomach.

Sigerson had halted just inside the doorway. In front of him, splayed out across the carpet, lay a man's legs encased in neat pin striping. A revolver rested close by one shining shoe.

A dark-eyed woman with olive skin sat cradling the remains of the man's head, rocking to herself, expressing her grief with ululating cries. She did not appear to notice the men standing at the door, or the blood and matter that covered her hands and clothing.

"Zeki?" Sigerson asked softly.

Zeki knew what he wanted. "Yes, that was Jamal."

Behind them, voices expressed queries, concern. Shuffling steps approach the doorway.

"We cannot afford to linger," Sigerson murmured. "Von Stein will be here any minute."

He turned away.

"You did not find this place by accident, did you?" Zeki asked, his voice emerging from between his knees.

The place he referred to was their dubious shelter. Night had fallen not long before, but the shadows were long by the time Holmes had led Zeki into the abandoned palace overlooking the Bosphorus. They had camped in a big room with high arched ceilings and wide double doors all along one wall. The floor was littered with rubble and the cooking fires of previous short-term tenants. Discarded items of clothing and rubbish lay everywhere on the floor.

Holmes remembered a more graceful state of affairs here. The palace had seen better days.

They had the room to themselves that night, although numerous piles of cold cinders told him that it was not always unoccupied.

Holmes had pulled one of the remaining doors off its hinges and broken it up for firewood. Now a small fire burned between them, while Zeki sat with his back against the wall, his knees pulled up tight against him, and his arms wrapped around his legs.

"You did not search for this place. You led me straight here," Zeki pointed out. "You've been here before."

Holmes let his gaze rake across the arches of the ceiling and the crumbling walls once more. It was like rubbing an irritable tooth. "Yes, I've been here before," he admitted.

Zeki shivered a little, and clamped his legs tighter. "You know Constantinople."

"A little."

Zeki grinned, his dark eyes narrowing. "A lot," he corrected. "You've lived in this city before, haven't you?"

"More or less."

"You lived *here*," and Zeki's gaze lifted to indicated the room they were in. "That's why you knew exactly where to come."

"This place was derelict even then," Holmes answered, and reached for his packet of cigarettes.

"That doesn't answer my question."

Holmes carefully lit his cigarette, concentrating on the task. Then he rearranged himself into a more comfortable position and studied the young man across the flames.

"And what of you, Zeki?"

"Me?"

"My brother's associate informed me you were a subject of the Ottoman Empire and a native of Constantinople. A fine young Turk. I was told you were willing to assist Britain's efforts in the war as His Majesty's government has shown sympathy towards your cause."

"Your brother's associate did not lie."

"Not knowingly. But in fact, you are no more a native of Constantinople than I, are you?" His tone was pleasant.

Zeki's eyes widened. "*Effendi*?" The Turkish title of respect sounded unforced.

"If you had grown up in this city, you should know the streets intimately. Yet twice this morning when we were making our way to Fairuza's, you could not name the compass bearing we were heading in until you had checked the sun—yes, boy, I saw your quick sighting look."

"I was rolling my eyes with exasperation! You were driving me mad!"

"You covered it up almost perfectly, I give you that. You are extremely skilled at dissembling. But I am better. I've spent a lifetime exposing the truth. I have seen all its guises. And I know you did not know your way about the streets this morning."

Zeki shook his head, his curly hair dancing. The riotous curls were part of his camouflage. They gave him an innocent air that made him appear even younger than he was. "It is true—I did not know where I was this morning, but that does not mean it is all a lie! Constantinople is a great city. A big city! I do not know every square and fountain, not even every mosque! It is impossible to know a city in that way. Do you know London . . . every single cobblestone of London?"

"Almost. Enough to know I would not have been bewildered this morning had we been in London. I have made it my task to know every cobblestone. We are in Constantinople, however. Yet I was not lost, even here, and my familiarity with this city comes from six short weeks, over twenty-five years ago."

Zeki licked his lips. "You confused me with all your questions and demands . . ."

"Granted, everything you say might be true, although I doubt it. You are a quick thinker, Zeki, or you would not have survived so long in such a demanding role. But that does not explain the photograph."

"The . . . ?"

"There was a photograph on your windowsill. I moved it last night when I checked the catch. And I spent some time studying it from the table while you were writing your list. The people in it . . . they are your mother and sister."

Zeki's mouth opened a little, as did his eyes.

"Your room has no personal touches in it anywhere. You have quite properly arranged things so that you might abandon everything in that room at a moment's notice, save for the photograph. You were irritated when I brushed it aside so callously. Your irritation told me the photograph has some personal value to you. You are too young and too adventurous to have already married, therefore the women in the picture are most likely your sister and the older woman your mother."

Holmes leaned over the flame and extracted a burning splinter, which he used to light another cigarette, before continuing.

"It is quite a picturesque background, too. A holiday,

was it? The sea behind them looked most inviting . . . all that sunny sparkle."

Zeki's eyes narrowed, and this time there was no smile to accompany it. "I do not understand."

"Come, it is simple enough! They are your sister and mother, yes?"

"Yes."

"The men in the background are wearing multicolour cummerbunds and loose shirts. And your family stands in front of a sea which sparkles in the sun."

"I suppose . . . yes."

"You have stared at that photograph innumerable times. What else is on the sea besides sunlight?"

"I . . . I do not recall."

"There is a boat. Towards the horizon, and almost out of the frame, but you can clearly see the fisherman on it casting his net. Fishermen cast their nets early in the morning. And the ground behind your mother and sister is shadowed by their long silhouettes. Morning, with the sun on the sea. A sun that is obviously behind the camera operator. Was that you, Zeki? A box Brownie, perhaps?"

Zeki shook his head a little, his mouth opening as if he were about to speak, but nothing emerged.

"I see I shall have to complete the picture for you. You were standing with your back to the sun, boy. You were facing the sea. A western sea. The western seas near here are either the Sea of Marmara, the Mediterranean, or the Black Sea, which laps upon the shores of Georgia. It can't be the Mediterranean, or the men would be wearing *dishdashahs*, and the boat would have a triangular sail. Neither are the men Turks, as they would be if that were the Sea of Marmara. It is the Black Sea. And your family, and you, Zeki, are either Georgian or Armenian."

Holmes lifted the revolver in his hand to point it at Zeki across the flames, and cocked it. "You are not who you say you are."

Zeki sat motionless for a silent, strained moment, staring at the gun. He had grown pale.

"Someone told the Germans where to find Fairuza. It could not have been Jamal, as his fear of them was so great he killed himself rather than face their retribution. It was not I. It could have been you, Zeki. You are posing as someone you are not. How deep that double identity reaches remains to be seen."

Suddenly Zeki leapt to his feet, cinders crunching beneath his shoes, spun to face away from the fire and sprinted for the solitary external door, at the far end of the room.

Holmes watched until Zeki was halfway towards his destination before aiming and firing the revolver. The bullet ricocheted off a large lump of masonry barely a foot in front of Zeki's position, leave a long white scar on the rough face. Chips and powder flew into the air, and Zeki threw his arms up in front of his face, protecting it. He came to a sliding halt on the pebble-strewn floor, a gasping exhalation his only expression.

"I've picked out smaller targets than that rock from twice the distance. A target the size of your head will present me with no problems at all." Holmes spoke calmly.

Zeki remained very still, his back turned, and his arms still raised.

"If it was you who betrayed those agents, Zeki, do not expect the slightest leniency from me, for your betrayal may have cost my brother his life. I warn you."

Zeki lowered his arms very slowly, and the slightest murmur came from him.

"What?"

"They're all dead!" he cried, turning to face Holmes. "They're dead, all of them. Don't you understand?"

"Your family?"

"They took them away. Put them in trucks. Too many, too many of them."

"*They?*"

"I was hiding, you see. I was scared . . . I didn't want to go. And I watched them put Mama and Karli into the truck. They pushed them in, even though there was no room. They were screaming. Karli was afraid. Even my mother was afraid. And I knew if my mother was afraid, then it was very, very bad, and that's why I hid. I didn't want to face what scared my mama. . . ."

Startlingly, tears appeared on his cheeks, and slid quickly down to his chin.

Holmes lowered the revolver, de-cocking it. "You speak of the Mehmedchiks?" he asked quietly.

Zeki wiped his cheeks with two violent swipes of his hand. "I tried to find them, afterwards. They were driven to a staging post. Then they walked. To the camps in Syria." He was staring at the flames of the fire, speaking to himself. "I followed them, always too far behind. There were bodies on the way. Graves, markers, and sometimes no grave at all. There were children, and old people, and further on, even young ones. Whatever territory they marched through, there was an enemy that swooped on them. Kurds, Syrians, Bedouins . . . all of them encouraged by the Turkish pigs!"

Holmes put the gun on the floor beside him. "Sit down," he ordered gently.

Zeki shuffled towards the fire, and sat down heavily. He sniffed.

"You are Armenian." It was not a question.

Zeki nodded. His eyes were glazed, their focus turned inwards, upon memories.

"The Turks forced your people from your homeland, to the camps in Syria, and killed so many of them. That is why you serve Britain?"

Zeki was still staring at the flames, and after a moment of contemplation, he shook his head. "I serve Britain because Britain fights the Turks, and this is the only way I know how to fight them, too. I fight for my mother. For Karli. Because I was afraid that day and did not fight for them then." He glanced quickly at Holmes, then dropped his chin and gazed at his knees. Shame oozed from his rounded shoulders.

The silence between them grew and stretched, emphasized by the crackle of the little fire.

"Were you aware that Fairuza and Jamal knew each other?" Holmes asked at last.

Zeki's head came up. His eyes began to gleam. "They could not have . . . I did not let any of them meet each other. Ever."

"They both grew up in this city, did they not?"

"Yes, but even if they knew each other from before, they could not have known their secret was one they shared."

"Those who make the best agents have an innate ability to thoroughly understand people. Perhaps they met one day, and in the course of conversation, Fairuza learned enough to suspect Jamal. If Jamal was a true friend, then suspicion would be enough. When Fairuza had the chance, she took it, and telephoned Jamal to warn him. It did not matter if her suspicions were correct. She had no need for Jamal to confirm them."

Zeki huddled closer to the fire, obviously feeling the cool night air more than Holmes, who had come from the depths of an English winter, did. "If Fairuza had been free long enough to make a phone call, then she might have used that moment to escape."

"Indeed. She sacrificed the chance to warn another, then fought her captors every step of the way to delay their pursuit of Jamal." Holmes dropped another handful of timber scraps on the fire, and it sparked and spit back. "You chose well when you chose Fairuza. She is apparently a quick-thinking woman of rare courage."

"Allah be with her," Zeki murmured. He stirred and

shifted, glancing at Holmes. "Who betrayed us, if it was not Fairuza or Jamal? There is no-one else."

Holmes threw the last of his cigarette into the fire and sat up. "There is one other possibility. I had to eliminate all the other alternatives before I could afford to settle my attention upon this last one, for it will be no easy task to unearth him."

"Who is he? I'll slit his throat myself!"

"Peace, Zeki. Your task in this arena is best served by a clear mind, not one fouled with strong emotions."

Zeki scowled. "Fairuza was a friend of mine, too."

"You will serve your friendship with her better if you remain calm." Holmes stared at the young man until he shrugged and rested his chin on his knees, staring into the fire.

"I believe the fresh light of morning will be a better time to talk of the man we seek," Holmes said. He let his gaze wander over the ruins picked out in soft moving light and shadows. "We'll let the night draw between us and memories."

Zeki shivered again. "As long as I survive the night," he muttered.

SOMEWHERE IN THE long hours that followed, Zeki fell asleep, although he was only aware of the accomplishment when he roused and felt the roughness of stone beneath his flank. The fire still crackled in front of him, and he was aware of extra warmth over his shoulders. There was an aroma that came with it, that his sleep-clouded mind took a moment to identify.

It was tobacco smoke. Specifically, Black Russians.

He blinked a little, then heard the quiet sound of a footstep, crunching in masonry debris and cinders.

It was possibly this sound that had woken him.

He moved his head slowly until he could see beyond the fire, in small movements that would not draw attention.

The far one third of the long room was a series of tall, floor-to-ceiling arched windows, separated by elegant columns. Any glass in them had long since been broken or fallen foul of the elements. Beyond them was a narrow terrace that overlooked the Bosphorus but was made private by a filigree screen carved from stone. A little starlight and what remained of the moon shone through the intricate screen, enough to show Zeki Sigerson's silhouette.

The older man stood in the frame of a window, leaning against it. The light showed he was without his jacket, but he did not seem to mind the cold. The small breeze that drifted from the river brought with it the smells and sounds of Constantinople late at night, unnaturally hushed by the contingencies of war.

After a moment, Sigerson's head dropped, bringing his gaze to his feet.

The pose was unnaturally still, and Zeki shut his eyes, uncomfortably aware that he was witnessing a deeply private moment, one he knew Sigerson would not want to share.

He settled his head back on his bent arm, and composed himself for sleep.

THE NEXT MORNING Holmes prodded Zeki awake, and they breakfasted on the contents of Holmes' hip-flask, which warmed them even though it did little to ease their hunger.

They brushed the dirt of an uneasy night from their clothing, then climbed out of the ruined palace to mingle with the stream of pedestrians heading for Galata, the commercial district of the city. Holmes took the lead.

The dawning day was bright and sunny, but cool, for winter held the city in its grip. As they walked, the pair exchanged a few comments in Turkish, to all appearances another pair of clerks on their way to their appointed positions for the day.

Eventually Holmes murmured to Zeki in Arabic, "The building on your right—across the road. That is our destination."

Zeki glanced casually at the low, one-storey building, a disinterested pedestrian.

"The Oriental Export Company? It seems too innocent a place to hide the one we look for." There were too many people in the city who spoke Arabic for them to risk speaking in plainer terms and perhaps being overheard.

"It is undoubtedly the place to begin our search," Holmes assured him. He crossed the busy road and turned the corner, then moved along the side street.

"You promised an explanation," Zeki pointed out.

"And you shall have it, young Zeki. But I prefer to give such explanation when we are away from casual eavesdroppers. And we shall be in that position very soon."

He was glancing up at the buildings beside him as he walked. Finally, he nodded in satisfaction. "Yes, it is manageable. A few fences to scale and roofs to cross, and we will be there."

Accordingly, several minutes later, they stood in a squalid yard enclosed on all sides by the solidly built rear elevations of shops and office buildings. It had taken the scaling of precisely two fences and one roof to reach this place. This was a busy, successful area, but the owners of the commercial ventures poured their resources into appearances on the main streets. The rears of the buildings were forgotten and decrepit.

A small corner of one dark brick building jutted into the yard. Barely five paces of wall emerged from the buildings on either side, but one of the walls was interrupted by a window. The window was opaque—possibly painted white on the reverse side. Thick iron bars protected it, and they were secured with a good, strong padlock threaded through steel eyelets, facing the window.

Holmes reached through the bars and gave the padlock an experimental tug, while studying the bars and window.

"This is the back of the export company building?" Zeki asked.

"It is," Holmes confirmed, reaching into an inner pocket. He withdrew a small, soft leather wallet and extracted two thin, oddly hooked probes.

"We are breaking in?" Zeki asked.

"It would seem that way, wouldn't it?"

"Observing the shop front from a distance would not be sufficient? Your agent will presumably visit these premises sooner or later, would he not? Isn't that why we're here?"

"I don't know the answer to that yet. And observation will not be sufficient. I'll explain once we're inside."

While Zeki watched, absorbed, Holmes pushed the probes carefully into the keyhole of the padlock and delicately twisted them.

"For a man like you, you have some strange skills, *Effendi*," Zeki said in an undertone.

"Skills a younger man acquired. Eons ago." Holmes twisted his wrist, the padlock audibly clicked, and the clasp sprang open. "But they serve this particular man quite well," he added, pulling the hasp away and swinging the bars aside.

He pressed against the frame of the sash window and stepped back, examining it. Then he rested his ear against the glass for long moments. "Silent," he declared. "And quite empty, I believe."

"Is there a wired alarm?" Zeki whispered.

"It would seem improbable when the window bears such strong bars . . . but a good long knife will soon tell us one way or the other."

Zeki reached into his trouser pocket, but Holmes was already reaching under his own jacket, behind his back. There was a quiet snick, and he withdrew a glittering knife with a long, curved blade.

Zeki's eyes widened. He watched as Holmes probed between the top and bottom frames of the window with the point. When the knife's progress was halted a little more than a third of the way across the width of the window, Holmes nodded.

"Yes, there's a wire," he confirmed, then took a better grip on the knife, and forced it down and sideways with a sharp, hard push. "But it no longer presents a problem," he added. He pulled the knife out, hid it away beneath his jacket, and glanced at Zeki. "Do you doubt now that this place is as innocent of purpose as you proposed? Bars on a window one can explain away, but bars *and* an alarm? That is overly cautious even for this district and these times."

"Are you ever wrong, Mr. Sigerson?" Zeki asked.

Holmes smiled a little. "More often than I can comfortably confess." He pushed the bottom window up a little, bent to peer inside, then pushed it up fully and indicated Zeki should climb in.

Holmes eased his way in after the agile man, and found Zeki standing barely two paces away, stock still, with his eyes closed, breathing deeply. His face held an expression of pure bliss.

Zeki stood in a narrow corridor of a large, high-ceilinged room. On either side of him were rows of bags, bundles, boxes and other anonymous packages. Most had writing stencilled on them, in a variety of languages. Holmes could see Arabic script, Farsi, English, French and German from his position by the window. There was very little Turkish script to be seen.

"Imports," Holmes murmured.

The packaging was anonymous, but the pungent

aromas that flooded the room told a far better tale. There was the unmistakable miasma of spices and herbs, and unidentifiable scents that spoke of exotic substances.

"Food!" Zeki breathed, swallowing.

Holmes slid the window shut, and refastened it. He walked to the end of the narrow corridor and looked around the corner. Another glass-fronted door stood at the end, and as Holmes looked, the shadow of a passerby crossed the frosted glass. He crossed to the door and tested the handle. It was locked. On the other side, letters were painted across it, and after mentally reversing the letters, Holmes made out the word *Ambar*. In Turkish, it meant storeroom, or warehouse.

He went back to Zeki, and found him sitting cross-legged on the bare floorboards, a package of dried figs in his hands. It had been ripped open and he was busy chewing on some of the contents, with the joy of a hungry child.

"You add theft to a tally that already lists breaking and entering?" Holmes whispered.

"I am hungry!" Zeki protested, his words distorted by the mouthful of fig. He chewed some more, and swallowed mightily. "There's some sultanas there, too!"

Holmes glanced at the gaping wound in the side of a carton sitting atop a tea chest. The script on the side bespoke Italian origin.

"Thank you, but I prefer more civilized dining," Holmes replied.

Zeki burrowed back into the packet in his lap. "Then tell me why we are here," he suggested, selecting another fat fig and biting into it with overt relish.

Holmes lifted his left forearm and slid the cuff back to display a bare wrist. He frowned and lowered the arm. "I believe we can spare a few minutes, and I promised you an explanation. We're unlikely to be interrupted in here, as the door is locked—and we would have plenty of warning.

Very well." He lifted the broken box of dried fruit aside and settled himself on the tea chest.

"I had very little time in London to investigate the man I now seek, but Mycroft had long ago researched and documented all the information to be had about him. This information was given to me by Mycroft's superior just before I left London."

"You have it here?"

"It is prudent when posing as a Turk not to walk around with documentation on English agents in one's pockets. The information is safely tucked away somewhere else. Its authenticity you will have to accept as established."

Zeki nodded. "And the man's name?"

"I don't know." Holmes rapped the tea chest with a quick little tattoo. "A cigarette would not go astray just now, but it would quickly lead to our detection, I fear. Alas . . ." He took a deep breath. "This man with no name has been feeding Mycroft information about the Ottoman Empire since before the war. Troop movements, German strategies and personnel, Turk policies, underground political movements . . . all excellent information."

"And Mr. Mycroft took such information from a man with no name, whom he had never met?"

"Not at first. The first package arrived in early 1913. It had been sent by penny post—just as all information packages since then have arrived. It was addressed to Mycroft personally, which was somewhat alarming, for Mycroft's position within the government hierarchy is not commonly known. The information itself was a treatise of the political and military positions of the Ottoman Empire and the German interests in those parts. It included biographies of key people and their weaknesses and strengths. The thing was a useful resource in its own right. After careful verification of some fifty or so facts in the document, it was assumed the balance was reliable, and the document became a key element in British war plans. However, the anonymous donor was still suspect."

"Then more packages arrived?"

"Yes. A steady, regular flow of them. None of them were as comprehensive as that first package. But all of them were rich in data that Mycroft could use and pass on and upwards."

"Did he?"

"Reluctantly, at first. But as his own circle of agents—your group, Zeki—grew and began to supply an alternative source Mycroft could use for verification, he did begin to rely upon it."

"Then why do you believe this agent was responsible for the attack upon Mr. Mycroft?"

"Mycroft himself came to believe the information was suspect. All your agents were supplying information which, between them, was verified. The faceless agent's data was just a little bit too different. It wasn't enough to cause alarm until an unknown person attempted to murder Mycroft."

"Why would the agent want to do that? It would tip his hand."

"I'm not sure of the motive yet, but Mycroft was meeting your Ottoman courier the night he was assaulted. Perhaps the courier had facts that pointed conclusively to the faceless one's duplicity. The messages the courier should have been carrying were taken, and Mycroft didn't have them. Perhaps the rogue agent wanted to learn the identities of those agents you had left. It's a curious coincidence that quite soon after Mycroft's attack, the remaining agents in your group are removed from the chessboard."

Holmes shrugged. "It doesn't matter right now why he did it, only that he did do it, and might do it again."

"Why do you believe that?" Zeki licked his fingers a little. "There is nothing there that says he will try again."

"There is nothing to assure me he will not. The rogue

arranged the attack on Mycroft, then finished off the courier, too. Since my arrival here in Constantinople he has seen to the complete disintegration of your entire network. Yesterday we established that the culprit was not part of your group, and last night I was fully satisfied that it was not you. There is no-one else we know of. The rogue agent is the last possibility."

Zeki waved his hand around the room. "And he is here? Why here?"

"The letters sent by penny post would normally be a perfect means of cutting off any trace back to the source. Mycroft, however, is crafty and had the full resources of His Majesty's government at his disposal. The letters were traced back to a company in London. Yet the paper and ink, as well as the contents, point towards a Middle-East origin. Therefore there is some sort of channel between the London company and the Middle East. The connection was not hard to find. The company, by name, is the British Occidental Export Company, established 1908, and doing a respectable business. They have branches in Alexandria, Constantinople, and Bahrain, with constant shipping and transport from the Middle East. The war has only slowed the pace of their commerce."

"And the Constantinople branch?"

"The address was this very building, Zeki. I memorized it before I stepped off the ship at Gaza."

"But this isn't that British company you named. It was . . ." Zeki frowned, obviously stretching to recall the name.

"The Oriental Export company. As opposed to the British Occidental Export company. The names are not dissimilar. And a company with obvious British connections would find trade difficult to come by here. A minor change of name would be prudent. And one cannot dispute the address, Zeki. The British company lists this address as their Constantinople branch."

"That means the agent, whoever he is, sends the information to the British company from this company." Zeki frowned. "Then he must have some sort of connection with this company. A stranger, even a regular customer, wouldn't be given such a regular, reliable channel of communication."

"Well done, Zeki. This very point was proven by Mycroft's investigators two years ago. They learned that regular packages addressed to the manager were shipped to the London company along with other exports. When the manager of the London company received such packages and opened them to discover another sealed package addressed to a Mycroft Holmes, he was to purchase postage for the package and post it. There has been a succession of three managers in that company since the information has been arriving upon Mycroft's doorway, but always, the orders are obeyed."

"Orders?" Zeki said sharply.

"Yes. Orders that have been in place since before the war. The original managers who would have put the orders in place have long since departed for overseas postings. With the outbreak of war, investigation in Constantinople itself—the next logical link—became impossible. And for reasons of prudence and security it was decided not to call you in to investigate on Mycroft's behalf. As the anonymous agent was theoretically a friend, not a foe, the investigation was dropped at that point, and Mycroft's people reverted to accepting the agent's facts at face value."

Holmes pursed his lips, as if suppressing a strong reaction.

"But *now* we investigate? Now my people have been sacrificed?"

"Your people . . . and my brother," Holmes said softly.

Zeki pushed the packet of figs aside and wiped his lips with the back of his hand. He got to his feet. "I am ready."

Chapter Six

MAJOR WILLIAM HÄFNER SET OUT FROM THE HARBIYE barracks with two junior officers, one of them behind the controls of Von Stein's motor car. It was half past eight in the morning, and a hard day's work lay ahead of him.

He enjoyed the weak sunshine passing through the window by his elbow and allowed his thoughts to drift a little. It was a rare moment when he could allow his guard to relax and his thoughts to wander, and he enjoyed the luxury for the length of time it took to negotiate the crowded streets between the barracks and the heart of the commercial district.

The address he was heading for was a business lying close by the Galata Bridge over the Golden Horn. The driver was soon pulling the wheel over and the tires bumped against the rough edge of the road.

There were more motor cars in Galata than anywhere else in the city, but motor cars that contained three German officers in the middle of the business district on a weekday was unusual enough to create a small stir of morbid interest.

Those businessmen watching them climb from the car

knew well enough why they were here. Possibly they had suffered through a similar visit in the past. Even if they had only heard rumours, they were still uneasy. The representatives of Imperial Germany were of chancy temper these days, for their mettle was being tested in ways these simple business folk could not possibly conceive.

Within the limits imposed by a war waged almost on their doorsteps, their lives—and the commerce that went with it—carried on.

Aware that he was moving into a dangerously philosophical frame of mind, Häfner shrugged his shoulders beneath his greatcoat, trying to dispel the mood. He crossed the road to the double-doored shop front. Peiter already had the door open and stood stiffly at attention.

Häfner stepped into the neat, clean front office of the Oriental Export Company and observed the secretaries' and clerks' startled expressions. Abruptly, all the typewriters fell silent. Surprise was swiftly followed by dismay, and just as quickly hidden.

The front office was large and airy. An expanse of dark green linoleum shiny with wax was split by a thigh-high railing that separated the public portion of the office from the group of secretaries' desks and the high clerk's desks at the back.

In the far back wall was a door with a frosted glass pane, which obviously led into the inner managers' offices and storerooms, but it was shut.

The office manager shuffled forward with a series of short quick bows that were almost comical. He pushed open the swing gate in the rails and stepped through.

"Herr General," he began, in bad German.

"Major, you idiot," Häfner snapped.

"Herr Major, I am Syed Mushtaq Ali, the manager of this establishment. Is there some way my humble company may serve the great German Imperial Army?"

He was a typical Turk—small framed, short, with dark

eyes. His black hair was oiled and combed smooth, with an unnaturally straight and perfect part in the middle. A red rose adorned his lapel and there was a red silk kerchief in his pocket. The eyes were wide, with the same curiously hurt and vulnerable look so many Turks seemed to have.

"Your company is an export company, Herr Ali."

"Certainly, Herr Major."

"It has come to my attention."

Ali lost the colour in his cheeks. "*Effendi*?" he said.

"What did you call me?" Häfner shot back.

"I mean . . . my apologies . . . I mean, Herr Major?"

"You mean what?"

"I—I . . . I mean . . . I meant nothing, Herr Major." He dropped his gaze to his feet. He was visibly trembling.

"An export company can be in a privileged position," Häfner continued smoothly. "You have opportunities the average subject does not. You have far-reaching contacts. Such power and opportunity could well corrupt a manager of such a business. He might use it to benefit himself and his friends. These are hard times, after all."

"This may be true, Herr Major, but I assure you, our business is honest. We work hard to bring pleasures and luxuries to simple folk . . . such as yourself. Whatever you have heard must be completely unfounded. We know it is by your good graces that we are permitted to continue our business."

"You speak wisely, but you do not reassure me. The information I have received about you and your company was very specific." He reached into a pocket and withdrew a single sheet of paper. "For example, you recently acquired a bolt of silk cloth from Japan . . . and failed to declare the importation to the customs officials."

"That is a lie!" Ali declared with bravado that could only have been a product of sheer indignation. He would not dare speak so if he was any less irritated.

"Really?" Häfner said smoothly. "A search of these premises would produce no cloth?"

"Herr Major, we have many such bolts of cloth on the premises, but I assure you they have all been properly declared and the appropriate taxes paid on all of them."

"It was a very expensive roll. Bright pink—a colour barely seen since the war placed such stress on economies and ladies' fashions. My wife, a brunette, looks wonderful in that colour, for instance, but I haven't seen her wearing it since 1913 . . ."

The little silence that greeted his words was pregnant with tension.

Finally, Ali cleared his throat. "As it happens, we do have such a bolt on the premises, although it could not possibly be the undeclared cloth you seek. I will show it to you, Herr Major, and you can inspect it for yourself. In fact, I will make you a gift of the cloth—for your wife, who must crave such pretty things these days. And then you will know that I am an honest merchant, yes? For I would not freely give you illegal merchandise, would I?"

Häfner reassembled his expression into one that showed cautious pleasure. "Well . . ." he began doubtfully.

"Perhaps, Herr Major, we could discuss this matter in my office?" Ali was sure of himself now. It was clear from his growing confidence he knew where the conversation was going, what Häfner wanted of him. He clicked his fingers, and one of the clerks hurried forward to open the door that led further into the building. Beyond was a corridor, with glass-fronted doors leading from either side.

Ali was waving Häfner forward. "I will have you brought an excellent cup of Turkish coffee—"

"I hate Turkish coffee," Häfner growled, not moving from the spot he stood upon.

"Of course you do!" Ali agreed, without batting an eyelid. "For a delicate palate such as yours, our thick brew is offensive. I have some African beans—delivered here only yesterday. Much lighter, a delight to the nose. Come, come, Herr Major." He waved to one of the clerks sitting at a typewriter. "Luise, the cerise silk organza to my office at once."

Häfner moved towards the corridor, and as if his movement was a signal, the five typewriters behind him began tapping out their messages once more. The atmosphere in the front office visibly relaxed. They were sure their manager had read Häfner right and that he would deal with the matter as swiftly and efficiently as usual.

Häfner knew Ali was indeed efficient. He was a wily man, who had managed to keep his business open and operating through dint of bribery of corrupt officials, a carefully built network of associates and friends in high places, and by keeping a painfully clean, law-abiding reputation and appearance at all times.

The corridor Häfner stepped into had six doors leading off it—two on the left, and four on the right. The door at the end of the corridor on the left had a glass front and the Turkish word *Ambar* in Latin script painted across it. There was a lingering mixture of scents, odd and intriguing. Häfner recognized spices, teas, coffees, dry goods and other exotic odours that beckoned, but he kept his attention to the matters at hand.

There were two clerks in the corridor, and one looked over his shoulder, saw Häfner's uniform, and stepped to a door and slipped behind it with startled speed. The other continued down the corridor, and opened the far left door. Häfner caught a glimpse of shelves of dry goods before the door shut behind him. Obviously that was the storeroom and the source of the wafting scents.

Ali opened the far right-hand door and waved Häfner into his office. "Please, sit down. The coffee will be here very soon." He shut the door, and Häfner eased himself onto the padded upright chair that stood in front of the desk.

The highly polished wood of the desk was unadorned except for a single telephone. Ali sat down behind the desk, spread his hands across the wood, and stared at Häfner.

"You bring news from Hadiya?" he said softly.

Häfner nodded and delved into his greatcoat again, producing a large buff envelope, which he placed on the desk. Ali slid it to the edge. He opened the drawer beneath and dropped the envelope into it, returning the desk to its pristine orderliness.

"The coffee should be here momentarily," Ali said.

"I'm sure it will be good . . . although I quite like your Turkish stuff—it is superior at the end of a long day."

Ali smiled. "Then you'll be relieved to know that is what you will be served. We have no African beans at all—the last shipment was absconded with by enthusiastic customs officials somewhere out on the Aegean Sea. Damned Greeks!" Ali scowled.

Häfner cocked his head sharply as he heard a minute noise at the door. He rose to his feet, but spoke casually. "You mean to say you serve my fellow German officials Turkish coffee and claim it to be African?"

Ali answered smoothly. "But of course."

Häfner moved silently towards the door.

"Half of them cannot tell the difference, anyway," Ali continued. "If I tell them it is African, they believe me, and declare it to be the best coffee they have tasted in a month. One claimed he could tell me where in Africa it came from . . . down to the nearest square mile!"

Häfner gripped the door handle, opened it very suddenly, and stepped out. He looked up and down the empty corridor, then shut the door again, puzzled.

"Someone was listening?" Ali asked.

"I don't know. Perhaps I'm just imagining things. We're all a little more nervous these days."

Ali smiled sympathetically. "I'll have this package on its way by midnight. Rest easy on that one."

"Hadiya will be pleased to hear it," Häfner responded.

The door opened again, and a clerk hurried in with a startlingly bright bolt of silk, and a second man behind him carried an armful of cigarette cartons and tinned goods.

"Ali, no . . ." Häfner began.

"You must take these," Ali insisted.

"Just the cloth. It would look suspicious if I did not . . . and Madeline will truly adore the colour."

"You must give the cigarettes and preserves to your men."

"They are obedient and do not question me."

"Then these will ensure their undivided loyalty." Ali waved his hand as Häfner opened his mouth to protest once more. "I am more familiar with bribery than you are, Herr Major. You must trust me on this."

"I will," Häfner agreed reluctantly.

"And you must promise to wave your armful of goods so that everyone on the street cannot fail to see them as you walk back to your lovely automobile," Ali added.

"To show all who see that you have successfully bribed another corrupt official?"

"But of course. I have a reputation as an astute businessman to maintain amongst my peers," Ali said smoothly. "And I wish to make them envy me just that much more."

Häfner gave in with a great gust of laughter.

ZEKI CLIMBED BACK into the yard and sucked the splinters from his fingers as Sigerson slid back out through the painted-out window, soundlessly shut it once more, swung the bars back over, and relocked the padlock. Zeki was breathing heavily, and his heart was thudding erratically.

"You scared me!" he accused Sigerson. "You order me to stand guard at the door into the corridor while you prowl around amongst the people out in the offices, spying on them. Then you duck back into the storage room like a startled goat—not once, but twice! And both times you send me flying! Then you push me out the window with no more ceremony than you would afford a . . . a sheep!"

"With all due apology to your fingers and hide, Zeki, I had rather more important matters to worry about on both occasions." Sigerson inspected the yard. "Eavesdroppers are not supposed to prosper, but we have had the greatest good fortune. It was inevitable, perhaps, that we should manage to be in this place at such a time." He smiled, and rubbed his hands together.

Zeki stared at him. "You make no sense!" he protested

"No? It's of no matter—we cannot stand here and discuss it, anyway. One question, Zeki. Does the name 'Hadiya' mean anything to you?"

Zeki frowned, and shrugged. "It's just a name."

"Is it a place? Or a person?"

"I know of no place called Hadiya. It's a man's name."

"Then we may well have found the name of the faceless one. A trip to the hall of records is in order."

"Hall of records? But . . . ?" Zeki stared at Sigerson, truly puzzled. There was an eagerness, an excitement emanating from him.

"I will explain it all in time. But first I must confirm the ownership of this company. Someone gave those orders in London, Zeki. Someone set up this form of communication in the first place. And they're still running things and giving orders, if I understand fully what I just heard. With luck, we'll find their name on the company papers. Or we will find a name that we can use to trace the German connection."

"*German?*" Zeki's voice squeaked in surprise.

"Yes, German," Sigerson confirmed grimly, and turned away. "Come! The hall of records!"

THE HOUSE OF central records lay in Stamboul, just on the other side of the Golden Horn. The journey led directly across the Galata Bridge and through the elegant, archaic roads and squares, past the beautiful fountains and pools of ancient Constantinople.

Zeki wondered what the passersby would think of the innocuous-looking man walking by his side if they knew he carried instruments for picking locks, a revolver in his pocket, and a wicked, gold-handled knife in a scabbard strapped to his belt, and that he could use all of them with experienced ease.

The hall of records was gaily decorated on the inside, rivalling the frescoes and artwork of the most magnificent mosques of the city. The atmosphere inside the echoing, vast chamber was equally dignified. Silent clerks scurried between the huge tables, carrying rolls of records from the stacks to the businessmen and officials who waited at the tables for their requested materials.

Zeki and Sigerson found an unoccupied table, and Zeki caught the attention of a clerk, who hurried over and nodded. "Your request?" he asked.

Zeki asked for the company ownership records for the Oriental Export company and gave the address they had visited. The clerk nodded again and hurried away.

They sat in the cool, dim room, waiting. Sigerson carefully avoided catching anyone's eye while appearing to be casually interested in his surroundings.

"What if the company is actually listed as the British one you called it? The name they use in London?" Zeki asked.

"We will simply ask for that company name, if this one produces no results. But it will—the people behind this scheme are thorough and have paid great attention to details and appearance. All will be in order. You'll see."

Zeki did not feel fully reassured. "Will you not tell me now what you heard in the corridor of the export company?" he asked.

"Not here," Sigerson said. "Later. Patience, Zeki. I can see the end to this matter now. And I will explain it all in time. These records will confirm my guesses, and then I will be able to give you facts, rather than suppositions."

The clerk finally returned with a bundle of rolls and spread them out upon the table—which explained the reason for the large tables. He nodded and moved away to give the two businessmen their privacy.

Zeki frowned over the Turkish script while Sigerson pretended an interest and held down the corners of the manuscripts.

"There are a lot of legal clauses," Zeki murmured. "Long ones."

"I see that aspect of business does not change from language to language," Sigerson replied. "Keep going. What is this document?"

After a moment, Zeki replied, "It's the setting up of the company, I think. Charters, limits of liability. Declarations."

He read a while longer, then pushed it aside. "There are no names on it," he explained, reaching for the next.

"Look for a board meeting, or a declaration of ownership," Sigerson advised, standing up and pushing the first document further along the table. "Registration of a public company even here must involve a declaration of who will be in control of that company. Trading would be hampered without that knowledge."

Zeki scanned the next document and pushed it away to reach for the third, while Sigerson stacked it on the first.

Immediately, Zeki pointed to the text. "There! President. Syed Mushtaq Ali."

"Hmmm . . . I thought he was too good to be a simple manager," Sigerson murmured.

"*Effendi*?"

"Never mind. Who else?"

"Board members. Al-Qishawi Abdulkarem. Al-AdarahAl-Ajleh."

Sigerson shook his head, frowning.

Zeki grabbed his sleeve. "Here!" he hissed. "Hadiya! Hadiya Adlparvar."

Sigerson surged closer. "Where?"

Zeki pointed the name out, and Sigerson shook his head irritably. "Spell it—Latin script," he instructed.

Zeki spelt the name aloud, slowly.

"Parvar," Sigerson murmured. Abruptly, he sat down again, his hands lying flat against the document. His eyes were distant, unfocussed.

Zeki found his heart was thudding just as hard as it had been when Sigerson had bolted back into the supply room on both occasions that morning, yet he did not understand why he should feel this sudden, terrifying rush of fear and excitement.

"What is it?" he hissed again, keeping his voice low. Businessmen did not shout at one another, after all.

"I have been utterly blind . . ." Sigerson murmured.

"Sir?" Zeki prompted yet again. Then, more urgently, "Sigerson!"

He stirred and looked at Zeki, and amazingly, he smiled and clapped him on the shoulder. "How would you feel about a hot meal, some coffee, and a big fire before which you can warm your toes?"

"Where? When?" The thought of food was more than enough to distract Zeki from his deep puzzlement over Sigerson's reaction to the name.

"Now. As soon as I hunt down a place to buy some supplies."

"The Grand Bazaar is a short walk from here," Zeki pointed out.

"Of course it is. Yes. Then to the Grand Bazaar we must go. And then, Zeki, back to our grand palace. With food and fuel and the good news I have to cheer us, you won't notice the drafts, I promise you!"

Chapter Seven

THERE WAS NOTHING OF THE MELANCHOLY MAN ABOUT Sigerson as they settled down in their camp for one more night.

The inwardly occupied person of the previous evening was nowhere to be seen in the energetic, cheerful one that moved about the campfire, producing an astonishingly good meal from one pot, a bagful of herbs and a small handful of goat meat.

The goat meat he had bargained for with the persistence and panache of a man long used to the ways of the bazaar.

There were some vegetables in the pot, too. A sweet potato, some dried peas, and an old carrot that Zeki would have pronounced as beyond use, but the long simmering Sigerson gave it brought it back to life.

The ingredients were the same as Zeki faced each day—a variety of foods had become harder to acquire as the war dragged onwards. Yet with the same ingredients, Sigerson managed to produce a palatable meal completely different from the depleted diet Zeki had been suffering.

He had never tasted a dish quite like it. The mix of

spices and method of cooking were strange. However, Sigerson seemed to be completely familiar with the process.

It was little wonder, then, that he had not hesitated to eat the spiced eel Zeki had cooked that first night. He was apparently used to stronger tastes.

There was more wood for the fire, and a blanket for Zeki's toes. The hip flask was produced once more. Along with a piece of aged cheese that Sigerson sliced with his spectacular knife, the contents of the hip flask finished off the meal to perfection.

Zeki sat cross-legged next to the fire, the blanket about his shoulders, feeling a rare contentment. "Food, fuel, and good news, you said," he reminded Sigerson.

"I have not forgotten," Sigerson answered. He was cleaning his knife, and he put it away carefully before lighting up a cigarette and stretching and leaning back against the wall. He smoked in silence for a moment, then, "What does the name Hadiya Adlparvar mean to you?"

"I know it means something to you. I have spent the rest of this day trying to understand what it means, but . . ." Zeki shrugged.

"I am getting ahead of myself, anyway," Sigerson said. "Let me explain it to you in the order it happened. At the premises of the Oriental Export company, I asked you to guard my escape route while I ventured out into the corridor to see what I could discover.

"That first time I returned to the room, I was only a dozen paces away from the manager of the company. He and his guest had stepped into the corridor."

"They saw you?" Zeki asked, startled.

"They saw another clerk going into the storage room, his back to them." Sigerson shook his head. "They saw something they expected to see and therefore dismissed it from their minds."

Zeki considered this. "I see," he said at last. "And the second time you went out into the corridor?"

"A moment. I have not related what I learned the first time I ventured into the corridor."

"You heard the manager's guest arriving?"

"Very good, Zeki. I was in time to overhear the arrival of a German officer. They did not give a name, and I did not see him, for there was a door between me and the front office. He's an unpleasant fellow, to judge by what I heard."

Sigerson repeated to Zeki the conversation he had heard that morning, both the one in the front office and the one in the manager's office.

"It's clear the manager, Ali, is forced to send these missives to England via his export channels, for whatever purpose the Germans have set up this complex scheme. And the Germans don't mind a little creative bribery thrown into the mix," he concluded.

"You were lucky you were there to see and hear all this," Zeki observed. "It is exactly the information you needed to solve the puzzle."

"Luck had little to do with it," Sigerson replied, with a wave of his hand. "Yesterday, the Germans picked up two of your agents. They may believe you have more of them out there, who observed or learned of their associates' capture. Therefore, they cannot fail to report back to Mycroft the disappearance of those two agents, at best possible speed. Naturally they were going to deliver a message to their courier channel this morning. Just as we were naturally following our own leads to the same place."

"And Hadiya is the double agent?"

"Most certainly. A German delivered the message that will make its way back to London, to Mycroft's replacement—a German who takes his orders from Hadiya. And the Germans allow the business to remain open despite the high risk an import and export company represents to their security."

"So you checked the company's records to see who owned the company . . ."

"And found the Hadiya they spoke of."

"It is the same one?"

"Without doubt." Sigerson threw his cigarette into the fire and put his hands behind his head, stretching out. "What do you know about the Divine Wind, Zeki?"

The change of subject was not the surprise it might have been twenty-four hours ago. Zeki was becoming accustomed to Sigerson's non sequiturs. They rarely were the complete departure they appeared to be. Willingly, he tapped his memory for the requested information.

"I know he is the leader of a band of Arabs that roams through central and eastern Anatolia. He and his band of guerrillas have been single-handedly responsible for slowing down the German and Turkish war efforts in that area. And I know the Germans would do anything to pluck him from Anatolia and thrust him into a cell in the darkest corners of the Harbiye barracks." He pulled his knees to his chin and rested it upon them, thinking.

"I know, too, that the Turks consider the Divine Wind to be Allah's hand, the deliverer of justice. The righteous one. And many of the Germans, who once thought the entire thing the work of rumour-mongers and mischief-makers, are beginning to think of the Divine Wind as the embodiment of their bad luck." Zeki grinned. "Although they are very careful not to say that in front of their superior officers."

"Just lowly Turkish clerks with long ears," Sigerson added, lighting another cigarette. "I have heard of the Divine Wind, too. I heard him described as the nurturer of justice."

Zeki nodded. "Yes, I've heard of him spoken that way, too."

"You have? It's odd, isn't it, that you've heard of that, and you have been speaking Arabic almost constantly for two days, yet you entirely missed the connection."

"I did?" Zeki felt his jaw loosen in surprise.

Sigerson smiled a little. "I am being a little uncharitable. When you use a language that has been a part of your thinking since birth, you aren't often aware of the literal meanings of the words you use. The average Londoner would be shocked to realize the *bloody 'ell* he drops so casually was once in part a knight's sworn promise to do or die *by my lady*." He paused to blow cigarette smoke with contemplative slowness, watching it rise to the cracked plaster above. "Or that my family were originally named because their ancestor lived near a holly tree," he added. "For you, Zeki, perhaps *Hadiya* is too commonplace. I did not grasp the significance of the meaning until it was coupled with the last name." He let the name roll off his tongue, patently savouring it. "Hadiya Adlparvar."

Zeki felt a touch of irritation. Sigerson was clearly enjoying his bafflement. "I do not understand," he said simply.

"Arabic, Zeki!" He switched to English. "What does *Hadiya* mean?"

Zeki frowned. "Decency? Justice?" He heard the word, and repeated it softly, wonderingly. "Justice . . ."

"The closest meaning is 'a guide to righteousness,'" Sigerson added.

"Allah be praised!" Zeki sat up straight. His weariness had abruptly vanished. "And Adlparvar?"

"It is a compound name. Created from a mixture of Arabic and Persian. *Adl* is Arabic." Sigerson's brow lifted and he looked expectantly at him.

Zeki sought the answer, and found it. "Justice. Again."

"And I know enough Persian to know *parvar* translates loosely as 'one who nurtures.'" He paused again.

Zeki strung the clues together. "The nurturer of justice. The guide to righteousness." His heart started to thud. "The Divine Wind," he concluded. The enormity of the secret bemused him. "Are you sure?" he asked Sigerson, his voice low. "The Divine Wind, a secret German agent, or . . . or . . . a double agent?" He frowned. "Working for the British? It . . . it is. . . ." Finally, he simply shook his head, his English failing him.

"It is truly too much to grasp all at once," Sigerson agreed, returning to Arabic. "And I felt much as you do now, when I realized the significance of the name. Yet it makes perfect sense. How better to hide than out in the open for all to see?"

"But wait," Zeki said, holding out his hand. "The Divine Wind *fights* Turks and Germans. He wounds them at every opportunity . . ."

Sigerson was nodding, a smile lifting the corners of his mouth. "Rumours. Gossip. Unsubstantiated tales. Do you know a single person who has directly been involved in any of the Divine Wind's affairs?"

"No . . . but the Germans genuinely hate him! They spend all their time searching out the Divine Wind's spies, the ones who they are sure feed all the information about the Germans' movements and strategies out to the Divine Wind himself. Von Stein—" He sat bolt upright. "Von Stein hates him. He spends all his time searching for the Divine Wind. And now, he searches for the Divine Wind's informants. He is obsessed with finding him. And if the Divine Wind *is* a German agent, it does not make sense."

"It does if the Germans here in the Ottoman Empire do not know he is one of theirs." Sigerson spoke calmly, with complete confidence, and the firm note made Zeki pause.

"How could they not know?" He was utterly baffled.

"Berlin does not tell them."

"But that is . . . crazy!"

"As crazy as running a double agent who feeds corrupt information back to the British? Who learns through that contact with the British about your circle of agents, and methodically eliminates them, one by one, reaching right back to London itself?" Sigerson got to his feet with sudden energy. "There is a good purpose for such subterfuge, Zeki. One never knows what one may learn when one's true identity is masked. You, yourself, have used that situation to your own advantage, have you not?"

Zeki's lips thinned. "Yes," he said, his voice low.

"I have proof the Germans here do not know the Divine Wind's true role in their affairs. I heard it this morning at the Oriental Export company. You heard me tell of what happened. The German made a great show of arriving there and extorting goods from the manager, who played the little scenario out with perfect cooperation. It could only be to disguise the officer's true purpose. And this was confirmed the moment the manager shut his office door. The first words he spoke were *You bring news from Hadiya?* Clearly, the Divine Wind—Hadiya—has only one or two trusted contacts within Constantinople. The real information is delivered to Berlin, from where it is dispersed with great thought and efficiency where it will do the most damage at the most appropriate time."

"But why be so secret about it that your own men must suffer?"

"Hadiya is apparently of such strategic value, they cannot afford to let his true role be known to too many people." Sigerson paused hesitantly. "It is not the first time I have seen this pattern of command used in Berlin," he added at last. "It ensures the greatest security, the least likelihood that secret identities will be revealed."

That Sigerson had been mixed up in this sort of covert operation before was not a surprise to Zeki. The man had more than adequately demonstrated his skill at the work over the last two days. That he had been close enough to

Berlin to be familiar with the hierarchy and operational procedures was less obvious, but it made sense.

"You speak wisely, I believe," Zeki told him. "But one point still puzzles me. Hadiya must be here in the city, yet the Divine Wind, if he is anywhere, is on the far side of Anatolia. If they are the same man, he cannot be two places at once. How does he control affairs here in Constantinople from his saddle in far eastern Anatolia?"

"Does London not control you and your affairs, Zeki? And is not London even farther away?"

Zeki nodded. "You are right on both counts, *Effendi*."

"Besides," Sigerson added casually, "Central Anatolia is only four hundred miles from here. I crossed it in eight days, and I was not hurrying. For all you know, Zeki, Hadiya might actually be controlling his little empire from right here in Constantinople."

Zeki stared at the man. "You? You crossed Anatolia? Alone?"

"You sound startled, Zeki. You do not think me capable of such a journey, then?" Sigerson was smiling.

"Well . . . no!" Zeki waved his hand at Sigerson's well-pressed suit, which showed little wear or dirt despite a hard night's accommodation amongst dust and mortar, and the immaculate neatness of his appointments. "The patrols would have taken one look at you and arrested you on the spot. You would stand out like . . . like . . ."

"Like an Englishman in a desert?"

Zeki felt his cheeks warm. "Yes!" he declared.

"Demonstrably, I was not noticed." Sigerson frowned. "By anyone," he added thoughtfully. "And yet every day I was out there, I had thought that this day I would be found by the Divine Wind or his men. Yet I saw or heard no sign of him or his guerrillas the entire journey. Curious . . ." He lifted his gaze back to Zeki. "More proof, perhaps, that the Divine Wind is nothing but air and rumour?"

Zeki shrugged. "I don't know what to believe any more."

"Perhaps it was as well I did not meet him, after all. I had assumed the fellow was an ally, one I could call on for help if I needed it. Now when I do look him in the eye I will know him for what he is."

"*When?* You mean, you are going to look for him?"

"Yes, of course. That is the sole reason I returned to Constantinople."

"You came here to discover the identity of the man who betrayed my people. You have the name, now. Why do you wish to confront him?"

"To see his face, Zeki. To know him. To know I am right. One look is all I need."

Zeki shook his head. "Madness."

"Perhaps. I thought you might want to come along. They were your people, too."

"Fairuza is still alive," Zeki pointed out. "While there's a chance, I can't leave her to the Germans. They will question her until they're sure they have it all, and then they will execute her. Until that time, I have friends, people who will help me, or help Fairuza—people who do not mind working against the Germans if the risk is small enough. Between us, we might save her yet."

Sigerson nodded. "You must do right by your people," he agreed.

"You will face Hadiya for me, instead."

"With pleasure," Sigerson replied.

"So . . . tomorrow you will go back out into the hills of Anatolia? To hunt down Hadiya?"

"Tomorrow I go to Ankara by the weekly train, to collect my remaining possessions and the horse that was given to me by a friendly Australian officer."

"You have papers that will get you past the German patrols?"

"Of course. I acquired them in Ankara."

"And then?"

"And then I return to the eastern peaks of Anatolia to catch the Divine Wind."

Chapter Eight

THE LONE RIDER ENTERED THE VILLAGE ONLY A FEW HOURS after the German patrol had left. Caspar missed his arrival because he was seeing to the rounding up of the goats the Germans had scattered to the four winds in their usual disregard for the natural order of things.

But he did not fail to hear the calls of the women, and the odd note in their voices. It was enough. Caspar walked as quickly as his tired old bones would carry him, back to the centre of the village.

The women, hussies all of them, were standing about the legs of the stranger's horse, while he spoke to them from his saddle. He was an Arab—a Bedouin, if judged by his dark flowing robes. He was muffled to the eyes by his head cloth, which he had tucked around his face against the cold wind that was blowing in from the north.

He was trying to talk to the women with a mash of Turkish and Arabic. The women clung to each other and shyly giggled, burying their heads against each other's shoulders when they became too self-conscious. It had been many months since they had seen a virile man who did not wear a German tunic and stomp all over their gardens.

Caspar stepped up the pace of his hobble, working the long stick he carried to pull him along a little faster.

The Bedouin saw him approach and climbed out of his saddle. As Caspar approached, he bowed in greeting, but he did not uncover his face. Caspar was pleased at this Bedouin sign of respect but was careful not to show it.

"You're a long way from your homeland, rider," he suggested, calling up his rusty Arabic.

"Many of us are, these days, *Effendi*," the rider returned in hesitant Turkish. "I am looking for . . ." And he hesitated, obviously searching for the word he needed.

Caspar remained courteously silent. It would not do to presume the man's purpose. And he had time to spare a stranger additional embarrassment, when he was plainly seeking assistance of some sort.

The man looked down at his feet, and spoke a single crude word in another language.

Caspar laughed aloud. "*Vous parlez français?*" he asked.

"*Oui, monsieur. Je fais. Mais le français n'ait pas une langue que je prévois à entendre dans ce domaine.*" He spread his hands and, still in French, added, "These lands have never been captured by the French, after all."

Caspar shook his head. "I learned it from the same people as you, I would guess. I spent much time in the Sahara in my youth. I mingled much with the Legions—they taught me how to fire a rifle, how to clean a rifle, and how to swear." He laughed again, and clapped his hands to catch Jammina's attention, waving her towards the house.

"You are looking for . . . ?" he prompted the rider.

"My group . . . my tribe. I have been long apart from them, fulfilling my duties. I'm looking for news of them and where they might be."

Caspar nodded slowly, keeping his smile in place, while caution slid through him. "Asking for news of anyone but Germans is a risky errand, is it not?"

The rider tugged at his robes, displaying them. "If I am not shot on sight, *Effendi*, I know I will be safe in asking my question."

"You have met those who shoot first, then?"

He nodded. "A few." It was a cautious answer.

"Germans. The Turkish army."

"Not always."

Caspar considered him. "Your way has been hard, has it not?"

The man's answer was slow to emerge. "I have been searching for news of my people for five days. They have not been easy days, no."

"Hmmm." Caspar considered this. "I have heard of the group you seek. They were north of Malayta, where the Tohma joins the Firat."

"The Euphrates?"

"They call it that. You know the area?"

"I have been there before. Many years ago. There are the remains of a Roman road there."

"That is the place," Caspar agreed. He tapped his chest. "I am Caspar . . . and it is my duty to care for this village. I am all they have left now the stronger men have gone to fight the southern threat."

The Bedouin loosened his head cloth, and pulled it aside, revealing a thin, pale face beneath the sharp eyes. "My companions called me Barakah when I was last in this place."

White one. Caspar understood the name. "Barakah, my house, my food is yours. Will you partake with me?"

"Gladly. But I must risk offence by leaving shortly thereafter. I will not bring the wrath of the German Empire upon you, as I would if I were discovered here."

Caspar liked this tall Bedouin who swore in French and was so far from home. His own sons and grandsons were somewhere in the Holy Land, facing the might of Britain and her allies, and he liked to think that some stranger would offer them the same kindness, perhaps. It was the way of things, often. One poured the seeds upon the waters and let them flow where they might, to come to rest and root in far-off places.

"Come," he told Barakah. "A meal, and food for your horse, and we will see you on your way before sunset."

"Allah will notice your kindness," Barakah murmured, following Caspar into the house.

"He knows I do this only to practise my French and to please Jammina."

Barakah laughed a little. "I believe you, Caspar, but He is not that easy to fool."

SEVEN DAYS LATER, the tall Bedouin called Barakah, who was known as Sherlock Holmes elsewhere in the world, lay on his stomach on the crest of a low, flat rise in the land. He was using a collapsible telescope and studying a sharp, deep gully below him.

The last seven days had been easy, straightforward travelling. The days before that he had been casting amongst villages and lonely dwellings in the wilder areas of north-eastern Anatolia, searching for any gossip or news of the Divine Wind. The village elder, Caspar, had given him information that ended his search and sent him like an arrow to this lonely gully in the middle of barren, craggy land. For he had been to this place before.

The gully was a remote one—far from any well-trafficked routes, which made it the perfect place to hide a camp from casual observers. At the end of the blunt gully, protected and half hidden by sheer, curving walls, lay the camp of the Divine Wind. In the fading light, the movements of the robed figures about the camp were wide open to Holmes' scrutiny.

At the back of the gully there was a large, rectangular

tent, larger than those that huddled about it. Most of the activity of the camp was centred there. The command post.

Holmes had been watching this tent for most of the afternoon. He had already identified a number of key people in the camp, by simply observing their movements in and out of the main tent.

There was the small boy who had only recently reached manhood, for he continually adjusted his *kuffiya* and *agal*-rope, scratching under the cloth as he hurried from the main tent to the outskirts of the camp. The messenger boy.

Hadiya had brought a harem of one with him, too. Late in the afternoon, the black-shrouded and veiled woman had appeared at the opening of the tent—the first person to emerge who had not first entered. She had looked around with the alertness of a tense rabbit and then made her way to the stream that trickled along the base of the west side of the gully, constantly checking over her shoulder and all around her.

At the stream she had turned her back to the camp and refreshed herself, her movements hidden behind the voluminous black robes and veiling. She had hurried back to the tent with the same frightened skip in her step, while every man in the camp studiously ignored her.

Just on sunset, Hadiya himself appeared.

It was unmistakably Hadiya, for the entire camp seemed to tense and their behaviour become noticeably self-conscious. The two guards on either side of the tent flap straightened up, their rifles snapping upright against their shoulders. The men laughed harder, worked more industriously, and moved with more purpose and speed, while their tall leader standing at the opening to the tent observed the activity with a watchful eye, his arms crossed over a thick chest.

Holmes readjusted the focus of the telescope with infinite care and studied him.

Under the head cloth he revealed the same black eyes and weathered skin as most Bedouins. The eyes were set apart, while the sharply hooked nose lifted with sharp enquiry as his attention shifted and refocussed. The face was a gaunt one, but it showed strength.

Under Hadiya's top robe was belted a holster, and Holmes identified the butt of a high-calibre Smith & Wesson revolver. It was an unusual weapon. The chill breeze blowing with the coming sunset lifted his robes enough to show English riding boots beneath.

English boots, American weapons, and Bedouin attire. The guards held Russian rifles, and Holmes had noticed English and French bayonets and rifles scattered across the camp. There was a plethora of goods from every corner of the globe with the glaring exception of Germany.

The omission was a flare signal of illumination.

After a few minutes, Hadiya turned and re-entered the tent, and the flap was lowered behind him, a clear signal to all that Hadiya had retired for the night.

Holmes slithered back down the gentle slope until he could stand without being seen and walked back to where he had tethered the horse. He drank tepid water from a flask and watered the horse with the last of the water in the water skins carried on the saddle. He fitted the horse with a nose bag of feed and sat on the thigh-high rock beside it, facing towards the sinking sun.

He did not eat. His own food supplies had run out two days before, but he had continued on. He would not have made it back to the last place he had acquired supplies, and his quarry lay not far ahead. Instead, he looked to be enjoying the last of the day's warmth—for the evening was quickly becoming chilled.

When the sun dropped below the rolling horizon, he wrapped his head cloth about his face, tucking the front corners over the *agal*-rope, slipped the nose bag from the horse's head, and climbed up into the saddle. He urged the horse up the gentle slope to the top, then onto the long, slippery lee side of the hill.

The horse's feet slipped and skated along the rough shale slope, sending up a cloud of a dust and a loud rattle of gravel and pebbles that rolled down ahead of them, declaring their arrival.

A shout announced they had been sighted, and suddenly the camp that had been settling for the night became a stew pot of bubbling activity—men diving for their rifles, bellowing at each other.

It was a muted alarm, diluted by curiosity, for Holmes' Bedouin clothing was unmistakable, and he carried no weapons overtly. That curiosity allowed him to ride right into the middle of the coalescing troop before their mass slowed the horse. Hands reached for the halter, anchoring the beast.

He was pulled down from the saddle, his *kuffiya* pulled aside and his clothing probed. The golden knife and the revolver were quickly discovered and confiscated.

Holmes held up his arms. "I have come to speak to your leader! I intend no violence."

"You are not a Bedouin," came the accusation. "You speak like a foreigner."

"A foreigner who apes us." There was anger in that voice.

"I wish to have speech with your captain," Holmes reiterated as the rough hands prodded his body experimentally, looking for more booty. The clamour they were making as they discussed him and speculated on his identity and purpose almost completely masked his words.

He filled his lungs and lifted his voice. "I am here to speak to Hadiya Adlparvar!" he shouted.

Total silence was his response, as every pair of eyes surrounding him grew wider.

THEY PUSHED, PULLED and pummelled him into the big tent, to drop him onto his knees on the carpets in the main section of the tent. A small folding table was before him, and the *ma'nad*—the curtain that divided the sitting place where Holmes sprawled from the traditional women's place—hung behind. There was no-one in the sitting area, and the men who had transported Holmes to the tent departed after dumping his knife and revolver on the table.

The two guards Holmes had watched from the top of the gully now stepped inside the tent, their rifles cocked and resting across both hands, wary expressions on their faces.

Hadiya slipped through the curtain, followed by a woman dressed and veiled in the traditional heavy black robes. Only her eyes were revealed behind the veil, and they were lowered, her head down. She moved to the corner of the sitting area, and stood silent, her head still lowered.

Hadiya picked up the knife on the table and examined it. He jerked his chin towards Holmes. "Search him properly," he said to the guards.

The smaller of the two searched Holmes' clothing and body with infinitesimal care, and added to the collection on the table a stale packet of Turkish cigarettes, a nearly empty packet of Russian cigarettes, a box of sulphur matches, a small notebook and gold propelling pencil.

Hadiya pushed the items around with a long forefinger, his expression thoughtful. "The horse?" he said shortly.

They brought Holmes' saddle bags inside, and withdrew the contents, laying them out on the table. The little amount of feed for the horse that remained was placed on the carpet. There was a tin pan, a spoon, some herbs twisted inside a cloth, and clothing. A box of bullets to go with the revolver.

The bags were tipped upside down to indicate their empty state.

Hadiya studied Holmes again. "No watch. No identification. Yet he knows the name Hadiya, and he speaks with an accent." He paused, considering. "Did you check the boots?"

The guard behind him removed Holmes' boots, and tipped them upside down and shook. Two fine probes, the pair that had successfully overcome the padlock on the window of a warehouse in Constantinople, fell silently to the carpet.

The guard dumped the boots and laid the probes on the table.

Hadiya's brows drew together, and he turned the probes over and around thoughtfully. Finally he put them aside gently and faced Holmes.

"You are not German."

"No."

He considered the short answer for a moment longer, then waved to the woman standing in the corner. "Vashti has a gift. She remembers every word ever spoken. I let her hear words I think I might need to be retrieved some time, somewhere. It makes things . . . official. You understand?"

The implied reasoning behind such a need for records was that Hadiya might one day be called upon to justify his actions. It spoke of higher masters.

But there was something else of greater significance in the man's words. Holmes was not the only one with an accent. For Hadiya spoke with the slightest inflexion—so minute it might have been missed by less-keen ears.

Holmes, however, had no trouble identifying it, for once upon a time he had lived with it for nearly two years and heard no other tongue.

Hadiya's accent was Persian.

Holmes thoughtfully donned his footwear once more.

"Your name?" Hadiya demanded.

"Barakah."

"And what are you doing here?"

"I came to find you, Hadiya Adlparvar."

The man lifted his hand for silence. Then he spoke quickly to the guards, and they stepped outside the tent. The flap was lowered.

Hadiya picked up Holmes' revolver from the table and checked it was loaded. He placed it ostentatiously just within reach of his hand. His own American gun he loosened in its holster.

"That is not my name," Hadiya said, his voice low. Without looking at the woman, he said, "Vashti. Tea."

The woman moved to another small table in the rear corner and poured him a cup of mint tea from an elegant samovar, which was kept warm with a gentle flame from a lamp beneath. She offered Holmes the small cup, which he accepted, then backed away and returned to her corner. Every movement was completed without lifting her gaze from her feet for a single moment.

"You have no right to hold me here," Holmes said, and sipped the tea. It was excellent. "I am a civilian."

"Have you not heard? There are no civilians. We are all soldiers in the eyes of the Lord," Hadiya replied.

"Praise be to Allah," Holmes intoned, his mind racing. "Why are Persians fighting a war so far from their homeland?"

The silence that greeted his question was as loud as a shout.

Finally, Hadiya said gruffly, "We are Bedouins. Surely, as you ape our ways and clothes, you know that."

"Your accent declares your lie. You are Persian. From the mountains, too."

Hadiya considered this a moment. "Bedouin. Persian. It does not matter," he declared. "We have all found a greater enemy on our doorstep. Tell me, gentle guest, why is a civilian combing the slopes of these hills, moving so carefully between the cracks of two mighty armies?" Hadiya smiled a little at Holmes' expression. "You were seen passing by one of my outpost sentries this morning. We have been aware of your scrutiny all along."

"I'm looking for Hadiya Adlparvar, who goes by the name the Divine Wind."

"The Divine Wind? I have heard the fanciful tales about this warrior. He doesn't exist."

"I'm sure he does."

"If he did, I would most certainly know of him."

"Exactly the conclusion I have drawn. I believe you know Hadiya Adlparvar far more intimately than any evening tale."

"You believe?"

"I have spent several weeks tracing Hadiya. Throughout my investigations, I have heard tales of the Divine Wind—as the guide to righteousness, the nurturer of justice. Last week I learned that the man I seek goes by the name Hadiya Adlparvar . . . a name which translates as the guide to righteousness and the nurturer of justice."

"A similarity in reputations. And you based your excursion to these parts upon this remarkable coincidence?"

"I did not tell you I came here from elsewhere when I learned the name. Why do you assume that?"

"You said you came in search of the Divine Wind because of an unlucky resemblance to a man you seek. Yet the Divine Wind was not your first target." Hadiya spread his hand. "This is a very large country. There is so little out here that would occupy a man of your . . . interests. And you do not carry the marks of a man who had been here for some time." He considered Holmes anew. "Why have you gone to this much trouble?"

"I give my reasons to Hadiya Adlparvar himself."

The man studied him, his face impassive. He said softly, "I do not know this man Hadiya Adlparvar."

Holmes shrugged. "Then we are at an impasse."

And then it happened. Hadiya's eyes cut away from Holmes, and he and the woman exchanged a glance.

Holmes felt his pulse race. A man looking to a woman in this land of female chattels?

Abruptly, all the new information he had learned in this short interview rapidly formed a new pattern and locked into place.

"It is small wonder no one knows this man Hadiya Adlparvar," Holmes said slowly. "He has managed to remain safely undetected and recognized because he is really *a woman*."

Again, there was a long silence.

The pair exchanged glances again. Then the woman held up her hand to the man and stepped forward. "Yes, I am Hadiya Adlparvar," she said, her voice low and musical, but with a rough note, as if she had been straining it lately.

"I have come a long way to speak to you."

"Why do you seek to find me?"

Holmes looked pointedly at the man and she raised a dismissive hand. "I trust Cyrus implicitly."

"But I do not. You must forgive a guest his idiosyncrasies, Hadiya, but I have nearly lost my life through treachery not once but twice while searching for you."

She considered him a moment, then exchanged quick words with Cyrus. It was telling that her trusted lieutenant left with barely any argument.

The tent flap dropped back into place, leaving him alone with Hadiya. She was silent and still, apparently in no rush to continue the interview.

Holmes reached for the revolver on the table. He cocked it and pointed it at Hadiya. "The game is over, Hadiya." He pulled off his head dress with the other hand. "I am a British agent, and I have been searching for you. You are the rogue who has betrayed and murdered my people."

She remained silent, pointedly not removing her own enveloping head gear. "British?" she finally asked, her voice hoarse.

"You have been under suspicion for some time now." Holmes considered her a moment longer. "Despite my origins, Hadiya Adlparvar, I am still able to feel the insult of not revealing one's face. I have done you the courtesy, after all."

When she still hesitated, he added, "Your anonymity has long since passed out of your reach. It is time to stop this silly game and reveal yourself."

His demand seemed to agitate her.

"You have no choice," Holmes insisted. "Come, Hadiya, for a military genius, you are very slow to recognize a point of no return. You can always kill me later. Or vice versa."

She considered him a moment longer. "On the contrary. I could no more kill you than slice off my own hand." She reached up for the face veil and slowly detached it and lifted it away. She dropped it to the table and added in perfect English, "As you well know, Holmes."

Recognition hit Holmes like a blow, and it took several seconds for his labouring heart to catch up the beat again. Through lips that felt numb he formed her name. "Elizabeth."

The revolver dropped to the carpet.

Chapter Nine

"I HAVE BEEN UTTERLY BLIND," HOLMES SAID, SOME TIME later.

They were in the women's quarters of the tent, where Elizabeth had brought him. She offered him a chair but sat upon cushions herself.

"Not totally blind," she answered him. "You found me, after all."

Holmes rejected the chair and lowered himself onto another cushion, and studied her.

She sat perfectly still, allowing him the study.

There were differences time had wrought. Beneath the black silky robes she was still as slim and supple as he remembered, but the steel strength that only he had known existed in her was a little more apparent now.

She wore the invisible cloak of command well, but there were a tension and weariness that told of harsh decisions and life lived on the edge. The green eyes were unchanged. They were staring at him, now, waiting.

"For once, I didn't foresee this," he said slowly. "And in hindsight, I should have at least surmised . . ."

"Why? You thought me dead," she said crisply. "Leave

it, Holmes—we don't have time. I have another appointment in twenty minutes. And there is much we must talk about." She pushed his cup closer to him. "Drink. And tell me—are you really an agent? Part of Stainsbury's system? Or do you, too, report directly and only to Mycroft?"

Holmes closed his eyes briefly. "You *are* Mycroft's agent," he said flatly. "And you are not working for the Germans, so—"

"You came looking for a German agent? Here?" Anger wove through the words.

"I had good reason."

"You usually do." She settled her hands in her lap. It was a calming motion. "Tell me what brought you here," she added quietly.

Holmes related the events since his arrival in the Middle East and Mycroft's assault in desiccated tones. He omitted no facts, and Elizabeth absorbed it all without interruption. When he had finished she remained silent, her gaze unfocussed. After a while she stirred and her gaze returned to him.

"I can see no errors in your assumptions."

"There are none."

"Yet you arrived at a completely erroneous conclusion." She smiled a little. "I am not a German agent, Holmes."

"I know. You would not harm Mycroft, even through a second party. But it may be someone else in your camp. The fellow who poses as Hadiya. Cyrus."

"Impossible. He has never set foot in Constantinople. And his men are loyal to Hadiya. To me."

"They are Persians? All of them?"

"Yes, all of them. Hand-picked by me. I know these men—I know their temper, and I know what motivates them. Your German agent is not of their number."

"Why are you so certain?"

"Because they fight for vengeance's sake." Elizabeth lifted her hand, palm up. "There is no greater prod to man than fear or desire. And they desire the blood of Germans. They want it to flow across the sand as their wives' and children's blood flowed."

"Abadan," Holmes spoke. "They are from Abadan."

"Not originally. But they were there, living and working for me, when the Turks—under German control—crossed over the border from Mesopotamia and blew up the refinery in 1915."

"Working for you?"

She smiled a little. "Does it seem so strange?"

"The Anglo-Persian Export company . . . it is yours?"

"It was, once. It is a public corporation now, and it spreads across the globe." There was a hint of pride in her voice. "One of the company's interests is oil. I have good, scientific research that gives me reason to believe southern Persia is rich with it, and have speculated to that effect. The refinery the Turks destroyed in 1915 was the first fruit of that speculation."

She waved a hand at the walls of the tent, symbolically including the whole camp. "These men were there."

"After four hard years, would they still thirst for vengeance?"

"Perhaps not, but their loyalty to me is unquestionable."

"Not entirely. I question it."

She pursed her lips for a moment. "They have been with me for the last thirteen years," she said softly. "Long before this war was an inevitability. These men, Holmes, once guarded and drove Sullah's goods trains across Anatolia and Persia, until real trains replaced that necessity."

Holmes remained silent.

"From Sullah's family business grew the export company," she added. "I was there right from the beginning."

"You *were* in Persia when Watson came looking for you. You were with Sullah all the time."

She hesitated again. Then she slid back the material of

her gown from her wrist and consulted a modern-looking wristwatch. "I must go. It is nearly time for evening prayers, and I have an appointment that cannot wait." She stood up. "I will have food brought to you at once. Your saddle bags were missing that item."

"And they have been empty of food for three days," Holmes admitted.

"Then I will delay your supper no longer."

LATER THAT NIGHT, when Holmes had dined well and long, Elizabeth returned. She spoke of nothing concerning her business, but instead sat on the same cushion as before, a cup of mint tea before her.

"I am recovered," he assured her. "Enough that my mind is free once more to concentrate on the problem at hand. I seek a man—a German agent—who has betrayed all of us. He is not you. And you assure me he is not one of your men."

"On that you must trust me," she added. "They have been with me a very long time, and I speak for them all."

"I will accept that for now My reasoning has been restored along with my full stomach, and I have come to some conclusions while you were gone."

"I will hear them."

"First, I must know how you came to work for Mycroft. I need a complete picture."

She sipped her tea before beginning, "Mycroft did not know it was me. All our dealings have been completely anonymous.

"Contact has always been indirect. I approached him, originally. When the war broke out I was . . . well, I was in Europe. I gathered some initial information together and channelled it through to Mycroft personally. I knew he'd take the information seriously. Heaven knows no one else would have given much serious thought to information dropping into their laps out of nowhere. I was right, he did take notice, and after a few more installments, he trusted me."

"And eventually used you."

"Yes. That is, after all, what I intended."

"No one knows of this . . . activity?"

"These men? No. They are concerned only with the activities of the Divine Wind."

"Then how does your information get to Mycroft from here?"

"I take it to Constantinople myself. From there it is couriered as a small, unremarkable package via the export company to London, where it is placed in the post and delivered to Mycroft by the efficient penny postmen."

"You have been very active. Very mobile."

"It has been to my advantage, my experience in travelling quickly and unobtrusively." She smiled. "No-one has beaten my times through the Alps. Not even you."

"Your record will continue to stand uncontested by me," Holmes assured her. "How do you come by your information, out here?"

"Observation. Deduction. And a carefully built network of gossip collectors and rumour merchants. The truth comes in many guises—one just has to pan for the gold amongst the detritus—" She grimaced. "Why do I repeat back to you a truism that you yourself taught me?"

"It's a truism that bears repeating," he said.

She smiled a little. "London's scandal sheets are, here, the women, servants and enlisted men of two empires. Between them they keep me floating upon a sea of fact and conjecture. That is where I had to go this evening. While Hadiya's men were occupied with evening prayers, I was sharing coffee with a woman from a village near here—a village close to the winter quarters of a Turkish military patrol. We camped here nearly a year ago, and I met her then. Tonight she had much to tell me about the excesses of the troops, the hardships her family are enduring, the handsome officers . . . including their names and ranks and duty rosters, which she has catalogued and memorized so that she might coordinate her leisure time with the off-duty hours of the most desirable of them."

"This explains why the Divine Wind is so well-informed. The Germans fully believe he is supplied his information from a source right amongst them. Another agent."

Elizabeth's smile broadened and became mischievous. "Perhaps they are right," she suggested.

The sound of rifle fire was unexpectedly loud—the single shot echoed against the rugged sides of the gully.

Immediately, there was a cry of protest from somewhere in the camp and return fire—many shots that blended together.

Elizabeth surged to her feet, and was gone even as Holmes was rising to his. He hurried through to the main section of the tent, just as Cyrus burst through from the outside, his gun in his hand.

"Germans!" he declared to Elizabeth, who was checking a revolver of her own. "Dozens of them."

The sound of firing was growing steadily.

"Tell the men to disperse—scatter as far as they can." She slid the gun into a hidden pocket within her robes, and looked up at Cyrus. "This is the mischance we thought might come one day."

"You still do not believe you have an agent among you?" Holmes asked. "One who directed them here the moment I arrived?"

Cyrus turned on him. "You brought them here yourself, English dog."

"Enough!" Elizabeth snapped. "Concentrate on the present, or all will be lost. There is still hope, Cyrus. Disbanding and running will give some of us a chance to avoid the Germans—they cannot chase us all if we are separated. And those they do chase will weaken their ranks by separating their numbers. The men all know to make their way back and meet here when the Germans have finally departed."

Cyrus gave a short bow, his hand to his heart, and whirled and slipped from the tent.

There was a muted *slap!* Elizabeth flinched a little. "This tent will be their first target. They're in range now. We must hurry."

It was then Holmes realized the little noise was that of a bullet punching through the material of the tent.

Elizabeth picked up a skin with a long thong that she slid over her shoulder. From the gurgling it made and the swollen shape, it clearly carried liquid. Water. For a long trek. She adjusted her veil, and looked at Holmes. "You must come with me."

"I will make you their prime target if I am with you."

"Holmes, they're not here for you. It's me they're looking for. The Divine Wind."

"You believe I brought them here?"

She moved to the back of the tent. "It is a curious coincidence that the Germans, who have failed to find us in over three years, suddenly discover us the moment you arrive. Did you bring them upon us? I do not know for certain." She reached for the bottom of the tent.

"I'm sorry, Elizabeth." The quietly spoken words, falling amongst the sounds of chaos and panic that seeped in from outside, made her pause and glance at him.

"I have brought danger upon you once more," he added.

Through the veil he could not see her expression, but her eyes narrowed as if she had suddenly smiled. "This is a danger I have courted for years. Do not worry for me. Cyrus willingly bears the brunt of their desire to find me. That is why I set up the operation this way."

"I would have done that for you. I tried to."

She dropped her gaze. "I know." For a moment she stared at her feet, until another bullet slapped through the tent, and ricocheted against the samovar with a sour whine. Then she gathered the loose long robes about her, and pulled up the edge of the tent.

"Come," she said. "We must employ the back exit."

THE TENT HUGGED the back of the gully, protected on three sides by unscalable cliffs. The walls of layered stone rose directly before them as Holmes and Elizabeth emerged from the tent into the blackness of a night without a moon. The camp was well lit with cooking fires, but into this pocket only shadows reached.

Elizabeth pulled at his jacket sleeve. "This way."

They moved towards the cliff, skirting larger boulders, keeping to the deeper shadows at the base. In their black robes they melded into the night.

Holmes sighted the narrow crevice ahead of them—another blacker shadow amongst shadows—when the bullet hit him. There was a sudden, sharp agony, and then he was falling to the unforgiving ground.

Elizabeth dropped the water skin and sank down beside him as Holmes clutched at his thigh, gritting his teeth. Blood welled slowly around his fingers.

She pulled off her veil, and quickly tore it into strips. "How bad is it?"

He grimaced. "The bone is broken . . . at least." His breath was uneven, his voice tight with control. The leg felt as heavy as iron, and ablaze with pain. Clammy perspiration broke out on his forehead.

Elizabeth looked around for any possible splints, but the rocky ground was barren. Moving fast, she pulled his robes aside and bound the wound over the top of his trousers as best she could with the strips of veiling.

"It's not a compound fracture. The bandage will stem the blood flow, but that is all I can do here, with no medical kit." She stood up and held out her hand. "Here."

"You can't carry me."

"I'm not leaving you."

"You must."

"*No!*" Her voice was low, intense. "There is a cave only a few feet ahead—it emerges into another valley far from here. We have only to reach it to gain a degree of safety. I will leave no-one to the Germans' tender mercies."

She lifted a finger in warning. "Don't give me any of your stiff upper lip, Holmes. If I leave you they will draw every last drop of information out of you, kill you, and come for me."

"Elizabeth—"

She grasped his wrists, and with a abrupt, strong surge, pulled him up onto his good leg. She slipped under one arm. "You'll have to help me."

Holmes ground his teeth together to combat the pain motion gave him, his consciousness swimming in and out of focus. After a small moment that stretched for eternity, he found his vision was whole again.

Elizabeth was patiently waiting, holding him upright. "Holmes?"

"I'm still here." It came out as a gasp.

"I warn you, if you faint on me, I'll throw you over my shoulder and carry you like a sack of potatoes, and your dignity be damned."

"I will keep that in mind."

He could barely hobble, hurry though he did. Elizabeth was carrying him more than assisting him, and his injured leg dragged uselessly. Every pebble and rock the loose foot bumped over sent hurtful waves through the leg.

An eon passed before they reached the cave, but Elizabeth did not stop. Coal-black darkness enveloped them, and cold brushed their faces.

He thought they had changed direction a little when she halted and picked up his hand and guided it to touch the rock wall. "I need both hands," she explained. Even though she whispered, the cave picked up the sibilant and echoed it endlessly.

He supported himself against the wall and listened to quiet movements, the rustle of her robes, and the clink of glass against metal. "You have a lamp here?"

There was a furry scraping sound and a sulphur match flared in the dark, illuminating her face beneath the black head cloth. "What use is a bolt hole if one can't see the way through it?" She smiled a little. "We'll have to risk light even though we're not deep enough inside the cave to avoid detection. The way becomes . . . challenging, further in." She lifted the kerosene lamp with the wire handle and held it out to him. "You must carry this."

He took the lamp in his free hand and she ducked beneath his arm again, and took his weight once more.

"How far?" he asked.

The cold was seeping into his bones now, and he shivered once.

"Far enough to know we cannot afford to dally," she said quietly. "You least of all, in this cold."

They began their peg-leg progress again, the lamp swinging wildly from Holmes' hand in response to his drunken gait.

The narrow way they were following abruptly opened out into an enormous cavern. There was a rustle and stir in the air and Elizabeth came to a complete halt. "Shut your eyes!" she commanded, and shielded her face by twisting and tucking her chin to her shoulder.

Knowing what was coming, he obeyed.

Abruptly, cold air fanned his face in a steady, blowing stream, accompanied by thousands of quick clicking noises.

Bats, disturbed by the light of the lamp and the noise of the humans' arrival, were leaving the cavern in an elongated cloud. They would pass out through the long slit Holmes and Elizabeth had just traversed.

"They'll let them know where we are!" Holmes said, lifting his voice a little.

"Not if we're no longer here when they arrive."

The current of air against his face slackened, and he opened his eyes, and lifted the lamp. "Where are we going?"

"You cannot see it from here. The lamp will not reach that far. On the other side of the cavern there are a number of cracks and holes. Only one of them leads to the next valley."

She pushed him into forward movement across the sandy floor of the cavern.

They walked for long minutes until the swinging arc of the lantern began to radiate off stone, ahead. When the walls were fully illuminated, Elizabeth paused.

"I must check my bearings," she explained, and her voice was low and a little breathless. She studied the walls. "Could you lift the lamp?"

Holmes obliged and a moment later she said, "Yes, now I have it."

They hobbled forward again, their direction slightly adjusted. The sloping, broken wall ahead of them held three fissures at ground level, and another four at various heights.

"Which one?" he asked, his own breath ragged.

"The lower one, thank goodness."

The slot she led him to was tucked into the crease of an outcrop of the wall and was the least obvious of those on the floor level of the cave.

Inside, after a few paces, it enlarged into an irregular, down-sloping path.

"This will lead us almost directly to the next valley over. We'll go steadily downhill now. It's quite a distance." She looked up at him from under his arm.

"You should rest when you need to," he told her.

She shook her head. "There's nothing stopping them from following us, and the way is level and wide enough that they could use horses if they wanted to."

"The opening is narrow—they could only pass through it one horse at a time."

"One man with a rifle is all they need. And we're barely moving a mile an hour. Resting is not a luxury we can indulge in."

They began their long walk.

Silence, broken only by the sounds of their exertion, was their companion until they broke from the mouth of the breach and found themselves in a dried-up stream bed that led into the narrow valley ahead.

Elizabeth doused the lamp.

Compared to the unbroken blackness of the cave, the night was ablaze with starlight.

They worked their way clear of the stream bed and began the hard trek down the valley, heading for the way a mile or so ahead where the cliffs dropped away and the valley opened out. Until they escaped the narrow valley, the chance of being overtaken by the Germans was all too real.

They had been travelling for twenty minutes when Holmes sensed a reverberation beneath the one foot in which he still had feeling.

"Cavalry," he said.

"I know," Elizabeth said between deep breaths. "Coming up behind us. About . . . five minutes away."

"And we're still in the valley," he added. "The slopes?"

"It's a fifty-degree slope, Holmes. I'd be foolish to attempt the climb unaided even on my good days."

"How far to the end of the pass?"

Elizabeth concentrated on her footsteps for a beat. "We'll be lucky indeed to make it."

Their speed increased a fraction, as the sounds of pursuing horses grew louder. The tattoo of hooves was a frenetic heartbeat pounding at them.

"We're not going to make it," Holmes said calmly.

"Shut up!" she said flatly.

Two more broken steps.

"You should leave me. You could reach the end of the valley without me."

She did not answer.

"I'm a single British agent. I will tell them very little of affairs in this corner of the world, and they will believe I know no more. You know too many people, too many secrets, to risk that exposure."

The thudding of horses was distinct now. They could hear the riders calling to each other.

Their calls were in German.

"They knew which crevasse to use because my blood showed them the way," Holmes added. "And I am bleeding still."

Elizabeth's silence continued, as did her dogged progress.

"Elizabeth . . ."

"No!"

"Elizabeth, you must leave me here."

"Not this time."

Holmes pulled his arm from her grip and pushed her away from him. He sank to the ground. "This time, I make the choice," he said. "Go. They're almost here."

He knew she understood the priorities that must power her decision. She was a leader of hard, uncompromising men, and such decisions came naturally to her.

She sank down beside him. "I will get you back to London," she said softly. "This is not the end of it."

"I know."

Her hand rested against his cheek, and her lips touched his. Then she flexed herself back to her feet, and was gone into the night with the suddenness of a fleeing deer.

Holmes wiped her tears from his cheek and sat back on his hands to await the arrival of the Germans.

Chapter Ten

VON STEIN REFLECTED UPON HIS GOOD LUCK AND BECAME even unhappier.

"This matter grows more complicated by the minute," he growled, sinking his chin into his hand and staring out the window.

"Sir?" Heinz ventured nervously. He was sitting on a straight-backed chair, highly polished boots square, knees together, clipboard straight and pencil poised.

"Again, run through it for me," Von Stein ordered.

"All of it?"

"The highlights will do, but start from the beginning."

Heinz cleared his throat and looked down at the clipboard. "As you know, sir, Berlin issued orders that we were to find and follow a man of a certain description who would be arriving in Ankara on the weekly train. If we were to follow him carefully, without giving ourselves away, he would lead us directly to the Divine Wind."

"Which we did."

"Which we did," Heinz agreed. "You sent your best hunter, Richenburg, and a small troop of men, with orders to commission reinforcements from the post at Ankara.

Then Richenburg found the man on the train and followed him. The man did not appear to know he was being followed. Nevertheless, Richenburg very nearly lost him on at least three separate occasions, for the man used a series of loops and cut-offs designed to throw off any pursuit.

"The man proceeded to a country hostel on the outskirts of the city. He disappeared inside and emerged a day later dressed as a Bedouin. He had a horse, well laden with supplies, and while Richenburg contrived to follow him by borrowing a vehicle, the major in charge of the troop requisitioned mounts and supplies from the base, and waited for Richenburg to report in.

"Richenburg successfully followed the man to eastern Anatolia, to a camp of Bedouins. At the camp, the man was taken into the tent of the leader and did not reemerge. Given what we know about the Divine Wind, it was presumed this was the Divine Wind's camp and that the man had reached his goal.

"The major brought the troop within rifle range of the camp and ordered them to attack."

"The first mistake," Von Stein murmured.

"Yes, sir," Heinz said expressionlessly.

"You do not agree?"

"Oh, it was a bad choice *strategically*, sir—I do not argue with you. But I can guess at the temper of the men. Three weeks without action, following an erratic wanderer, would not have endeared them to him. And then to be within hailing distance of the Divine Wind—the man who has caused so much grief amongst their fellow soldiers over the last few years? If I had been told I must walk away, leave the Divine Wind in peace, after suffering three weeks of discomfort to find him, I am not sure I would have been especially pleased."

"*Especially pleased*? That is a beautiful understatement, Heinz." Von Stein's mouth curled a little. "You have a point. Besides, the major was a long way from his command. Under the circumstances I believe we can forgive him for giving the order to attack."

Heinz nodded and glanced back at his clipboard.

"During the running battle that followed, some Bedouins were captured. But not many—not as many as should have been caught. They were good fighters, and they know the trick of blending in with the sand and disappearing. They slipped away like water from the hand."

"Of course they are good at escaping us, Heinz. They've been practising it for three years."

"Yes, sir." Heinz checked his clipboard again. "Richenburg had seen their leader emerge from the tent a few times, and examined both the prisoners and the bodies, but none of them were the Divine Wind."

"And now the Divine Wind and his men are dotted about Anatolia and will be impossible to pick up unless we hunt down each of them, one Arab at a time."

"However, Richenburg did follow the trail of the man who had led them to the camp. He had apparently been shot at one point, and a blood trail lay through a cave system that gave access to the next valley. In that valley they found the man himself. He was in such a state that he could not have made his way there unassisted, yet his helpers had deserted him."

"And no-one knows who the helpers were."

"Richenburg suspects, and the major concurs, that it was probably the woman the Divine Wind kept in the tent with him. She was not captured, and the tent was quite close to the cave system. As she dropped her water skin during her escape, they are confident that she will perish in the desert. Besides," and Heinz smiled, "they had a better prize on their hands."

"The injured man," Von Stein added.

"Indeed. There is a Turkish outpost not far from the camp, and they took him there for emergency treatment.

His wound was attended, and his clothes and all he carried examined. The Divine Wind had apparently begun the same task, for they found the traveller's saddle bags inside the command tent, and they examined these also."

"And that is how they discovered the man is English," Von Stein concluded, "which makes the entire expedition extremely messy and complicated."

Heinz frowned. "I'm not sure I understand how uncovering an English agent could be considered messy."

"Because it brings Berlin into it. When I was informed of the man's nationality I, in turn, informed Berlin. In response, I was treated to a flurry of wires which insisted I bring the man to Constantinople, treat him like I would my own brother, and wait for Berlin to deal with him." Von Stein sighed. "They're sending someone to take over the man's interrogation."

"It would appear the *Englisher* is more important than we first realized," Heinz concluded.

"He had no identifying papers on him at all?"

Heinz pursed his lips as he consulted the clipboard. "Only Turkish travelling papers for the name Raki, which we assumed were false. But the western clothing beneath his Arab robes was tailored in London, and other possessions were of British manufacture."

"It's the details that trip a man up," Von Stein observed.

"I do not believe he thought he would have to stand up to close examination."

"Possibly not, but it was careless of him. What of the hostel he used in Ankara?"

"The major got word to the base in Ankara and a few men were sent to investigate. The house was empty, the owners fled. Richenburg says the *Englisher* would have told them to go away for a while, as a purely precautionary measure. It is what he would have done under similar circumstances."

"So we cannot follow that path of investigation. The

owners would have learned by now that Germans were in their home. They won't come back."

"Which leaves us with the *Englisher* we are not permitted to speak to," Heinz summarized.

"Oh, we can speak to him," Von Stein returned.

"Sir?"

Von Stein swivelled away from the window to properly face his desk and Heinz. "Berlin won't tell me who this *Englisher* is. Very well. I will find out for myself. He has been in the city at least once—that much is clear, as he was on the weekly train from Constantinople. It's possible he is the source of information the Divine Wind has been using to track German and Turkish troop movements and activities. I would confirm that before I put the man into the hands of higher authorities."

He tapped his desk thoughtfully. "Do you speak English, Heinz?"

"No sir . . . and the *Englisher* does not speak German or Turkish."

"I need to find someone with English—outside the barracks. None of my usual translators. I want to keep this quiet. No word, no rumour must reach back to Berlin."

Heinz frowned. "If it is discretion you want, then perhaps . . . well . . ."

"What?" Von Stein snapped.

"I hesitate, sir, because it is a most unconventional proposal."

"Yes, yes."

"Sir, Madame Häfner, I believe, speaks English well enough."

"Madeline?" Von Stein frowned. "How odd."

"She learned it as a child, for she had an English nanny. Although Major Häfner had the grace to be embarrassed when he admitted it."

"She has been ill—indisposed."

"William says she is well again, and I saw her myself,

sir, this morning. She used the car. Some dressmaker appointment—she was excited about a fabric shade she'd acquired . . ."

Von Stein pursed his lips, then nodded. "See to it, Heinz. Have Häfner ask her, or do it yourself. If we do this correctly, and can get the *Englisher* to talk, then we may finally learn more about the structure of the allied agents' network in the city."

"The woman—Fairuza—was of no use?"

Von Stein grimaced. "She's strong, that one. I'm beginning to think we won't get anything from her. Not now."

"But now we have the *Englisher* . . . ?"

"Yes, the *Englisher*. He's important. Berlin's frantic activities tell me that. I want to learn his secrets. I want to open up the secrets of this entire city." He grinned. "That would make a prize well worth all the messiness and complications, Heinz."

THE OFFICER CALLED Von Stein appeared on the fifth morning of Holmes' incarceration at the barracks of Harbiye.

He strolled into Holmes' cell with the casual pace of a passer-by. Holmes had seen lions at London Zoo pad about their cages with the same loose gait, and his sense of caution leapt high.

This man was not to be dismissed nonchalantly.

He was looking around the moderately sized cell with mild interest, inspecting the appointments.

The fold-down bed was semi-comfortable, the thin mattress clean and free of vermin. The stone floor and walls were smooth and unmarked, although in the early morning hours a chill seeped from them that the daylight and warm air from the tiny barred window high up in the outside wall did little to disperse.

During those hours, Holmes wrapped the blanket from the bunk about his shoulders.

Because of the splints and bandaging on his leg it was more comfortable to stay on the bunk. There was no other seating in the room.

Von Stein stopped in the corner and turned to face Holmes, his hands behind his back. He glanced at the crisp white fresh bandaging. "*Könnte ses sein daß sie einen kleinen Unfall gehabt haben?*"

Holmes did not look down at his leg. "I don't speak German." He gave a little shrug.

"*Kein Deutsch? Wie günstig.*"

Von Stein stepped to the door, opened it and called out in German: "Please request Madame Häfner to attend."

"Yes, sir!" came the response.

"And get two chairs!"

"Yes, sir!"

Two hard straight-backed chairs were brought to the cell, and Von Stein arranged them facing Holmes. He sat on one, watching Holmes. "I am almost certain you do understand German, my friend. But I will play out your whimsy."

Holmes stared blankly at him.

Light footsteps in the passage heralded Madame Häfner's arrival. Von Stein stood and watched the door expectantly.

Holmes looked up as the door opened to reveal Madame Häfner. She was a dark-haired, perfectly coiffed woman in her forties, dressed in a shimmering, expensive dinner dress, a fur stole, and glittering jewels. Tall, slim, with sharp, intelligent green eyes.

Holmes fought to keep his face expressionless, overriding the natural reaction of deep shock with sheer, iron will.

It was Elizabeth!

Von Stein held out his hand. "Madame Häfner . . .

Madeline . . . I am so sorry to interrupt your evening meal and card game."

"You can make up for it later, Alexander," Elizabeth told him with a smile. "By escorting me back for *schnapps*."

"You must forgive me for asking this of you. I am well aware of your abhorrence for the gruesome side of my trade. You must take that as a measure of my great need."

"Heinz did convince me of this necessity, Alex."

"I will spare you as much of the unpleasantness as I can."

"Alex . . . enough. We are at war. I want to do my part."

He smiled, and kissed the back of her hand.

Only then did she look at Holmes, her face completely neutral. "This is the Englishman?"

"He's not much to look at, is he?"

"He is older than I expected." She glanced at Holmes' cast. "You've been rather careless with him, haven't you?"

"Not I. His comrades left him at our feet in that condition."

"I see they are loyal to a fault," she said dryly. "I suppose it is a little better than shooting their wounded if they slow them down."

"For this man, it is worse. He is something of a prize catch, Madeline." He handed Elizabeth to the chair. "Would you like to see if he is willing to talk?"

Elizabeth gave a dry laugh. "You are ever an optimist, Alexander." She looked at Holmes, settling her hands in her lap. "Good evening, *Englisher*," she said in English threaded with a light German accent. "Generalmajor Von Stein wishes to ask if you are willing to tell us about yourself." She leaned forward. "I would advise co-operation. Von Stein, I have been told, is very clever and inventive at extracting information."

Holmes shook his head. "I'm afraid I can't."

She glanced at Von Stein. "No," she told him.

"So I gathered," he replied, watching Holmes with eagle eyes. He sighed. "We're in for a long night, Madeline."

"That's all right, Alex. I was losing anyway."

MUCH LATER, VON STEIN lifted the woman's hand to his lips. "Madeline. Thank you so much. Your help has been invaluable."

"I am sorry you did not get what you were looking for. He did not speak . . . not even when you roughed him up a little."

"That is to be expected."

"What will happen to him now?"

"Oh, we will continue to question him . . . if I can presume upon you as the need arises?"

"Of course." She frowned, her mouth pouting. "Alex, I do not have a very good imagination, but it seems to me that to make a man reveal information he does not want to part with would require more than simply questioning him."

"You are correct," Von Stein agreed.

"You must have an entire arsenal of methods for doing just that, yes?"

"Madeline, you surprise me. Your questions show an interest in those nasty areas you profess to detest."

"Oh, I do detest them! And I am not asking for details. But it seems to me that more is required in this situation than simple questions, and I am wondering why you are stinting yourself. Is it because of me?"

"Partly, my dear."

She bit her lip, frowning. "You cannot speak to him without me. If you must do unpleasant things to make him talk, then you should do that. I will help you. I can be brave, Alex."

"I am utterly sure of that." He placed his hand over his

heart and bowed. "Your patriotism is laudable, Madeline, but that is not all that stays my hand. I'm sure Heinz explained that I am moving against direct orders from Berlin. Those orders also insist that the *Englisher* be physically cared for. As for some of my—what did you call it?—my arsenal of methods, yes. They can be somewhat intrusive, so I must practise a little restraint."

"That is a pity," she returned.

"Oh, it's merely a temporary inconvenience," Von Stein assured her. "One must become more creative when faced with unexpected difficulties."

She shivered, and wrapped the fur about her more tightly. "I believe that is all the detail I can stand, just now," she added.

Von Stein opened the cell door. "I will see you from the building."

She stepped out of the cell, not even glancing in Holmes' direction.

The cell door shut behind them.

Von Stein escorted her towards the reception area where an *Unteroffizier* manned a small desk and kept record of who entered or left the holding cells.

"Madeline, you are an astonishing delight. What an unexpected performance!"

"I said everything you wanted me to say, about there being worse to come, and so on. I was sufficient, then?"

"You were *brilliant*, my dear. You have my deepest admiration for your performance. You were utterly convincing."

She smiled a little. "That is because I spoke only the truth, Alex." They stepped out into the reception area, while the *Unteroffizier* studiously studied the wall beside him, his pen capped and sitting unused on the table.

Von Stein picked up her hand one more time, and kissed it properly. "You may well find some of it uncomfortable to watch, but I ask out of deepest need."

She nodded. "I understand. Call me when you need me again."

"Please give my regard to Häfner. I gather he has no objections to my borrowing of his lovely wife?"

"Only when he is winning, Alex. How can he have any complaints? When I am here in this accursed town, at his side?"

"Devotion and loveliness. Goodnight, Madeline, my dear."

"Goodnight, Alexander." With a sweep of silky skirts, she turned and left, while Von Stein watched her, admiration on his face.

For a small moment he had wavered in his decision to use her as a translator, but need had genuinely overcome his reluctance. Now, watching her lovely, mobile face and her sparkling green eyes made him consider what the impact might be upon Madeline herself. What if he was forced to maim the *Englisher*? Could she remain calm enough to translate whatever he said? Would she carry the image to her night-time pillow, as so many of them did?

She had spoken nothing but truth in the cell, she had just said. That meant she was willing to participate no matter what lengths he went to.

He had his answer, and once more marvelling at the power of loyalty to the Fatherland, he returned to his office.

"THERE HAS TO be a way!" Elizabeth railed, pacing the oriental carpet with quick, angry steps, the taffeta swishing along with her.

William Häfner remained seated, with an outward calm. She had rarely seen his demeanour change from this placid state but right now, it merely increased her anger. She yanked the irritating fur from about her shoulders, and dumped it upon the couch as she passed by.

"Well?" she demanded, as his silence stretched on.

"You know the facts as well as I, now. You want to extract a prisoner from Harbiye Barracks—the largest barracks this side of the Horn and the Bosphorus, which just happens to be jammed to the rafters with Turks and a crack German cavalry brigade. And you want to pull that prisoner out in such a way that your identity is not revealed, and there will be no pursuit. A prisoner who is, in all practicality, immobile."

"I have inside help. You. And now I have access to the barracks myself, too."

"Only when Von Stein calls for you."

"They are genuine advantages."

"Granted. But they are our only advantages. Elizabeth, you set up this operation for information gathering, and that is all. Military strategies that you are asking me to dream up for you require resources we don't have—men and equipment being the top two."

"Then you will have to make do with a woman and ingenuity," she snapped. "We have to get him out. As soon as possible. He will not let them break him, and I won't let him die because of it."

"Why not?" Häfner asked reasonably. "You've made harsher decisions than that before now."

She paused her pacing, and stood head down, her arms wrapped about her, staring at the coloured tufts of the rug. "He's there because he came to Constantinople in search of me."

"He came for Hadiya, not you."

"I am Hadiya."

"There is a difference to him," Häfner argued.

"Not any more. Von Stein wants him broken and spilling his secrets and that's exactly what Holmes won't do, because one of those secrets is me. And that's why I have to get him out."

"Are you sure he won't break, Elizabeth?"

"I know him. He will not break. He will not entertain even the possibility of it."

Häfner considered this. "You would be risking so much to get him out. If you're so sure he will not betray you, then perhaps you should not take that risk."

"You mean, leave him there?"

"Why not? If he does not break, then Von Stein will ensure he is dead, instead. Dead men tell no tales."

Thoughtfully, Elizabeth resumed her pacing.

Chapter Eleven

It was a perfect place for an execution, Von Stein thought, looking around.

He was studying the secondary parade square at Harbiye, a small, intimate one enclosed on all sides but one by buildings. The south side was bordered by the rear of a sprawling building that had a wide upper balcony conveniently built to overlook the square. This is where Von Stein stood, soaking up the winter sun and enjoying the view.

The door to the balcony opened, and Madame Häfner stepped out. She was dressed in sombre grey, which took some of the zest from the sunny day. Her hat shaded her face.

"Madeline, what are you doing here?"

"I heard you were going to execute the agent this morning, Alex. I felt I had to come."

"But why? This is no place for you, my dear. And you have been working so very hard for me these last few days . . . you deserve your rest. And on such a splendid day, too—you should be sunning yourself somewhere where you can be waited upon hand and foot."

Beneath them, a line of soldiers carrying rifles marched around the corner of the building and across the quadrangle, where they lined up squarely in front of the most central stone pillar that supported the roof of the building on the west side of the square.

Major William Häfner accompanied them, and once they had formed ranks, he began handing out bullets, one per man.

"Is this really necessary, Alex?" Madeline asked, grasping the stone balustrade with both hands as she watched the soldiers load their rifles. "You've done all you could and achieved nothing. Why this?"

"It is the way of things," he said. "Spying is a capital crime, for it undermines our country. Germany is weakened every time an agent passes on information to our enemies. Such a heinous activity merits a suitable reward. So."

"But agents are working for their own countries, are they not?"

"Not always. But soldiers work for their own countries. They work openly and honourably. They do not hide. They do not steal." He curled his lip with distaste. "They face a proud death, yes?"

"I suppose so."

"Your own husband is one of them."

She looked down at the square where Häfner stood to one side of the ranks, waiting, and did not answer.

"You see?" Von Stein said. "If the soldier risks death fighting for his wife and children, then so should a spy. And for a dishonourable duty, an ignoble death is proper."

She sighed.

"Perhaps you should return home, Madeline."

For a moment she considered. Then, "I will stay. I will see it through—so that I can understand."

"Very well. That is your choice, but I did warn you."

"Yes, Alex."

Von Stein rested his hand briefly on her shoulder.

At the door the noise of another's arrival sounded, and both of them turned to face it.

Through the door came a chair, followed by the soldier who carried it, his rifle slung over his shoulder. He placed the chair in the corner of the balcony, while another two soldiers slowly emerged.

Between them they almost carried the English agent, his splinted leg dangling heavily between them. They dumped him on the chair and took stance close by him.

"Why did you bring him here?" Madeline demanded, watching the Englishman settle himself more carefully.

"An object lesson," Von Stein told her. "If he watches one of his own being executed it will remind him of what he faces himself, if he does not cooperate."

"You mean, if he does cooperate you will not shoot him?"

He hesitated, then answered honestly. "No, he will still be executed. Confession does not redeem him of sins of this magnitude. But he will experience leniency, an end to the unpleasantness."

"Does he know this?"

"Probably."

"But then why this game?"

"You would be amazed at the illusions one's own mind can maintain when in a tight corner. He may know it, but when the desire to stop the pain becomes overwhelming he will convince himself that confessing will remove all his problems, including his pending execution."

"That is . . . nasty, Alex."

"It is all part of the game. I am just helping the illusion establish itself."

"He looks sick," Madeline murmured, studying the man on the chair, who watched the parade ground below with disinterest. He frankly leaned against the balustrade, his splinted leg thrust out to the side. The posture looked weary, drained. He hadn't glanced at them or shown by any reactions that he might understand what they were saying. The Englishman had grown thinner and listless. There were fading, yellowed bruises on his face and neck, and a fresh dark one on his temple, but there was no sign of any other physical damage.

"He looks fine to me," Von Stein answered. "A little bruised, perhaps, but nothing that will cause Berlin to protest. Considering the limitations I have been forced to work with in this case, I am satisfied that I have delivered the most persuasion possible without causing damage."

Madeline shivered. "Why don't you give the man a pair of crutches or a cane, instead of making our men practically carry him?"

"Crutches would give him mobility, the means to escape if he had the opportunity. I'd rather tax our men than provide him with that chance."

"You think of nothing but your work, Alex. It drives your every decision—agents and betrayals and the constant looking over your shoulder. Does it not end? Do you not wish to return to being a simple, honourable soldier?"

"I long for that time," Von Stein said honestly. "And just maybe, the end of all this is near." He looked down to where Madeline's husband stood waiting. "You may begin," he called to Häfner.

Häfner saluted, then looked towards a door in the building they faced and waved.

"How is that possible?" Madeline asked. "Would there not be agents still roaming about the Ottoman Empire, replacing those you have found?"

"One day far in the future, perhaps. Building a ring of agents is the lengthiest process imaginable. You can't recruit just anyone. And I have discovered the man in Constantinople who does the recruiting and manages this particular ring."

"I thought the agent had not spoken?"

"Neither of them has uttered a word of any significance."

"Then how . . . ?" she asked, bewildered.

He smiled grimly. "I seem to have a guardian angel in Berlin. Another wire arrived today. It was most illuminating. Enough to make what few assets I have on hand completely redundant."

Another prisoner was brought forth, between two soldiers. This one, despite having the use of both legs, also dangled helplessly between her captors.

The two soldiers strapped her to the column, her arms spread, and her hands belted around the column. She submitted to the process without struggle. Her head remained lowered and her body slumped, although Von Stein had been assured she was still conscious and aware of what was happening to her.

Her understanding pleased him. He had been free to deal with this one without constraint and, when faced with no limitations in that way, it was extremely easy to get carried away and reduce the prisoner to the point where they could not communicate and were not attentive to their circumstances. Von Stein had managed to walk the fine line between maximum persuasion and unconsciousness throughout the weeks of interrogation.

Even so, the woman had remained silent and even now spoke no last words, no protestations of innocence or justifications.

"With this one gone, tomorrow when we pick up her controller, we will have completely disabled the allied information systems in this city," Von Stein declared.

Häfner called off the command to ready, and fourteen rifles were cocked and lifted.

"Aim!"

Von Stein heard Madeline draw a deep breath.

"Fire!"

The volley was incredibly loud in the confined square, and rolled like thunder for a small moment. Von Stein studied the body of the Turkish woman dispassionately, consoling himself with the thought that failure was to be expected sometimes.

There was a sickly moan beside him, and he turned in time to see Madeline sag, her knees buckling.

He reached for her, but she was falling the other way, towards the agent, who was trying to get his injured leg out of the way.

Madeline crumpled against the splinted leg, and the agent clutched at his thigh, almost lifting himself off the seat in an effort to alleviate the burden. He groaned and began jabbering at her. Judging by his tone and the expression on his face, he was furious with her, and was venting his anger with the ugly vowels and unmusical sentences of English.

The two guards leapt to help Madeline back to her feet and prop her against the balustrade.

She shook her head, trying to clear the mustiness, while the Englishman collapsed back, panting. Perspiration appeared on his high forehead, and by the feeble soothing movements he made to the bandaged leg, it was clear he was in agony.

Von Stein felt a vast amusement. Madeline's swoon had pointed the way towards cracking the Englishman. As the wound he bore had already been there when they captured the man, Berlin would not notice if the degree of injury were increased.

He glanced into the yard where Häfner's men were taking away the body.

One failure, but there was a greater success to come.

Yes, it was a beautiful day.

"Madeline, are you alright?" he asked.

"I'm so sorry, Alex," she murmured. "I thought I could stand it, but I couldn't. I'm sorry." She cupped her face in her hands.

"Nonsense, Madeline. It happens often, especially the first time."

"I hope there is never a second!" she declared, her voice muffled by her hands.

Von Stein pulled her hands away, and lifted her chin. "I did warn you, my dear."

"Yes, you did."

He relented a little. "Come, I will take you to our wonderful refectory for some restorative brandy. I'm sure that is much more to your taste."

ELIZABETH BURST INTO the house, already opening buttons and fastenings on her grey ensemble as she strode through the marbled foyer. She went straight up the sweeping staircase and down the wide corridor to a room on the right.

Just inside the door she halted, surprised. "William!"

Häfner sat on the delicate stool that matched the dressing table beside it. There was a glass in his hands, two-thirds full of golden brown liquid, and a crystal decanter at his side, which was half full. He was in shirt sleeves. His uniform jacket lay in a crumpled heap in the far corner of the room. It looked as though it might have been flung there.

"Are you all right?" she asked him.

"I'm getting there." He took a gulp from the glass. "I got back here just in time to be comprehensively sick. Now I'm getting better."

"I see." Elizabeth moved through to the wardrobe, and pulled the drape across.

"I ran out of whisky, so I came looking for yours." William's voice was muffled by the curtain.

"You know you're welcome to it." She stepped back out into the bedroom, carrying a jacket.

William blinked and took another mouthful. "You know what we did today?"

"Yes, I know," she said quietly.

"We stood by and watched—"

"I know."

"And I was the one who gave the orders!"

"William, don't do this to yourself. You know there was no real alternative."

He took another drink, silent.

Elizabeth put the jacket on the bed and crossed to the dressing table and opened a drawer there. "You know you can halt this any time you want," she said quietly. "Your cause is won now. Your reasons for undermining the German army have gone." She rested her hand against his shoulder. "You should consider going to St. Petersburg. That is where your heart is, after all. And Trotsky could use a good leader like you."

"And what would you do?" he said dryly. "An officer's wife alone in Constantinople?"

"I can manage. There are ways. A quiet, but public divorce, and a new lover—a Turk perhaps. That would be a reason for Madame Häfner to stay in the city. It would cause a scandal, but . . ." She shrugged. "You're free to go, William."

He considered this, drank, then shook his head. "You need me. I could still be of use."

Her hand tightened for a moment. "Yes. I don't deny it." She turned back to the drawer.

William studied her, the men's trousers and shirt she wore, and her hair bound tight to disguise its feminine length when she donned the hat she was holding in her hand.

"Where are you going?"

"Von Stein knows where Fairuza's controller lives. He's going to pick him up tomorrow. Holmes told me where to find him, so I'll go tonight and circumvent Alex."

She reached into the drawer and picked up a revolver, which she dropped into her trouser pocket.

"Circumvent?" William blinked. "You mean you're going to kill the controller?"

Elizabeth paused, her gaze on the dresser top.

"You are!"

"That is what Holmes told me to do."

"But why?"

"I don't know. He didn't have time to explain. It was risky as it was—one of the guards might have known English, and I don't think Von Stein is as ignorant as he pretends to be, either. But Holmes used slang and a Cockney accent—it made it harder to follow."

"He specifically told you to kill this man?"

"Yes."

"But he's an agent. One of yours . . . ours, yes?"

"Yes. But Holmes obviously knows something we do not, that he could not pass along."

"And based entirely on his unsubstantiated instructions, you are going to kill the man?"

"I trust Holmes. He would not have told me to do this without reason."

William sat there, plainly baffled.

Elizabeth picked up the jacket on the bed and shrugged into it.

"He wasn't just a friend, back in London, was he?" William said at last.

She took a long moment to answer. "No, he wasn't."

"You told me you have never been married."

"That is the truth. I have never been married."

"I see." William gulped back the rest of the glass and poured himself another. The decanter lip chattered against the rim.

Elizabeth picked up the dark hat hanging from the corner of the mirror and put it on, adjusting it carefully to cover as much of her face as possible.

"You'll need to dye your hair again soon," William said. "I can see red."

She smiled, and patted his cheek. “Bless you, William. What would I do without you?”

“You’d do fine.” His tone became bitter. “You always have.”

She thrust her hands into her pockets. “I have to go.”

“Yes.”

“I don’t know how long I’ll be.”

“I’ll survive.”

She hesitated. “You’re worrying me.”

“I’ll be fine,” he assured her. “I’ll finish this up, think about today some more, throw up again, then stagger off to bed. And tomorrow’s headache will remind me of the reasons I keep doing this.”

“I wish my day’s work would rest as easily on my mind,” Elizabeth replied. “I envy you.”

“That’s a comfort to me.”

“I thought it might be.”

William cocked his head at her and his mouth lifted in a small smile. “I know I hate my lot right now, but I’m glad I met you, Elizabeth Sigerson. You’ve changed my life.”

“I thought Trotsky did that for you?” Her tone was light, amused.

“He showed me other ways to think about life. You showed me how to make those changes happen. When I get to St. Petersburg, they’ll have an excellent officer because of you.”

“I’ll send them my bill.” She touched his arm again, lightly. “I have to go.”

“Do you want help?”

She picked up his glass and handed it to him. “You couldn’t hit a target even if you were standing on it, William. Get drunk some more, and if you don’t quite make it to bed, I’ll tuck you in when I get home.”

HEINZ WRAPPED HIS dressing gown around him and opened the door, blinking in the light that blazed from the dormitory corridor.

Von Stein stood there, legs apart, hands behind his back, his uniform as fresh and pressed as it had been when he donned it that morning, twelve hours before.

"Asleep already?" Von Stein rapped.

"It has been a long day, sir," Heinz pointed out.

"It's about to get longer. I've suddenly become uneasy, Heinz. My instincts are twitching. I want to go and pick up the man called Zeki tonight. Not tomorrow, but now."

"Your instincts, sir?"

Von Stein frowned. "A hunch. Nothing specific. A nervous feeling that I'm missing something obvious. I've learned to rely on these feelings before. Let's go, Heinz. Get dressed. Anything dark will do. It's a dark night's work, after all."

Chapter Twelve

ELIZABETH TRIED TO PRETEND SHE WAS SIMPLY OUT FOR THE evening on a stroll through the streets, enjoying the mild air, but the gun in her pocket bumped against her thigh with every step, spoiling the illusion.

She repeated in her mind the address Holmes had gasped to her. It was in an area she was familiar with, an apartment house just off the elegant tree-lined boulevard she walked along.

The street was full of cracked, ancient stairs—she could see the beginning of it just ahead, on the right.

He must die. No less.

Holmes' words still delivered a little shock with every repetition. They troubled her. But disobeying the command was unthinkable for it was *Sherlock Holmes* who gave it: the one person she trusted unquestioningly.

A car drove past her, and she realized it was slowing down. In the darkness she saw the black blobs of three people in it, silhouetted by the backwash of illumination from the car's headlamps. The car came to a sudden, jerky stop opposite the street she had been directed to, and she ducked behind the wide trunk of a tree, alert and wary.

As all three occupants stepped out onto the street, she recognized the car. It was Von Stein's beast, and two of the men walking across to the steps were, by their shapes, Von Stein and Heinz. The third was distinguishable by the rifle hanging from his shoulder, and his peaked cap.

She pulled back behind the cover of the tree, her heart racing. What was Von Stein doing here? He'd said tomorrow. Why would he change his mind? It wasn't impatience—the man had inhuman self-discipline. He'd have spent the night enjoying the anticipation of catching another agent to add to his trophy collection.

She tried to draw some answers from what she knew but there were too many variables. She simply had to play it out for now and think later.

She pulled out her revolver and broke it open to check the load, then reassembled it and let it hang loosely from her hand, while she watched the steps. It was messy, but she would have to deal with Fairuza's controller from here.

The distance was not a problem for her aim, but it put her too close to the car. With three Germans as witnesses, she would have to run for her life. She would give anything to be standing another one hundred yards away and holding her rifle instead. It was tucked into the saddle bags of her horse, on the other side of Anatolia, and not even a king's ransom would deliver the rifle to her now. Even William's clumsy, inaccurate army piece was sitting in the rifle rack back at the house.

There was the sound of voices, low, intense, and she prepared herself; bracing herself against the tree trunk, and leaving her gun arm loose and ready to swing up.

Four people stepped down into the boulevard, and Elizabeth quickly picked out the new one. Her heart leapt hard. He was walking freely, chatting with a low voice.

Answers came quickly, then, for this man was not a reluctant prisoner, he was not simply cooperating. He was *one of them*. If Holmes knew this address it was because he had been here, and possibly even revealed his true name.

He must die. No less.

Of course . . . of course! The controller knew who Holmes was, and if he was a double agent, then Holmes' identity was in jeopardy.

The gun came up of its own accord. Elizabeth deliberately recalled the execution that morning. All her reluctance fled under the dawning realization that this man was probably—no, definitely—responsible for Fairuza's capture.

"News from Berlin," Von Stein had described his cable the day they had gone to pick the woman up. The controller reported directly to both London and Berlin, and Berlin fed the information back to Von Stein. And today he had spoken of another illuminating cable . . .

From Berlin, Von Stein had learned the identity of the British controller and come to pick him up. The controller must have revealed himself as a double agent. It would be enough to give Von Stein pause, but he would still cautiously bring him to the barracks to establish fully his true identity.

She took deliberate, careful aim at the Turk's chest, going for the safe heart shot rather than a head shot.

She fired.

The controller went down, clutching his shoulder. She had missed.

Her heart pounding, she took aim at the figure lying in the middle of the road, ignoring the rifle-carrying soldier running towards her.

Her second shot ricocheted off the old cobbles, missing him altogether. And she would not get a third shot, for the soldier was nearly upon her, unslinging his rifle. He was the most dangerous of them all right now, and she had to deal with him.

She shot the man through the thigh, and he went down

with a grunt, clutching his thigh, barely a dozen paces from her tree. His rifle clattered onto the stones.

Heinz was checking the controller—his health was of primary importance. But Von Stein was unbuckling his revolver.

Moving fast, Elizabeth picked up the rifle, to keep it out of their hands. She kept her eye on Von Stein. The street was dark enough and she was far enough away that the chance of being recognized by either of them was very low. Heinz had barely looked up, and the men's clothing would focus Von Stein's thinking. He would see what his eyes reported: A slim man wearing a hat.

She slung the rifle strap over her shoulder and carried it pointed and with her finger on the trigger, pocketed her revolver, and ran for her life.

"WELL?" VON STEIN snapped.

"He'll live," Heinz pronounced. "The bullet shattered the arm bone, but it came out through the shoulder. Nice clean entry and exit. He's just passed out, that's all."

Heinz got to his feet, and looked down the street. "The fellow took the rifle. But he was on foot. We can probably catch him, even now."

"There's no need. I know who it was," Von Stein said quietly. "Help me get these two into the car. We'll drop them off at the barracks infirmary on the way."

"On the way to where?"

"To the prison cell, first. You heard the name used by friend Zeki. The agent we're holding is none other than Sherlock Holmes himself."

"The name means nothing to me," Heinz confessed.

"He is the agent who so badly embarrassed Von Bork in 1915, and it is rumoured he has been the culprit behind a dozen other incidences since then. Is it any wonder Berlin want him for themselves?" He pushed at Zeki with his toe. "This one is beneath contempt in comparison, Heinz. Demonstrably so—they tried to kill him as a means to keep Holmes' identity secret."

Heinz picked Zeki up with a grunt, and Von Stein opened the back door of the automobile.

"Who is 'they'?" Heinz asked.

"There is one last agent out there, and now I know who it is."

HOLMES WAS WOKEN by a minute scratching at the cell door. It was still dark, but the quiet sounds coming through the grill over the window told him it was late—the barracks had shut down for the night.

The scraping sound was replaced by the sound of a key being fitted into the lock, but whoever had the key was having enormous trouble fitting and turning it in the dark. Finally, the tumblers turned over, and the door swung open.

Holmes was sitting up by then, but no-one stepped through the door immediately.

After a moment, a German officer peered around the door, barely visible in the small light coming from the high window. "Are you leaving?" he asked Holmes in badly accented English. The accent was made worse because the man was patently drunk.

Holmes remained silent.

The head withdrew. Then the officer stepped carefully into the cell. "C'mon," he said, waving in a wide "follow me" gesture. The arm movements made his entire body sway like a pendulum.

Holmes swung his legs over the edge of the bunk. "Where are we going?"

"Home, off course!"

"Of course," Holmes agreed. "Home. How stupid of me."

The man straightened up a bit. "I am Major William Häfner," he pronounced. "But you've never heard of me."

"On the contrary . . . I've met your wife on several occasions. And you were in charge of the firing squad this afternoon, weren't you?"

"My wife . . ." Häfner hung his head, apparently thinking hard. "She's terribly smart, you know. But three days, she can't work it out. And I thought, easy! And here I am. You see?"

"Yes."

He cocked his head. "I am making no sense, no? I'm drunk, you should know," he confessed candidly. "I'm making sense to me but I'm probably not making sense to you."

"You're making more sense than you know," Holmes told him gently. "Why are you taking me home?"

"For 'liz'beth."

Holmes considered this. "I'd like to go home with you, Häfner, but you can't just walk me out the barracks gates. They will have objections to that. And besides . . ." He tapped the long splints on his leg

Häfner cocked his head again, letting Holmes' words sink in. Then he muttered in German, "Imbecile!" and he stepped very carefully to the door, bent over, and picked up a black bundle, which he thrust at Holmes. "Iz mine, but I'm a major, too—just like you were . . . in Berlin," he said, still in German. "I thought of it. 'liz'beth told me, and I remembered. Clever, no?"

Holmes held up the clothing Häfner had given him to the light for inspection. A major's uniform. And boots.

"Very clever," he assured Häfner quietly. "But I never told Elizabeth. How did she know?"

"Guessed. When you were working in Berlin. Your name—*Major von Karnch*—on papers that came out here.

She saw them and laughed. And laughed. The name gave it away, if you thought about it, she said. I remembered." He pointed to the uniform, making himself sway again. "So . . . fellow officers, and all that. Parties, pretty girls, dancing."

"I understand."

". . . because I can't act sober right now."

Holmes patted his shoulder. "We'll just have to manage."

THEY CREPT DOWN the hall, Häfner supporting Holmes, who, because of his splinted and useless leg, staggered as badly as Häfner. But the too-large trousers disguised the splints and bandages, and the greatcoat hid the tunic that Holmes did not fill as fully as Häfner did.

At the entrance foyer a single light burned. At the desk in the corner a clerk lay sprawled across the sheets of paper he had been working on.

"What happened to him?" Holmes asked.

"Hit him," Häfner declared.

"Did you kill him?"

"He'll just have a headache. Like me."

They moved out of the building and into the small, deserted parade ground. The central column they passed was clean and starkly white in the light from the new moon. But there were chips and gouges in its surface that spoke of its secondary purpose.

Holmes rested his hand against it as he passed.

Halfway across the square, he said, "Do you have a flask, Häfner?"

"Got two, right now. Inside breast pocket."

Holmes delved into the borrowed great coat. "Ah! Excellent." He passed one to Häfner, and with his hand and teeth, unstoppered the other, pocketed the cap, and drank deeply.

"It's terrible brandy," Häfner said, swallowing a big mouthful, himself.

"It's the best brandy I've ever tasted," Holmes assured him. "Know any drinking songs, William?"

"Dozens!" Häfner said proudly.

HANS WAS FREEZING.

He'd swapped late night guard duties with Dieter, who was taking an exotic Turkish woman to a dance. It had been Hans' turn last week, and Dieter had covered for him without complaint, so he would do the same now. But late night duties always stretched so endlessly, with so little to do. And it was warmer in the sentry box than moving around, so he could not relieve tedium that way, either.

The officers on duty at the gate house, half a dozen paces away, had not spoken to him all night. They kept themselves tucked up in the gate house, sitting over a stove, and Hans knew Zimmerman had a bottle of *schnapps* hidden away that he would only share with the other officers.

That didn't help improve Hans' mood, either.

The faint sound of singing reached him.

Hans strained to hear more. Yes. Singing. Two voices. Coming closer, too. He listened for a little longer, a smile forming as he recognized the song. It was not an approved marching song . . . in fact, it was a bawdy ditty with a lively tune that had Hans' toe tapping as he listened.

He didn't know who was singing it, but he liked their enthusiasm and spirit.

The volume and direction made it clear they were heading his way. Smiling, Hans stepped out of the box and waited to catch his first glimpse of the rowdy pair. They couldn't be officers, he decided. Not with that sense of humour.

When the two did loom up out of the dark, staggering into the circle of light falling from the lamps on the walls of the gatehouse, Hans was a little shocked to see they were majors. They were holding each other up, silvery hip flasks flashing in their hands.

They paused to finish the song off properly, before staggering on to the gate house. One of the officers inside the gatehouse stepped out, his arms hugging his chest against the cold of the outside. He snapped off a salute when he saw they were superior officers, but there was a scowl of disapproval there.

"Major Häfner, and Major Von Karnch," the older one announced, with the careful pronunciation of a man who has had his fair share to drink.

The other one was digging in his pockets for papers, with no success.

Earhart, the gate officer, drew himself even more upright.

Hans suddenly knew he was about to make things unpleasant for the two majors. Even though they were superior officers, as the keeper of the gate, Earhart could insist on papers, and formalities, and force them to stand in the cold for many long, bumbling minutes while he inspected them—and Hans knew as well as Earhart that all that was necessary were names, which Von Karnch had already given.

He remembered that Earhart refused to share the *schnapps*, too.

Deliberately, Hans slung his rifle, and leaned on the counterweight to lift the boom gate. Then he snapped off a salute to the majors.

The younger one blinked, then shuffled to try to stand to attention, but failed. His acknowledgement was wavering. He tapped the other on the shoulder, and pointed.

Still supporting each other, they made their slow, happy

way out onto the street, and up the road towards Galata and the Golden Horn. Fifty paces away, they began singing again, a rousing chorus of a beer hall song.

Hans returned to his cold sentry box. He was still smiling.

ELIZABETH HURRIED INTO the house again, dumping the borrowed rifle in a dark corner by the front door, and rushed upstairs to change out of the trousers.

William was not in her room and the brandy decanter was gone, so she quickly changed out of the male costume, donning a vivid pink silk organza gown that lay waiting on the bed. She turned, intending to find William and ensure he was safely abed, and halted, smothering a shriek with her hand.

Von Stein stood in the doorway, a revolver dangling from his hand. He was leaning heavily against the frame.

"Good evening, Madeline."

"Alex! You scared me!" She frowned, and added stiffly. "And why are you here, in my bedroom?"

He straightened. "I seem to have misplaced a prisoner, my dear Madeline." He lifted the revolver and pointed it at her. "Is it Madeline? What *should* I call you?"

Chapter Thirteen

IT WAS VERY LATE IN THE EVENING. THERE WERE FEW PEOPLE on the quiet residential streets of Harbiye, and all of them carefully avoided the two German officers sitting on the edge of a small rectangular raised pool.

Holmes rested his leg while Häfner bathed his face with the chilly water and took a moment to clear his head.

"It won't be long before the alarm goes up at the barracks," Holmes said, continuing to speak in German.

"I know."

"We're not far enough away, yet. If they give chase . . ."

"From the gate I headed south towards the Horn. When he is asked, the gate guard will send the pursuit in the wrong direction."

"I was aware we had turned around and were heading north again," Holmes assured him. "But the deception will delay us from reaching the house by many minutes."

"We're safely out of the barracks. We'll get there," Häfner growled, holding his head.

"We're not safe until we reach the house," Holmes assured him. "If we are seen on the streets, we are both in bad trouble, for neither of us can run, right now. I would prefer we spend as little time as possible exposed in this way—especially wearing these uniforms."

"They allow us to walk around freely," Häfner pointed out.

"They're also what will get me shot for impersonating a German officer," Holmes added dryly. "Are you ready?"

Häfner groaned and got to his feet. "I should have gone to bed as Elizabeth said."

"Why didn't you?"

Häfner hoisted Holmes to his feet, and they began their slow walk again. After a few paces, Häfner answered, "She shamed me. I could not let her go to her grisly night's work while I slept off a moment of weakness. Besides . . . she was worried about you."

The silence stretched another few paces.

"She has picked her people well, I see," Holmes murmured.

VON STEIN SHOVED Elizabeth towards the dining chair. "Sit."

She pulled it away from the table, and sat.

Von Stein dropped the dark man's suit onto the opposite end of the table. Her revolver, which he had found in the pocket, he emptied of bullets and dropped on top. He pocketed the bullets, and stood in front of her, his big hands loose at his sides.

"Where is he?" he asked.

"William? I assume he's asleep."

Von Stein lowered his head, apparently disappointed with her answer. Without warning he struck her, backhanded.

The blow drove her out of the chair to sprawl across the hard marble floor. As she lay, dazed, she heard the chitter of the birds in the solarium, on the other side of the arch. Their noise was obscenely cheerful.

Von Stein caught a handful of her hair, and pulled her back up into the chair. A few hairpins scattered, with tiny musical chimes, across the floor.

Elizabeth licked her lips. One side of her face was numb, and she could taste blood. And her scalp at the back of her head stung where it had taken the strain of his grip. She looked up at Von Stein. "I don't know whom you are talking about."

He leaned over her, and she saw a heavy, visible pulse in his temple. "Of course you were the only person who speaks English here. You *are* English. Just as he is. It must have been a delicious irony, being my interpreter. Does he speak German?"

She hesitated. "I don't know—"

That was all the denial he allowed her.

This time, the blow knocked the chair over backwards, and she fell with it, her head rapping on the floor. Dazed, her head and shoulders throbbing, she felt his hands on her shoulders, grasping folds of her gown. She was hauled to her feet, and the gown ripped. He righted the chair.

"Sit," he told her grimly.

She lowered herself onto the chair, holding onto the edge of the table to do so. Her hair fell around her face.

Von Stein leaned very close to her. "I will accept nothing but direct, candid answers," he assured her. "Denying anything merely wastes my time, which I resent. Yesterday at the execution only you and the *Englisher* heard me say I was going to pick up the last agent tomorrow. And somehow you contrived between you to deal with the Turk. That weakness of yours, when you stumbled against him, and he cried out in protest—it was a beautiful piece of play-acting, my dear. But it has marked you indelibly."

She swallowed, and contrived to speak. "There were three guards there, too."

Von Stein looked at his left hand, which rested on the brown suit on the table. "But you were the one who came to deal with the Turk."

In the moment when he was bringing his gaze back to her she threw her head forward, sharply. Her forehead smashed into his face, striking hard. The blow straightened him up and threw him backwards, exposing his chest and abdomen. She pushed herself to her feet with a strong surge of power, and used the momentum to drive her fist up into his diaphragm.

Von Stein's entire body lifted, and the torso and head snapped forward over the blow.

Doubling her fists together, she swung them in a big circle around and up, to hammer into the bottom of his chin.

The impact took his feet out from under him, and he landed on the unforgiving marble floor squarely.

She stepped around him, and hurried into the foyer, moving unsteadily. "William!" she called, her voice weak. "William!"

There was no answer, and when she attempted to open the front door, she found it locked. The key was missing. She rattled the handle angrily, and turned away. There was a back door she could use.

Von Stein walked slowly into the foyer, staggering a little. He was not hurrying, not pursuing her. "Did you think I would not search the house and secure any exits? Do you think I don't know Häfner isn't here?"

William's absence was news to her, and she hid her dismay. She looked around, searching for anything useful, and saw the rifle she had propped up in the corner a short while ago.

She lunged for it, as Von Stein closed in on her. She whirled to face him, lifting the rifle up to point at him. She cocked it.

He stopped. "If you kill me, there will be no mercy for

you. My officers will hunt you the rest of your days. And they will find you and kill you, and all of your family."

She swallowed hard. "You are not the first madman to promise me that. I'm still here." And she pulled the trigger.

A dry click sounded.

Sickened, Elizabeth broke the gun open and stared at the empty chamber.

"Did you think I wouldn't have the sense to disable any weapons you might think fit to use?" he asked softly.

She looked up, backing away from him.

He reached into his holster and pulled out the revolver. "Mine, on the other hand, is loaded."

He fired.

EVERYTHING CAME BACK into focus with terrible slowness . . . until she moved, and excruciating pain jerked her senses to full alertness immediately. She couldn't prevent the tiny cry that escaped her. The pain centred on an icy, hot black area above her left hip, and to one side.

"You shouldn't have tried to shoot me," Von Stein's voice explained to her.

She looked around. She was back on the chair in the dining room, her upper body resting on the table. She straightened into a sitting position with slow, infinite care.

Von Stein was sitting in the chair next to her. He had turned it to face her. A glass of port rested on the table, and the decanter from the sideboard was at his elbow. The revolver lay next to his glass. He had one foot resting on the tapestry seat of another chair he had pulled out to one side.

"If there had been doubt before you pulled that trigger, madame, there is none now. You understand?"

"Yes."

She inspected her side gingerly. There was a lot of blood, which hindered her analysis. She thought, from the lack of difficulty she had breathing, that the bullet had grazed across her ribs, taking a good furrow of flesh, but doing little other damage.

"Where is he?" Von Stein asked. "I want him for myself."

"I truly don't know," Elizabeth told him. "The last time I saw him was this afternoon on the balcony."

"Where you stood and watched an associate die," Von Stein concluded. "Remember it, Madeline. You'll be standing on that spot in a few days' time."

She grimaced. "Elizabeth. Call me Elizabeth."

"Very well. Elizabeth. Is that your real name?"

"Yes."

"And Häfner?"

"What about him?"

"Is he part of this?"

"Why don't you ask him that?"

"Oh, I will, when I find him. Is he with the *Englisher*?"

"I don't know." She held up her hand, even though he hadn't moved. "I really *don't* know. I expected him to be here when I got home tonight. He wasn't in a state fit to walk."

She was light-headed. The urge to close her eyes and sleep was overwhelming. She clawed her wits back together. This was not the first time she had been shot and she recognized her body's response to the shock of it.

She deliberately reached for the wound on her side, and pressed it. Sharp tines of silvery pain speared her. The urge to sleep fled. She sat up.

Von Stein was studying her thoughtfully. "I think it is safe to believe you don't know where Häfner is. You ran into the hall shouting for him, which is not the action of someone who knows the house is empty. Very well."

He picked up the glass, drained it, and placed it back on the table while he studied her. "But you can guess, and I know your guess will be close." He poured himself another glass of port. "You are clever, Made . . . Elizabeth. I've always known your mind was quicker than those around us. So I know you could tell me the most likely place to find Häfner. And I suspect I will find my English agent right there with him. So where should I look? Where is he?"

"I will not abuse the intelligence you award yourself. I could guess, yes, but it would be against my interests. So I will not pretend to think about it, and I will not insult you by speculating aloud about the most unlikely places you will find him. You will not bother looking in those places."

"You know me well."

"We both know that if William is not here where he was expected to be, and your English agent has disappeared, then there is most likely a connection. Now you know as much as I about this business."

He sipped the fresh glass thoughtfully, then picked up his revolver again.

"I don't believe you."

She nodded. "Understandable, under the circumstances."

"You see, I know you are not being as candid as you might be. You're deliberately withholding key information from me, while trying to look as cooperative as possible."

She stayed silent.

"You've carefully avoided telling me the identity of the *Englisher*. I know you know it. You would not have done his bidding so willingly yesterday had you not known and trusted him."

"If I were to give his name, how would it benefit you? You already know all you need to know about him. He is English, and he is an agent here in Constantinople."

"Indulge me." His voice was smooth, gentle.

"If his name will convince you I am being candid with you, then I will tell you. His name is Sigerson." She shrugged. "You see? It is of no advantage to you at all."

He considered this a moment.

"Elizabeth, you are disappointing me," he said softly. "Just before your bullet knocked him senseless tonight, Zeki had already told me the name Sigerson."

"Confirmation disappoints you?"

"Zeki told me that was his pseudonym. He has another name. His real name. And if Zeki knew it, so must you."

"We worked independently. I didn't know Sigerson was in the city until you caught him."

"Yet you obeyed his order to shoot Zeki without question." Von Stein shook his head. "You know him," he repeated.

"As a fellow Englishman, yes. But that is all."

"This is quite a minuet we're dancing through, is it not?"

She licked her lips. Dry. She was thirsty. Another symptom of the bullet wound. She must watch her words most carefully, for it was easy to fall into thoughtless speech when the body was behaving this way.

"I don't think you quite understand your role here," Von Stein said quietly. "We've established that you are an agent—a very clever agent, who is probably working for the British, as you have just revealed you are English, too. You're resourceful, and you do not falter at cold murder. That makes you dangerous, and I do not underestimate your role in this little charade we're going through.

"But you are wasting my time, Elizabeth. Do you think I am sitting here, forcing Heinz to wait in a cold car, on a whim? I could avoid significant aggravation by simply taking you to Harbiye, processing the paperwork and having you shot on the morrow, but I do not. Why?"

"You want Sigerson," she said dryly.

"Yes, and so does Berlin. That puzzled me until I met friend Zeki. Do you know what he told me, Elizabeth?"

"I'm afraid I do," she said softly. "Zeki gave you his real name."

"Precisely. I know that name, and I know why Berlin wants him. The great Sherlock Holmes embarrassed them before the war began." He shrugged. "It is of little consequence to me, for I have greater issues to deal with in my own territory. Berlin's interest in him simply confirms what I have grown to suspect. Holmes is the key agent who has been feeding all my most delicate information to the Divine Wind.

"I've long suspected that there was a single conduit between the city and the Arab who has been harassing me for the last three years. Now I know I'm right, and I know who he is. And when I find him again, I will trace that conduit to the Divine Wind and rid myself of the troublesome guerrilla once and for all."

Elizabeth frowned. "And where do I fit into this?"

"You've been systematically milking me for information ever since Häfner was posted here. Since before the war. I assume you and the others like you passed it on to Holmes, who channelled it eastwards to the Arab. The woman—Fairuza—was one, too."

She felt a smile forming and suppressed it.

"I'm impressed, Alex," she said softly. "You have deduced so much from so few clues."

"Naturally. And I have no intention of handing you over to the army's administrative machinery until you tell me where I can find Holmes. I want the Divine Wind, and I will do anything to find him. Anything, madame. You, and then Holmes, are merely stepping stones that will let me reach him."

The urge to laugh suddenly gripped her. Dizzy relief was part of it, but the irony in Von Stein's passionate mission struck a deep chord of amusement in her.

He picked up the glass, tossed back the contents and got to his feet. The revolver was still in his hand. "So, I repeat. Where is he? Where is Sherlock Holmes? I know you know. I want your answer. Tell me where he is!"

The wave of laughter that swept her was silent, but her shoulders shook with it, and she was helpless to prevent the wide smile that came with it.

Von Stein's eyes narrowed, and his face darkened. "You laugh at me? You dare to *laugh* at me?"

She shook her head a little, not prepared to speak and risk vocalizing the laugh. But the laughter was not going away. If anything, it was swelling, growing deeper, as she repeatedly acquainted herself with the biting paradox.

Von Stein struck her across the cheek again, the gun still wrapped in his fist, doubling the solidness of the impact. She was thrown against the wall.

The impact ejected her laughter, but the hilarity did not evaporate with it.

Von Stein hauled her to her feet, and forced her to look at him by pulling her hair back. "Tell me where he is!" he shouted.

She smiled. "I don't know."

He shook her, his face turning a dark red, the veins through his temples swelling and beating visibly. "*Tell me where he is!*"

She thought anew of the absurdity of the moment, and this time she laughed aloud, venting her mirth.

Von Stein became a mad creature. His hand slapped across her face, sending her to the floor again. He followed the blow with a kick that landed on her thigh, making her cry out, all the while swearing at her, proclaiming his obsession with the Divine Wind, his determination to find him, and everything he would do to her if she did not give him the information he wanted.

She scrambled across the floor, trying to anticipate each blow from his heavy boots as he followed her one step at a time, kicking her with each step. She found herself in the corner of the room, and knew she had no way out. She dragged herself to her feet, taking three or four efforts to achieve it, as Von Stein's kicks took her feet out from under her each time. Finally, she gained her feet, and turned to face him.

He had halted and was staring at her. His chest was heaving as he panted heavily. His face was contorted with rage. "Tell me!" he cried, as he lifted the revolver to point at her and deliberately cocked it.

She wiped the blood and spit from her mouth, and winced as her ribs creaked with protest. "Kill me, Alex. Go ahead. Kill me, and you will never find your Divine Wind. I guarantee it." And she deliberately smiled, although all her humour had evaporated.

He visibly quivered with the dilemma, and his face writhed with it. She thought he might even stamp his foot in frustration. *"Where is Sherlock Holmes?"* he screamed.

"Behind you," came the quiet rejoinder.

Standing at the top of the two steps into the dining area stood Sherlock Holmes, dressed in a German officer's greatcoat. The splinted leg was thrust out a little to one side. He held a revolver of his own, and it was pointed at Von Stein.

Von Stein turned jerkily, like a puppet answering to the pull on strings. As soon as he faced him, Holmes fired.

The shot took Von Stein in the heart and he was flung back against the wall a few feet from Elizabeth's corner.

She stood very still and watched him die at her feet.

WILLIAM TIED HEINZ to the newel post on the stairs and took Von Stein's body up to the bathroom. He was moving slowly, but he seemed to be more sober than the last time Elizabeth had seen him.

Elizabeth lay on the table while Holmes sat before her and doctored her wounds, following her directions, and using the supplies from the comprehensive medical kit William retrieved from her bedroom.

While he worked, Elizabeth told him of all that had happened since the execution that morning, her tone dry and quiet.

Häfner returned and sat on another chair, listening intently.

When she had finished, there was a small, reflective silence.

"It is the end of Hadiya," Holmes remarked. "He will not survive this night's work. And Häfner must depart, too."

"William intends to go to St. Petersburg."

Häfner, who was frowning as he followed the quick exchanges in English, nodded. "*Ja.* St. Petersburg."

"That is where you go, too?" Holmes asked Elizabeth.

"I must go east and find Cyrus. The unit will have reassembled by now."

Into the little silence that followed, William said, "I don't . . ." and his frown deepened, as he searched for the word he wanted. Then he grimaced, and switched to German. "I don't understand why Von Stein wanted to find the Divine Wind so badly that he would defy Berlin to do it. It makes no sense. He was not interested in Holmes at all beyond his use in leading him to the Divine Wind."

"The Divine Wind killed his son." The voice was Heinz's.

They all turned to look at him, with a range of surprised expressions.

Heinz shook his head. "You should not have used German," he explained. "The sound carries too well around this echoing hall."

"Explain yourself," Elizabeth demanded. "I thought Von Stein was childless, or else his children were tucked away in Bavaria. He never spoke of an adult son."

"He only had the one child. There were complications, and the mother will never bear again. In 1915, his son was barely eighteen but threatened to enlist with the infantry fighting in France. Von Stein thought he could minimize the boy's danger if he got him a posting in Anatolia. William died in a raid by the Divine Wind, barely a week after arriving there." Heinz shook his head. "He never spoke of his son again, but Von Stein's drive to find the Divine Wind became . . . relentless."

"You give information to the enemy most freely," Holmes observed.

"It is harmless information. And I offer it to garner goodwill." Heinz licked his lips. "I know too much. It would not profit you to let me live, but I would bargain with you for my life."

"You would not die for the Fatherland?" Häfner asked, his lip curling.

"No more than you would," Heinz shot back. "I was not given a choice when I was posted to this place. For four years as Von Stein's assistant I have been . . . riding a tornado. And the Turks are losing. Soon, all will be lost and the allies will take Constantinople. I would like to be able to go home."

Elizabeth slid off the table, and walked gingerly toward him. "Why would we risk leaving you behind to wire ahead of us and have troops waiting for us at the next checkpoint?"

"You must trust me."

She stood before him. "I do not."

Heinz pursed his lips thoughtfully. "I will sign travel papers for you. They will serve you if you're stopped and questioned. And by signing them, if you are ever caught I will be implicated with you. It would be in my best interests to see you are left free."

"That does not prevent you from having us arrested. You could always say you were coerced."

Heinz dropped his gaze to his knees. "I just want to go home," he muttered.

"Elizabeth," Holmes said quietly.

She turned to look at him.

"Let him sign the papers."

"It isn't a full guarantee," she protested.

"He is not alone in the desire to return home. Take his papers. His word will be enough."

"A gentlemen's agreement? The world does not work that way any more, Holmes. Ask any man in the trenches. The unwritten rules no longer exist. There is nothing to stop him from betraying us the moment we leave the city." She shook her head. "His word is not enough."

"Then shoot him where he sits," Holmes said. "If the world has changed that much, then you must shoot him now."

She considered Heinz for a long, silent moment, then dropped her gaze. She turned to face the others. "I want to be a good twenty miles from the city by daylight. Hurry. We have much to do."

Holmes held up his hand. "Wait! There is one thing Heinz can do for us."

"What?"

He grimaced. "Actually, it is for me . . ."

Chapter Fourteen

ZEKI'S ROOM AT THE BARRACKS WAS MOST COMFORTABLE, IF somewhat bare, but he didn't mind the bareness. It was clean, and the electricity worked, and then there was the food.

In the few short hours he had been lodged here, awaiting Von Stein's return, he had ventured out to the refectory four times. There, he could feast on the huge quantity and range of food, and no-one stopped him, and no-one asked that he pay.

His wounded shoulder had been tended, and he didn't even mind the armed guard who accompanied him. Von Stein had assigned the guard before he left, and Zeki understood the necessity. He had not proved himself, yet, and until he did, Von Stein would ensure he was kept comfortable and secure.

Heinz found Zeki in the refectory. It was his fifth visit, and he was dining lightly on fresh white bread and an aged, redolent cheese. A pat of creamy butter sat to one side, a pot of Turkish coffee with it. He considered it breakfast, as the sun had just risen.

Heinz glanced at his watch. "I've come to collect you," he told Zeki.

"Von Stein has returned?"

"I am finishing up the affair."

"He found Sigerson?"

"Oh, yes, he found him."

Zeki gave a sigh. "Good. So now he believes me?"

"You have proved your status as a double-agent. Now all that remains is to prove that you actually work for us, and don't intend to switch back to the English side should it prove more convenient sometime in the future."

"I have only ever worked for Germany." Zeki felt a little hurt.

"You were recruited by the English, first."

Zeki curled his lip. "For the honour of fighting for my people. That is all they were prepared to offer." He spat. "You Germans, though . . . you understood. Money is the real power. Much money will you give me. Why would I switch sides?"

"Why, indeed? I had not realized the bargain Berlin struck with you was for money. I did wonder what could possibly hold an Armenian's loyalty to us."

"Now you know. And you can have no more doubts about me, no?"

"No. No more doubts," Heinz agreed softly. His lips curled up a little, as if he had tasted something disgusting. Then he looked at his watch. "Come. You're expected."

Zeki dabbed his red lips with a napkin, delicately, with his good hand, and rose and followed Heinz from the refectory, out into the painfully bright sunrise. The morning was crisp and cool, but the sun carried a touch of warmth that made it refreshing to be outside. Zeki caught up with Heinz as he tramped across the square. Zeki's guard followed along the regulation one pace behind.

Heinz reached the end of the parade ground, and halted. He delved into his greatcoat. "I forgot. Would you like a cigarette?" he said and offered a packet of black Russians.

Zeki reached for them. He would be able to smoke black Russians whenever he wanted, now, so refusing them would be silly.

Heinz lit the cigarette for him, and Zeki caught his gaze above the match flame. There was something cold and hard in the little German's eyes that puzzled him.

That was when an invisible sledgehammer slammed into Zeki's chest, throwing him backwards.

He died trying to fathom what had happened to him.

HOLMES EJECTED THE spent bullet jacket and watched as Heinz and the guard and another passerby gathered around Zeki's body. The line of fire here had been as clear as Heinz had promised.

His splinted leg was beginning to throb, pushed backwards as it was, and he swivelled awkwardly in the seat to put the rifle on the floor of the vehicle and lift the injured leg onto the seat. Elizabeth and Häfner were watching him.

"For Mycroft, for Fairuza," he said. He looked at Elizabeth. "And for you."

She looked away.

"It is done?" Häfner asked.

"It is a good rifle. It is done."

Häfner started the engine, and drove Von Stein's car carefully into the light early-morning traffic. The silence inside the car was deep and thoughtful.

ELIZABETH DECIDED TO use Von Stein's car to take them to Ankara. After that it would quickly become a liability, but for the journey to Ankara it would allow Holmes to rest his leg, and it would let them avoid the train system, which was a natural bottleneck.

An hour after leaving the last of the city behind, they found a quiet spot well off the road, and there Elizabeth used the medical kit to dress Holmes' wound and re-splint and bandage the leg again.

"The bullet wound is healing nicely, but you're risking permanent maiming by using the leg as much as you are." She grimaced. "But you know that. It's the doctor in me speaking, not the strategist."

"Doctor?" Holmes asked sharply.

"A courtesy title only. You know I learned from Watson, and I've kept up with developments since then. And my field surgery experience is very extensive." She delved into the medical kit again. "Is the pain very bad? I have some morphine . . ."

"No." He shook his head, emphasizing the refusal. "Don't offer it again." He looked at her. "Please."

She nodded a little, understanding.

AFTER THEIR STOP, Elizabeth took over the controls of the car, and Häfner settled into the passenger seat to sleep. Holmes sat in the rear with his leg extended.

The way became dustier and drier, although Elizabeth was a good driver, alert enough to avoid the worst of the bumps and holes. She was concentrating on watching the road ahead when she felt a warm hand on her shoulder.

"You have suffered because of me, again," Holmes said, and his thumb touched the bruised and swollen corner of her mouth.

She glanced a little over her shoulder. He had leaned forward to speak quietly. She returned her gaze to the road ahead.

"This time, Holmes, I'm alive because of you."

"I've done nothing but ruin your operations out here, and led the Germans right to the tent of the Divine Wind."

"Heinz was right, Holmes. The Turks are losing. They won't last much longer now, and then my role as Hadiya and as the Divine Wind would be over anyway."

She shook her head a little. "But it was because you are who you are that Von Stein could not see the truth just beyond that fact. He was convinced you were the one who has been feeding information to the Divine Wind throughout the war. With an agent of such stature to focus upon, he did not entertain the possibility that I could be more important to him than as a way to reach you."

"And this saved your life?"

"Yes. Von Stein would have killed me instantly had he even suspected my true identity."

"You're trying to comfort me. Thank you."

"I'm just telling you the truth."

"Ah, truth. It has been a rare commodity these past few weeks. Secrets within secrets, within more secrets. Everyone wearing two or three faces. Including me. I grow weary of it all."

Silence stretched between them.

"Why did you do it, Elizabeth?"

She knew he was not asking about her activities in Anatolia or Constantinople, and her heart started beating hard despite having prepared herself for this question ever since Holmes had ridden into camp ten days before.

"Is it," he added softly, "that you could no longer abide living in danger, as you were forced to because of me?"

She shook her head. "I wasn't running away, Holmes. I was searching for something I needed. Something even you could not give me, that you would not have been able to provide even if I had asked for it."

"Ah . . ." His exclamation told her he had leapt ahead of her to the answer. "Your freedom." And after a long moment, he added, "You are right. I would not have been able to let you go."

She nodded, feeling sadness well inside her. "I'm sorry, Holmes."

She heard him settle back into his seat. The silence stretched on.

THEY REACHED ANKARA that night but chose to camp on the outskirts rather than risk the military gauntlet they would inevitably face somewhere in the city at night.

They found a well-protected gully and drove the car right into it, breaking an axle over the rocks. The car was to be abandoned the next day, but it would provide some shelter for the night.

Elizabeth insisted on watch duties, and Häfner volunteered for the first watch. As soon as they had eaten, Holmes and Elizabeth settled down to sleep, while Häfner found a comfortable spot far enough away from the fire not to spoil his night vision.

Holmes insisted on second watch, which gave Elizabeth several unbroken hours of sleep.

She awoke naturally some time later and checked her watch by the light of the fire, which had been recently stoked. It was almost time for her watch duty.

Holmes had found a smooth piece of ground to spread his blanket upon and a small rock to lean his back against. His leg was thrust out before him. She could see his dark outline against the lighter night sky, blocking out stars.

Elizabeth gathered up her own blanket, moved to the rock and sat down beside him. She pointed to where Holmes faced.

"East, yes?"

"East," he confirmed.

"You still contemplate life while watching the sun rise and sink?"

"It helps me think."

She made herself more comfortable. "I thought, perhaps . . . you might want to know what happened in 1903. With Moran."

"There are things unanswered from that time," he said. It was a cautious agreement.

"And you cannot tolerate a mystery."

"This one I have tolerated for fifteen years. But I would rather have the answers."

"Very well." She paused, searching for a place to begin.

"He abducted you—took you from Baker Street," Holmes said helpfully. "I traced his movements as far as the tiny Indian hostel near the river. Watson and I even examined the room he kept you in. We found signs of you, including the warning note written in your own blood of the ship that he intended to leave England upon. But when we found the ship, and Moran, you were not there, and he refused to speak of your whereabouts. He hinted, instead, that if I did not let him go, you would be killed."

"Did Moran die when the ship blew up?"

Holmes lifted his brow. "You know of what happened?"

"I heard some details. What happened to Moran?"

"When it was clear he no longer held you captive, I killed him." Holmes looked away. After a moment, he cleared his throat. "How did you get away from him, then? That is a question no-one and no clue could answer for me."

"That matter was simplicity itself. They were injecting me with morphine . . . did you know?"

"We learned that much."

"Moran's sister would visit, change my dressings, and give me a dose of morphine . . . I had been shot in the arm, but the morphine was used as an inhibitor rather than for any relief from the wound, which was minor. Beatrice was sweet and gentle. I don't know how Moran convinced her to work with him, but she was quite patently an unwilling co-conspirator."

"Unwilling or not, she assisted him."

"Yes, and I think that was his mistake. She was a nurse and knew she had no business deciding doses and injecting patients with a medicine that can easily kill. I learned that Moran had insisted she deliberately give me too much, so that I would be in a stupor and useless.

"She was too cautious, and her doses were underestimated to help avoid any mistakes. It meant that I was recovering from the dose sooner than either of them anticipated. I was careful, and pretended I was still euphoric, hoping that an opportunity might occur that I could take advantage of. And with each further dose, I emerged from the fog a little earlier as my body began to build a tolerance for it."

She heard him draw a deep breath. He reached for a cigarette.

"In one of my more lucid moments I heard the name of the ship that Moran awaited and managed to write it on the base of the bunk above me."

"We found it."

"I thought you might," she responded. "Shortly after that I listened to Beatrice and Moran arguing. She wanted to cease the morphine injections, but Moran wanted me tame and controlled until his ship arrived. I learned that it was expected at any time. It was only then my mind could pull the facts together, and I knew my time to do anything about my situation was running short.

"Beatrice gave me an injection—he browbeat her into it. The next time it was the same; Beatrice would argue and Moran would demand her cooperation. Only this time when Beatrice pointed out that she stood a good chance of killing me with deliberate overdoses, Moran showed his true nature. He told her he cared little whether she killed me or maimed me, that my use as a hostage was limited and shrinking each day. It was of no consequence to him if she made a mistake with the dosage—it would serve his ultimate purpose anyway."

She took a breath. "I had suspected from the beginning that Moran never intended to let me go, but the confirmation was alarming, and that alarm was just what I needed.

"Beatrice would push everyone from the room when she ministered to me, and this time, when she leaned over me to inject me again, I acted."

"You fought her off?"

"I was aware enough to know the sounds of fighting would bring Moran and the guards to investigate, so I dazed her with a blow from my head against her temple, then tied her mouth and hands and feet with bandages from her medical bag. She watched my every movement and did not try to cry out." She shrugged. "I think she wanted me to escape and was glad to see me go. I took her coat and purse, and anything else useful in the room. There was a window there, a small one—" She sensed a small movement from Holmes. "What is it?"

"That window. I know it well. I had been sitting out beside it not long before you wiggled through it."

"I wiggled, yes, and then very gracefully dropped to the ground and winded myself. And while I was lying there recovering, I tried to think of where I must go next, what I should do. Even though I had gained my senses, my mind was still not fully my own. All I could think of was that I must keep moving, keep searching for freedom. During the time I had been in the grip of the morphine I had been plagued with memories, and many of them were of our time in Constantinople and Sullah's people . . ."

She sighed. "I went to Tayisha, Sullah's daughter. She was in London, studying, do you remember?"

"I recall Watson telling me that, yes."

"She took me in, and for the next two days she became my nurse, for I was very sick indeed. Between bouts of illness I managed to impress on her that she should not tell anyone where I was, and my condition worried her enough that she obeyed, for fear that contacting you might give away my location to the people who had inflicted this upon me."

She felt his hand on her wrist, a tight grip. "I know what you suffered through," he said quietly. "I would not wish that curse upon anyone."

"It was a curse, indeed, and I was only lightly brushed by its power. The release from its grip was truly a gift. But while I lay sick, my mind was active once more. It seemed I could do nothing but think. And my thinking returned to those memories of peace and pleasure and freedom I had enjoyed when the world had thought me dead. And here I was again, cut off from everyone, and possibly thought dead again."

She hesitated.

"You made a decision," Holmes said.

She nodded. "And today I tried to explain why I made the decision I did. I knew I could not let you know I was alive, for you would find me. And . . . I knew you would not want to understand."

The little silence whispered a strained aria between them.

"Go on," Holmes said at last, his tone neutral.

"I borrowed money from Tayisha. A great deal of money, actually. She knew her father considered himself to be permanently in my debt, and she insisted I take it, for Sullah would be angry if she failed to help me in this way. In return I told her everything concerning Moran and my decision, and swore her to silence—a silence I know she kept.

"For eight months I wandered around Europe, anonymous and unfettered . . . and it wasn't enough. Slowly but surely I was being drawn east. And finally I found myself upon Sullah's doorstep.

"It was a sad reunion, for he was dying. But he saw my arrival as a sign from Allah, for he had been fretting about the family's welfare once he had gone. His first wife had died a year before, and Tayisha was married and living in England. His sons were working for him, but none of them showed the leadership necessary to control and guide the future development of the big family enterprise that Sullah had developed out of his annual carpet migrations."

She shrugged.

"He asked you to do it," Holmes interpreted.

"Asked? No. He assumed that my timely arrival meant the succession was pre-ordained. Written in the sand."

"And you did not dispute him," Holmes added.

"No. I knew I had come home, as soon as I saw the mountains and the people. I could be anything I wanted, there, and they would accept it. And here was a place for me—being thrust at me. It gave me purpose and meaning.

"For the next few years I worked harder than I have ever worked since. I took over the management and supervision of the annual trips to the Mediterranean coast and to Constantinople. There, I would behave like a European, which eased business considerably.

"But Constantinople gradually became a hard place to earn a living. Too many bribes, and the Ottoman economy was collapsing. We had trouble getting along with the Young Turks coming up through the ranks. Many of them were still idealists and couldn't be bribed. Others were greedy and wanted too much—they didn't understand the old way of doing business.

"In 1910 I was caught up in a confrontation with one of these belligerent government officials. He dragged me before the Grand Vizier's assistant, and they were discussing confiscating my stock, and levying taxes and duties on what they could estimate had been our profits for the last ten—no, let's make it fifteen—years of trade. It was quite ridiculous, especially as they were going to guess at those profits, and I'm sure their guesses would have been extraordinarily high."

"How accurate would they have been, though?" Holmes asked.

Elizabeth smiled a little. "Close," she said modestly. "We had been increasing profits exponentially for years. But we had been careful to keep a humble face on the operation, to avoid drawing attention to ourselves. I had been confronted by suspicious officials on a few previous occasions, but this time I could not seem to shake them from me.

"The German military had been posted in Constantinople for years, and they had a finger in most of the affairs of the empire. One of their junior officers had been attached to the Grand Vizier's administrative wing, and he stepped into the scuffle.

"After listening to both sides—and you can be sure I made a most pathetic and hard-done-by case for myself—the officer suggested that as they only had hard proof of my revenue for this year, they would be best to tax me on this year's, and every year after that—and he extracted from me a promise to report to this office the following year when I returned to the city."

"Of course you promised," Holmes said dryly.

"Of course I did. The officer took me to the bazaar for coffee and explained to me that although he was sure I could creatively minimize my revenue reports, I would be best to report in faithfully next year. That, in his experience, the greedier of the officials did not last for long—they overreached themselves sooner or later, and with luck, when I reported in next year, there was a good chance there would be no-one there to report to."

"It was Häfner, wasn't it?"

"Yes. William is one of those people who can calm a room of mortal enemies by walking into it. A peace maker. A deep thinker, and a philosopher.

"I did report in the next year, and William was there, forgotten by Berlin, but the official had gone long ago. I learned more about William's politics, which leaned towards the proletariat. We did not meet very often—I was too busy, and we knew it would not look good for a German officer to be friendly with an odd, eccentric Englishwoman, but we became friends.

"My business became more legal and protracted in the city, as the year before I had incorporated the whole company and expanded it into an international concern.

"The work I was doing, work so unsuitable for a lady, was exposing me to a world of experience, and a world of people with different perspectives and ideas. Gradually, as the blinkers and channels wore away the limits I had habitually imposed upon my future, I learned to think in bigger, more ambitious plans.

"After my run-in with the Turk in Constantinople, I made a business trip to London. I took two of Sullah's sons with me—I chose them because they had been educated in Western universities and understood English business law. I registered the family company as a British company and put them in as managers.

"For the next four years I strengthened the Anglo-Persian interests. I was in and out of England often and used Tayisha as my representative when necessary.

"I also started exploring more diverse sources of income that I could channel back through the company. I began studying the future of oil exportation and spent some speculative funds on test oil wells in the southwest corner of Persia. I had the ideal workers, too. Sullah's sons and the men he had employed for years to bring the caravans through any conditions and problems safely back home—they were trained for harsh conditions and hard work. They trusted and obeyed me, and they knew how to work together. I sweetened the project for them by offering a percentage of any future profit to be shared among them—it was an idea I adapted from William's Bolshevik philosophies—and it worked with greater efficiency than I had suspected.

"Between the oil wells and London, and the offices in Constantinople and Mashhad, I spent a lot of time travelling. My contact with people from all corners of the globe, and the whispers and rumours I had begun to hear, hinted of war to come. A great war, that would draw in the entire world. And I could see how it might happen, given the alliances and treaties in place. I had only to draw on my experience with German control in Constantinople to see how most of Europe would go up in flames with a single match to light it."

"You were not wrong there," Holmes observed.

"I had learned how to think ambitiously by then, and I made new plans, designed to take advantage of my unique position in the Middle East. If war was to come, I had no intentions of hiding and idly watching it go by from a safe corner in Persia. The family had too many interests that would be in jeopardy.

"From what William had told me, and from the stepped-up activity of the German military in Constantinople, I knew the Turks would ally themselves with Germany. When the archduke was assassinated, I knew it had begun. I put the plans I had made into action and sent my first packet of information to Mycroft, using the export company as a channel."

"And Häfner? How did that come about?" His tone was still neutral.

"William could see what was about to happen as well as I. He wanted to abandon his commission and make his way to St. Petersburg. I convinced him he could be more effective here, working covertly. Accordingly, at the first declaration of war, William announced to his superiors that he would feel happier if his wife joined him in Constantinople, and a few days later, I dyed my hair black, and 'arrived' upon the Orient Express."

There was a long silence while Holmes slowly extracted a fresh cigarette and lit it, drawing deeply.

"Hadiya Adlparvar . . . how was he born? The Divine Wind?"

"You know about Abadan. Enver, a politician in Constantinople, allowed the Turks to cross the frontier and sabotage and destroy the oil wells there. My people, my men, wanted blood, and would not sit still for the stance of neutrality that Persia had taken. I knew I could not afford to ignore their lust for vengeance. It would slip and cut me to the quick if I did.

"I had heard about the British plans to incite the Bedouins to fight against the Turks for them. It was simplicity itself to have everyone pose as Bedouins. I moved them north to Anatolia, where they would do the most good harassing the Germans and Turks there—for that was the area for which I obtained the best information. Cyrus, Sullah's son, is steady enough in a pinch to lead them while I was not there, so long as he had goals and directions.

"So I began to split my time between Constantinople and the hills of eastern Anatolia, shuttling information and orders, and I have been doing it ever since."

"With a great deal of success, to which Von Stein's obsession testifies," Holmes said. "And the name? Where does the name come from?"

"That was William's idea. He thought I should have a layer between me and any people I dealt with for covert purposes. We invented Hadiya, who took over the operations in Constantinople, but whom people never got to meet, and had him listed as a member of the board, falsifying the records so he looked as though he had been a founder of the company. It gave him verisimilitude. And it meant I was simply taking orders from someone higher than me, should anyone try to trace the source.

"The name itself was also William's idea. He has a fondness for subtle jests of that sort. It was a natural extension of the reputation the Divine Wind was already engendering. The Divine Wind was the name Cyrus' group invented for themselves. It was a collective name, with me as the titular head and leader of it."

She laughed a little. "You share that penchant for names with William. That is how I knew you had penetrated the high command in early 1915. It was the name, filtering through from Berlin on orders and papers. *Von Karnch* is unusual enough, but its literal translation made me wonder. *A tall, thin man with long legs?*" She laughed again. "When von Karnch disappeared without notice, and with William's contacts in Berlin being very tight-lipped about his disappearance, I did not need any more confirmation that it was you."

The silence, this time, was protracted. Elizabeth allowed him the time, watching the sky before her gradually show the first signs of coming morning.

The streaks were unmistakable slashes in the inky blackness when Holmes spoke again. "Had you stayed in London, fifteen years ago, you would not have been able to achieve all that you have achieved here." She saw him breathe deeply. "I would willingly give you anything I could, but this . . . unconditional arena where you have been able to achieve so much—this, I could not have provided. Because of who I am, I would have failed you in that."

"I didn't see it as failure," she said softly. "It was because of your teaching that I had the courage to be and do all that I have done. Otherwise, I might still be working as a typist in a London office, a frustrated and sour spinster."

After another thoughtful moment, Holmes nodded. "Yes, there's that," he agreed, dryly.

Elizabeth laughed a little.

"And what now?" he asked. "Your affairs in Constantinople are delayed until the end of the war."

"The Divine Wind still has work to do. The Allies are pushing for Damascus now."

"They are breaking their knuckles upon Amman."

"But they will persist and wear the Turks down, and they will win through to Damascus," Elizabeth assured him. "The Divine Wind and his people should be there." She hesitated. "What about you?"

"London, and then, home."

"Why don't you stay with me?" She touched his arm, gently. "With us? You know you can be happy in this place. You were once before."

"That was a long time ago. Things have changed since then. Not just us, Elizabeth, but the whole world is changing. Even here I see it. What I liked here is disappearing and the West is moving in. I won't recognize this corner of the world in a few years' time. This war has caught so many people by surprise for it has been fought as a modern war, but it will force those changes to come about more quickly. No," and he shook his head firmly, "I would rather remain where I know what to expect. Change, in Sussex, is slow to occur. The people there will fight it every step of the way, and I will be one of them."

Despite knowing what his answer would be, Elizabeth felt a jerk of disappointment. She kept her face still and neutral.

Holmes lit a cigarette. "Age has given me a modicum of wisdom and perspective, which means I know myself too well. I am not happy unless I am the centre of my world. And you, my dear Elizabeth, are the shining epicentre of yours. I would never sit at your feet as Cyrus and Häfner are content to do."

"I would not ask that of you."

He glanced at her, and in the growing light she saw him smile a little. "You would ask it because you are who you are. I know—for I had a hand in making you."

She stared at the ground beside her, blinking.

"Besides," Holmes added quietly, and his tone had changed, and grown harder. "There is still something I must do to end this affair. In London."

Chapter Fifteen

The next day they acquired horses and supplies and donned Arab clothing before heading north-northeast into the dry, rocky lands beyond Ankara. After six days of easy travel they sighted the coast of the Black Sea, and here, William Häfner parted company with them, for his destination lay far in the north.

After their farewell, Holmes and Elizabeth travelled on a more southerly route, and after four days began to search for word or sign of the Divine Wind and his men.

Elizabeth's contacts in this part of the world were extensive, and hard news soon reached them: They would find the Divine Wind near Samsat.

Elizabeth was pleased when she heard this. "Cyrus has been moving further south. Good. They have itched to do some real work beyond petty raiding and sabotage. And the real work lies south."

Another three days brought them into the camp itself. Their way was more cautious, for as the Turkish front was pushed north, the countryside grew busier with the movements of troops and civilians.

Elizabeth's welcome was a reserved and respectful one,

but showed genuine warmth. Even Cyrus, when they stepped into the command tent, threw his hands up and said, “Praise Allah! Your timing is perfect as usual. I am faced with a dilemma only you can answer.”

Later, he spoke of the night of the German raid. “We lost five men—either killed or captured. Our casualties were so light because we scattered so quickly. The Germans destroyed the camp, of course, and left before sunrise the next day. By sunrise of the day after that, most of the men had trickled back into the camp. We stayed another two days waiting for stragglers and to finalize the tally of those missing, then moved far north into the no-man’s plains up there, where not even the Turks will go. When I thought the Germans had truly lost interest in us, I started bringing us south again.”

“You’ve done well, Cyrus,” Elizabeth assured him.

After two days, Holmes announced his intention to leave.

“But we’re travelling south, anyway,” Elizabeth pointed out. “And it’s safer travelling with a group.”

“A group of Bedouins amongst growing numbers of desperate Turks? I believe I would be able to travel faster and less conspicuously on my own.” He shook his head. “It’s time, Elizabeth.”

He was given supplies and gifts, clothing and whatever else he requested. Two horses—one as burden-bearer, the other the same horse he had been given by the Australian captain, east of Jerusalem, weeks before.

He left at sunrise the next day, and no-one stirred in the camp save Elizabeth, who emerged from the tent wrapped in her modest Bedouin woman’s disguise, but with her veil removed.

Holmes stood before her. “Thank you,” he said simply, and took her hand and kissed it. Then, moving more freely with the help of a roughly hewn crutch, he clambered with practiced awkwardness into the saddle and stowed the crutch. He turned the horses southwards and departed.

"SIR? CAPTAIN! ARE you awake? Captain!"

The exhortations brought Cameron Rowe slowly awake to find his sergeant standing over him.

He sat up slowly, as the aches and bruises of a dozen days' hard fighting reminded him of their presence. There was a steady throbbing from the bullet wound in his shoulder. He would have to have it seen to again. All of it was a weary reminder of the grim odds they were battling just now.

"What is it, Hughes?" he asked the sergeant. "And what time is it?"

"Just gone two in the afternoon, sir."

They had been out on reconnaissance the night before, and Rowe had fallen onto his camp bed only a scant three hours before. He groaned.

"I've got a fellow being held on the sentry line. He's asked for you by name, sir, or I would have tossed him out on his ear."

"Why does he want to see me? Did he give you his name?"

"That's just it, sir. He says his name is Sigerson, but the bloke's one of those Bedouin raiders or I'm a monkey's uncle. Injured, though."

Rowe stood up. "I'll see him." He reached for his coat, and stepped outside, to where the table and pair of camp chairs sat. His office.

He could see where the guards were standing, bracketing a tall Arab dressed in dusty, filthy robes. Hughes waved to them, and they pushed the fellow forward a little. He was using a crutch, and despite his maimed hobble, he covered the ground quickly. As he got closer, Rowe studied the eyes above the folds of the head cloth wrapped around his face. They were the eyes of the man he had spoken to, several weeks ago, just outside Jerusalem.

As he got closer, Sigerson pulled the head cloth loose, revealing his face.

"Sit," Rowe said, as soon as he reached the table.

"Thank you, that would be appreciated," Sigerson told him, sinking into the chair, and propping the stiff, splinted leg in front of him.

"You're still not travelling the easy path, I see," Rowe observed.

"The difficult way is often the most rewarding, haven't you noticed?" There was an air of humour, almost joy, emerging from the man, but it was so faint, Rowe thought he might be imagining it. A contained man, but one much changed since the last time he'd seen him.

"You found what you were looking for, in the north?"

"Oh, yes. I found answers, indeed." And this time, Sigerson did smile. He reached into his robes, withdrew a stiff packet of papers bound with an elastic band, and placed them in front of Rowe.

"You'll find in there the disposition, placement, strengths and numbers of most of the Turkish troops in and around Amman, and everything within striking distance to the north that could be brought to bear upon the allies."

Rowe looked at the packet, stunned. After a moment, he said slowly, "Do you know how valuable this information is? Do you know how we have been rebuffed twice at Amman?"

"Yes."

"It is precisely because we are not certain of the disposition of Turks in and around Amman that we have come to grief."

"Now you are certain, aren't you?" He tapped the packet. "I would appreciate it if you would pass this on to Chauvel and Allenby. They could use it, I'm sure."

"I don't doubt it," Rowe said dryly. "But you should give it to them yourself. They would want to thank you, even if they could do nothing else."

"No. I have lingered around Amman longer than I should, gathering this information. I did it not for praise from generals, but as thanks to you and your men for your help in December. You should pass this on, and there's no need to mention my name."

"I could not falsely claim this as my own work."

"Then say it was a native of these parts, who has since returned to his home. It will be close enough to the truth."

"You are going home? To London?"

"To London, yes, where I must deal with the last few tasks I have remaining. Then home, to Sussex."

"And the native of these parts . . ." Rowe pointed to his dusty robes. "You have lost all your reluctance," he observed.

"If you face the truth squarely, captain, it draws the sting. After that, there is no need to fear it any more."

Rowe smiled a little. "I won't profess to understand you, sir, but I'm glad to see you survived your excursion to the north."

Sigerson got to his feet, thrusting the crutch under him. "I have returned your horse. I suspect you might need extra mounts in the next few months."

"That we will." Rowe got to his feet again. "Get yourself some supplies from the canteen before you leave, Sigerson. And thank you. Your gift may just make the difference." He touched the packet of papers.

"That was its intention. I have a personal interest in ensuring the Turks are driven far from here."

Rowe held out his hand, which Sigerson gripped readily. "It has been a pleasure to meet you, Mr. Holmes."

Chapter Sixteen

Queen Anne Street
April, 1918

Watson was startled out of his reverie when the doorbell chimed, for no-one in London knew he was back. He had deliberately not announced his return, and even the tradesmen and suppliers weren't aware that he was home.

He answered the door curiously and found Sherlock Holmes standing upon his doorstep, leaning heavily on a handsome walking stick.

"Watson, my old friend. You don't think you can possibly slink back into London without my knowing about it, do you?"

"I should know better, I suppose," Watson said slowly, still dazed and puzzled. "Holmes . . . what on earth are you doing here? And where have you been? You've been knocked about a bit, I see."

"It's quite a tale, and one you deserve to share. I have a car waiting and a small adventure to finish. It's only the dénouement, I'm afraid, Watson, but would you like to be in on it? I can bring you up to date on the way."

Watson felt a small flare of enthusiasm, the first spark of a positive emotion he had felt in many long weeks. "I wouldn't miss it for the world," he said simply, and reached for his coat.

"And bring your revolver, Watson!" Holmes shouted, already several yards along the pavement.

WATSON WAS STARTLED to find Chief Inspector Tobias Gregson sitting next to the driver in the luxurious vehicle Holmes led him to.

"Good grief," he muttered and held out his hand. "Gregson, you haven't changed."

"Good to see you, Watson, and I wish I could say the same for you. You look . . . ill-used, old man."

"Yes, yes, there have been some trying times," Watson agreed awkwardly and turned eagerly to Holmes as he settled beside him, the stiff leg jutting awkwardly. "Where are we off to?"

Gregson murmured directions to the driver, who got the car under way.

"I've only just returned to London myself," Holmes replied. "I have to report in to my superiors."

"That would be Mycroft, then?"

There was a small silence.

"I see I shall have to start at the very beginning," Holmes said, and proceeded to tell Watson of Mycroft's assault and the events that propelled him aboard a boat for the Middle East.

Watson listened to the narrative with growing wonder.

"And is Mycroft still alive?" he asked hesitantly.

"I saw him myself, late last night, and they say he is doing well."

"And did you discover who was responsible for this assault?" Watson demanded.

"I did," Holmes assured him.

"Who?"

"Ah . . . well, you must indulge me for a while, Watson. I'd like to play this one out. Besides, I have yet to report to Lord Stainsbury, and the tale is a long one. I'd rather not weary myself with telling it twice over."

"The Holmes of old," Watson observed wryly. "I have missed these little dramas of yours."

"Yes, the Holmes of old is back," he answered. "Ah, here we are!"

The motor car pulled to the curb, and they exited, Holmes using the walking stick and taking the weight off his injured leg almost completely.

Watson observed this and cleared his throat. "I'd like to look at that when you have time, Holmes. It doesn't look good."

"I've been using it too much, I've been told," Holmes said cheerfully, "so I have been favouring it as much as I can, when I can. But later, Watson."

Watson contented himself with Holmes' implied promise, and followed him into the smart, modern commercial building, with Gregson behind him.

In the foyer a clerk came forward and asked their business.

"Lord Stainsbury is expecting me," Holmes declared. "Tell him Sherlock Holmes is here."

The clerk hurried away, and shortly afterwards, a man taller than Holmes himself appeared. He came towards them, his hand outstretched. "Holmes, it's good to see you. I must say that after months of silence I'm astonished you're here. I had expected you to send regular reports."

"They would have defeated the purpose of my going out there in the first place," Holmes said dryly. "How should I have sent the reports back to you?"

"Through the normal channels . . . ah! I see your point. The normal channels were already compromised."

Stainsbury shook his head ruefully. "Forgive me, it is anxiety that forces me to such lack of thought." He looked past Holmes. "Gregson." A nod.

Holmes turned a little. "And this is . . . my doctor, Watson, just lately returned from the western front himself."

Again, the nod; then Stainsbury glanced at the cane in Holmes' hand. "Trouble?"

"Much of it, my lord," Holmes said with a smile. "But let's not stand about in the entry hall discussing king's business."

"No, of course not," Stainsbury agreed, and led them down a wide corridor to a large office with mahogany furniture that glowed with care and polish. A deep, button-back leather couch provided seating for Gregson and Watson, while Stainsbury settled himself against the front of his desk.

Holmes pulled both visitor's hard chairs out, and rearranged them to his satisfaction before lowering himself to one of them, then carefully lifting his splinted leg to the other. The cane he rested against his hip.

"I am naturally agog," Stainsbury said. "Your assignment was successful?"

"I have discovered the turncoat and have dealt with him."

"Good. It is as Mycroft thought? The anonymous donor was the blackguard?"

"Not at all. It was the coordinator of the group who was to blame."

"The Turk! I find that hard to believe. I met the fellow when he was here. Young, retiring, eager to please."

"And he was quite genuine when you met him, my lord. The Germans got their hands on him not long after that, and I believe they bought his loyalty. Even in the short time I had dealings with him I noticed Zeki's fondness for the luxuries of life." Holmes pursed his lips. "I shall tell the tale as it occurred so that you understand my every deduction and conclusion."

And so he did. Watson listened, fascinated, as Holmes described his journey to the Orient and his return to Constantinople. The unravelling of the clues astounded him and, very discreetly, Watson withdrew a notebook from an inner pocket of his coat and began to make notes, the habit asserting itself almost unconsciously.

Lord Stainsbury interrupted. "After Zeki's confession that he was Armenian, you were completely happy that he was genuine?"

"Certainly," Holmes responded.

"Then you had no reason to question his loyalty again, and certainly nothing to justify your assumption that he was actually working for the Germans."

"On the contrary," Holmes said. "The events that occurred shortly after that proved conclusively Zeki was a German agent. After establishing the connection between Hadiya and the Divine Wind, I set out the very next morning to search for the Divine Wind, and when I found him, ten days later, the Germans attacked the camp. By that time I had confirmed that Hadiya and the Divine Wind were the same man."

"You spoke to him?" Gregson interjected, surprised.

"Certainly. He was at the camp of the Bedouins. And he was enraged that I had brought Germans upon them when the Germans to that point had failed to find them despite constant hunting. And he was correct. I *did* bring the Germans upon them. I was shot and captured during that raid, and on the long trip back to Constantinople, I had time to think it through. I must have been followed from Ankara."

"That was careless of you, was it not?" Stainsbury remarked.

"I took precautions against being followed," Holmes returned. "But I believed at the time that the chances of having someone upon my trail were so remote only cursory preventions were necessary. The Germans were clever enough to work around them and find me again. And they must have followed me into the heart of Anatolia, although I naturally never saw a sign of them. Again, I was lax in my precautions out there. I had told no-one but Zeki where I was going, and he had proved he was worthy of my trust. I was completely convinced by his tale, because it was true. I'm quite sure that, were you to investigate, you would find that Zeki's family were part of the forced Armenian relocation. The horror Zeki suffered was genuine, but his love of money proved superior.

"When I was outlining my plans to find the Divine Wind, Zeki explained he must stay in the city to help Fairuza, the agent who had been taken while we watched. I believe he was either Fairuza's friend or possibly her lover. That is how Von Stein found out about Zeki. Fairuza never spoke a word while in captivity, but her background would have been investigated, and Zeki's name would have emerged. His shock and distress over her capture were quite genuine. It was that authenticity that convinced me he wanted to stay in the city for altruistic reasons, and I let him stay."

"But how could he be genuinely shocked?" Stainsbury asked. "He must have turned her in to the Germans."

"Oh, they knew about her long before that. Zeki's entire network had been compromised from the beginning, and had been turned against us. It was only Hadiya's dissenting reports that tipped Mycroft off. Zeki reported to his superior, who either was part of the high command in Berlin, or else was closely associated with the high command, and it was Berlin that passed the information on to Von Stein when they were ready for Fairuza to come in.

"They timed it beautifully. As soon as I drew close enough to be a genuine menace, they pulled her in. They knew I could never be allowed to speak to Zeki's agents and start putting together the entire picture. They would have dealt with the last remaining agent in the same way, had he not seen to the task himself."

"But this is appalling," Stainsbury remarked. "The intelligence network out there was obviously a complete waste of time and resources."

"Not for the Germans. They could feed us any information they wanted us to know via our own network. It was a perfect situation for them. A direct conduit to the English ear, as good as a telephone, and far more trusted by both sides." Holmes dismissed the objection with a wave of his hand.

"The day I set out for Ankara on the weekly train, Zeki must have sent up the red flags, and Berlin shot into action. Von Stein was given his orders, and he obeyed immediately. Before I had even left Ankara, I must have had a tail. Zeki is the only one I told where I was going. It was he who betrayed me . . . betrayed all of us."

"It's a slim thread upon which to hang a man," Gregson pointed out.

"Ah, the legal necessities of proof," Holmes uttered. "You have a legitimate professional concern there, Gregson, and it is a concern I held myself. But Zeki's later actions were proof enough. Hadiya observed him chatting with Von Stein immediately after his 'arrest,' and Von Stein told Hadiya Zeki had given him my real name. That would have been enough for any mortal man, but Hadiya pointed out that Zeki may have been desperate to preserve himself and offered the information as a means of holding the Germans at bay.

"So I tested him. I had Heinz, Von Stein's assistant, ask him directly if he worked for Germans or the English. Zeki confirmed he worked for the Germans only, and the manner of his answer must have utterly convinced Heinz, for when he walked him across the square shortly after that I was watching through the sights of a rifle and saw Heinz offer Zeki a cigarette. It was the signal Heinz and I had previously arranged, and when I saw it, I acted upon it."

"'Acted'?" Stainsbury queried.

"I shot him," Holmes returned.

Watson found his pencil had paused. He looked up, shocked.

The silence in the room was profound, but it did not seem to ruffle Holmes. He stared back at Stainsbury with no hint of guilt or discomfort.

"You executed a man based on the word of a German?" Stainsbury said.

"On the word of a man who hated duplicity and wanted only to go home and escape the awful necessities of a war not of his choosing. Double agents are not to be trusted. Heinz knew that and gave the signal to me for the sake of his country."

"I suppose, given the circumstances, it was appropriate," Stainsbury said slowly.

"Zeki was a spy," Holmes said harshly, "and knew very well what he risked with his deceptions. The Germans had no compunction about executing Fairuza as soon as her use had expired. I merely returned the favour."

Stainsbury cleared his throat. "You appear to have been very efficient in the clearing up of this mess, Holmes. You've found the man responsible for Mycroft's condition and managed to sweep the board clean of black pieces at the same time. This Hadiya . . . he will continue to report as he has been?"

"Hadiya's time in the city has come to an end. He's a known factor now. He has returned to the Bedouins, and taken up his role as the Divine Wind on a permanent basis."

"I hope you thanked the man—he's literally saved your life, and saved England from further embarrassment. As you say, it was his independent reports that alerted us to foul play out there."

"Yet you were convinced it was Hadiya who was the turncoat," Holmes pointed out.

Stainsbury smiled. "Yes, that was rather foolish of me, upon reflection, wasn't it?" He stood up. "I must see to something rather urgent," he said. "It won't take a moment, if you don't mind," and he moved towards the door.

But Holmes, with his leg across two chairs, was neatly blocking the direct path to the door.

Stainsbury went to step around him, to move through the narrow passage between Holmes' chair and the wall. And Holmes' walking cane came whistling down in front of him. The end thumped against the wall.

"Actually, I do mind. Considerably so," Holmes said quietly. "I'd much rather you didn't tell Germany everything I have just revealed to you."

"What on earth . . . ? What is this?" Stainsbury declared, showing mild irritation.

"It is a curious omission you have made, my lord. You very carefully didn't ask me who Zeki's superior was, where he got his orders from."

"Holmes, I demand you let me through at once," Stainsbury demanded.

"Watson?" Holmes said, not turning his gaze away from the lord who towered over him.

Watson pulled his revolver out of his pocket and obediently cocked and aimed it at Stainsbury.

"Holmes, have you gone out of your mind?" Gregson spluttered.

"You should be examining Stainsbury, Gregson. He has carefully avoided my very direct question."

"Zeki's superior? You said Berlin was directing him," Stainsbury said impatiently.

"I didn't say that at all. Watson, I'm quite sure you have your notebook out by now. Did you record what I said?"

"I think so, Holmes. One moment." He turned back a

page, then another, then grunted with satisfaction. "Here it is, Holmes. You said Zeki reported to someone who either was part of the high command in Berlin, or else was closely associated with the high command."

Gregson stood. "Holmes, you can't accuse a member of the House of Lords, and a hard-working part of the war office of . . . of . . ."

"Treason," Watson supplied helpfully.

"Yes, treason!" Gregson finished.

"That is exactly what I am doing," Holmes replied, his voice low and intense. "I have proof that Zeki's superior was none other than you, Stainsbury. I suggest you sit down and listen."

Stainsbury's face had grown red with rage, and he did not step away from Holmes, nor did his gaze move.

Watson stood, too. "If you please, Lord Stainsbury."

The man glanced at the gun in Watson's hand, then returned to the chair behind his desk.

"You'd better make sure he doesn't have a revolver or two tucked within easy distance of his chair, Watson," Holmes suggested.

Watson searched the desk drawers, and withdrew a gun from the drawer, which he handed to Holmes. Holmes glanced at Gregson, who still stood, his eyes wide. "Do you find it strange a man such as Stainsbury should have a gun in his desk?"

"It's war-time, Holmes. Don't be ridiculous," Stainsbury said cynically.

"And this is London," Gregson said quietly. "The war is not being held on English streets. And even I do not keep a gun in my desk drawer." He sat down again.

"He does point out an uncertainty, though," Holmes agreed. "So let me prove my point quickly, and close the case. It has taken me much thought to put this together from the few tiny clues available. Stainsbury has been very good at hiding and made very few mistakes. Each mistake was miniscule, but it is enough to leave me with no doubt.

"Stainsbury had much to do with Zeki's original recruitment. He told me that himself, before I left London. It was, he said, the reason why he was sure Hadiya was the bad agent. I'm sure that during Zeki's orientation here in London, Stainsbury quietly bribed him into doing double duty while in Constantinople. It was a perfect system. Zeki would occasionally send a courier with actual messages and documents for Mycroft. Stainsbury would meet the courier privately and give him orders for Zeki, and the courier would faithfully return them to Zeki, believing he was passing along English orders, when they were actually German."

"I've heard nothing that resembles proof," Stainsbury growled.

"The night of Mycroft's assault, the courier from Zeki was also murdered. There was only one possible reason to ensure the courier's silence—to prevent him from revealing that it was not he who shot Mycroft. He became a handy scapegoat that pointed the way to Constantinople and ensured I got on that ship. But the courier's death also told me there was another agent in London.

"But why would he want you on the ship to Constantinople?" Gregson asked. "It doesn't make sense to send someone out there to examine a situation you'd rather left hidden."

"Because there was a rogue agent out there, spoiling things for him. Hadiya was independent, outside Zeki's influence. Neither Zeki nor Stainsbury could control the information Hadiya was sending back to Mycroft and, naturally, Mycroft soon noticed the discrepancies. Because Hadiya was the lone, off-kilter voice amongst a chorus, Stainsbury had no trouble convincing Mycroft that Hadiya must be the bad seed. That's when Mycroft brought me in, and he told me he'd asked me because Stainsbury had suggested it."

"But *why*?" Gregson asked.

"Because Stainsbury wanted to use me like a hunting dog. Hadiya was causing him problems. If he could point me towards Hadiya, he had no doubt I would flush him out. Zeki could then deal with him, and their problems would be over, for every other agent in the city was under Zeki's control.

"It must have disconcerted you when I refused the investigation, Stainsbury," Holmes added. He sighed. "My refusal led directly to Mycroft's attack. It is a heavy fact that I will carry for the rest of my days. Stainsbury wanted me in Constantinople. Mycroft must have told him the circumstances that prompted my first refusal, and he reasoned—correctly—that the death or near-death of my brother would overcome my reluctance.

"So Stainsbury cold-bloodedly came into Mycroft's office while he was absent, took the gun from the locked drawer—he would have known where Mycroft kept the key—and then calmly visited Mycroft upon his return. He engaged him in conversation, wandering around the room as they spoke. Then, when he was behind Mycroft, and Mycroft's attention was not upon him, he took out the gun and shot him, using the cushion from the divan to muffle the noise."

"Good lord . . ." Gregson murmured.

"That wasn't the end of it," Holmes added. "He locked the office behind him, then pretended that Mycroft was busy, meeting with the courier from Constantinople. The courier Stainsbury hurried to the docks to kill, too."

The silence in the room was complete.

"Speculation," Stainsbury said quietly.

"Deduction," Holmes said flatly. "Even on my way to London that night, I was handed the clues. Gregson told me Mycroft had been shot from behind with his own gun. And Mycroft's blood on the desk clearly indicated he had fallen forward onto the desk. Which meant he was sitting behind it at the time of the shot. How could the attacker have reached the gun if Mycroft was in front of the locked drawer? He could not have got the gun while Mycroft was sitting there. As Mycroft would never have allowed a courier free access to his office, *it couldn't have been the courier*. It had to be someone who could gain access to Mycroft's desk drawer without his knowledge. I suspected it was you, Stainsbury, before I even left London."

"And you still left? Holmes, how could you?" Watson cried.

"I had to play out the game. Stainsbury so badly wanted me in Constantinople he would shoot my brother to get me there. Very well, I would go to Constantinople and find out why. Mycroft was safe as long as I did not go near him, and you may have noticed, Gregson, that I did not suggest visiting him in the last rushed hours before I got on the train."

"Yes, I did notice," Gregson admitted. "But I assumed you were bent upon finding his attacker, instead. Family can be that way."

"Although I am certain that Stainsbury has been hovering by Mycroft's bedside every day since I have been gone, acting the concerned superior, while actually monitoring him to see if he would recover and reveal Stainsbury's secret."

"He has been," Gregson agreed. "I have seen him on both occasions I have been by to see Mycroft, myself." Gregson licked his lips. "After you explained to me that you had to go to Constantinople because the killer might try to finish off the job on Mycroft, I had two guards put on his bedside, around the clock."

"I knew you would," Holmes replied. "And that meant all Stainsbury could do was watch to see if Mycroft recovered or died. He would have been forced to attempt something if Mycroft had recovered, but that dilemma didn't arise."

"And while Stainsbury hovered, I rushed off to Constantinople to deal with the rogue agent he had primed me to find. And with Zeki's help I did find him. By sheer good fortune I learned that Hadiya was not the enemy, and Zeki was. You already know how I dealt with that."

Holmes lowered his leg to the ground and stood up, facing Stainsbury. "That leaves only you to deal with."

"You have no proof of any of this—it is all . . . circumstantial. Guesswork."

"Deduction from facts. Logic," Holmes countered.

"It isn't proof."

Holmes seemed to draw himself upright, challenging even Stainsbury's height. "My lord, when I realized you were what you are, I knew I was dealing with an extremely clever man, possibly one of the most audacious and cunning men I have come across in my career. Did you think I would confront you with mere logic and extrapolation as my shield?"

For the first time Stainsbury showed an emotion other than indignation. A tiny flicker of doubt shadowed his eyes, narrowed them. "This whole fairy tale is based on nothing but erroneous extrapolation," he said slowly, as if he were feeling his way.

"That is all I have presented you with until now," Holmes agreed. "Erroneous, however . . . that remains to be seen. If that was all I was offering, all of you would be right to doubt me. But I offer incontrovertible proof."

"Then offer it!" Stainsbury demanded.

Holmes smiled. "Verily, a witness!" he declared.

There was a small silence, a surprised one. "Impossible," Stainsbury declared. "If this deed I was sup posed to have committed took place in Mycroft's chamber, there could have been no witnesses."

"Ah, but there was!" Holmes exclaimed. "You overlook the one other person in the room beside yourself."

Watson felt his jaw loosening, and caught it up. "Holmes, you can't mean Mycroft, surely?"

"Yes, I do mean Mycroft," Holmes answered. "Stainsbury, surely you did not think that Mycroft would remain unconscious all these weeks? Did you not wonder at all?"

"You mean... he was pretending?" Stainsbury spluttered.

"Mycroft was too weak to defend himself, and he would have known without being told, and with absolute certainty, that I was searching for the proof needed to condemn you. All he was required to do was continue to let you think he was unconscious and unable to identify you as his attacker. Which he did with spectacular success."

Stainsbury's face turned the sickly colour of whey. He remained speechless.

"Last night when my train arrived in London," Holmes continued, "I slipped into Saint Thomas' in the small hours of the morning and spoke to Mycroft. He confirmed that it was you who shot him. And he confirmed that it was you who insisted he have me sent to Constantinople."

"Good god . . . !" Gregson muttered to himself.

The silence stretched for long moments. Stainsbury seemed incapable of a response, but the terrible, haunted expression on his face made no response necessary.

Holmes spread his hand a little, as one who was being completely candid. "I have recently been accused of depending on an outdated viewpoint in a world that no longer works that way, but some of those gentlemen's attitudes were useful." He picked up the gun that had been retrieved from Stainsbury's desk and broke it open to check the load. He removed all but one bullet, snapped it shut, and tossed it to Stainsbury, who caught it by reflex.

"You know what to do with that," Holmes said coldly.

"Holmes . . ." Watson murmured, alarmed, but Holmes lifted an imperious hand in the air towards him, silencing him. He did not shift his gaze from Stainsbury, who was staring at the gun with bewildered fascination.

Finally, Stainsbury stirred, and looked at all of them. "If you will excuse me?" he murmured.

Nobody responded.

Stainsbury turned and walked to the narrow door behind his desk, and opened it, revealing a small, private sitting room beyond. He shut it behind him.

The three remaining occupants of the room remained motionless and completely silent.

A few moments later there was the sound of gunfire from the sitting room.

Sherlock Holmes sank onto his chair with a long, deep sigh, and his chin fell to his chest, his eyes closed.

Gregson silently made his way into the sitting room, then re-emerged a few moments later and picked up the telephone on Stainsbury's desk. "Holmes, Watson, I suggest you leave. This is going to be an overnight sensation—a lord of the realm a German agent! There will be bobbies all over the place very soon, and the reporters will follow."

"It will be suppressed," Holmes answered, lifting his chin. "Stainsbury's peers will see to that. And perhaps it is just as well. Britain doesn't need this sort of blow to its self-esteem just now."

Watson tugged on Holmes' sleeve. "We'd best be leaving anyway, Holmes."

Holmes seemed to be stirring from the black mood he had fallen into. "Yes, yes," he murmured. Then he stood, leaning on the walking stick once more, and appeared to see Watson for the first time. "Watson! I am famished. Let's find a suitable eating establishment and dine together, just like old times." He limped to the door and opened it, and as Watson passed by he added in a murmur: "Besides, I have something to confess to you."

Chapter Seventeen

AFTER THE ENTRÉE AND BEFORE THE MAIN COURSE—AN excellent lamb joint with a fresh, tart mint sauce—Watson sat back in his chair and examined his old friend.

Holmes submitted to the examination with good humour.

"You haven't once made any remarkable observations about my domestic habits, my immediate past, or my intentions," Watson observed. "You're slipping, Holmes."

"I've had much to occupy my thoughts," Holmes said. He added, with a dismissive wave, "Besides, time spent in the trenches and a sickly bout with mustard gas, too little sleep and too little to eat isn't remarkable these days. Appalling, but not unique. I thought to distract you from your woes, not remind you of them."

"And you've done that with your usual miraculous ability to draw rabbits from hats and shock everyone within the general vicinity," Watson assured him.

"Ah, yes. I supposed if you had not experienced what I have experienced the last few weeks, this morning's revelations would come as a shock." He delved into his breast pocket. "I have several more revelations just for you, though, Watson." He withdrew a small parcel wrapped in brown paper and tied with string, and placed it before him.

Watson pushed at the small package with his forefinger. "Such a small package could only contain the entire treasures of the lost world."

"I bow to your superior cognitive abilities," Holmes responded. "And now you must put it away, unopened, as you have identified the contents."

Watson smiled, and pulled at the string. "What have you brought me from the wilds of the Near East?"

"This is not from me, Watson."

"No? Who is it from?"

"Hadiya Adlparvar. He gave me instructions to give it to you."

"Mycroft's loyal agent? Why would he be sending me a gift?" But Watson already had the string removed. He unfolded the stiff, waxed paper, and dropped his hand to the table to capture the tiny green object that fell onto the table linen and threatened to roll off the table altogether. A small, folded piece of paper fluttered from the brown paper to land next to his hand.

Watson unfolded the paper curiously, and read the short message there.

One life retrieved and returned to your care. E.

He studied the sparkling emerald on the tablecloth, as roaring noise surged in his ears, and his heart seemed to leap to outrace his breath, which was locked in his chest . . .

"Watson!"

Holmes' voice. From far away.

Then, blackness.

Watson recovered to find himself the attention of a whole room of diners.

Deep shame brought a flush to his cheeks, and he struggled to sit up from his prone position on the carpet.

Holmes helped him to his feet, and onto his chair, while Watson assured the milling people that he was fine, thank you very much, a passing moment only. Extreme hunger had caused a brief weakness, but it was over now. I am a doctor, I understand these things although I don't always abide by my own preventative advice . . .

Watson consumed an entire glass of water, his hand shaking, while Holmes reassured the manager that Watson would not embarrass his fine establishment a second time. Then he sat patiently while Watson sipped at a brandy brought by the waiter to aid his recovery.

Finally, Watson dared to speak. "Hadiya . . . is Elizabeth? She is alive?"

"Yes to both questions. You must forgive my love of drama, Watson. I could not resist shocking you. I didn't anticipate the degree of alarm I would induce in you."

"I would suffer through twice the alarm for news of this sort," Watson said truthfully. He fingered the emerald again. "No wonder you did not question Hadiya's loyalty."

"I thought you might notice that omission in my explanation to Stainsbury," Holmes replied.

"It comes from having watched you at work for so many years." Watson tapped the tablecloth. "So tell me the rest," he demanded. "What happened when Moran captured her that night?"

Holmes settled back into his chair, and told the tale, while around them the restaurant clientele eddied and thinned, then halted altogether.

Lamps were lit, and a fresh fire laid in the fireplace. Unobtrusive waiters refilled their brandy balloons and emptied ashtrays.

The short day was dying and night descending upon

the busy street outside when Holmes reached the end of his tale.

Watson sighed. "I wish I had been there," he said wistfully.

"No, you don't," Holmes said. "You're even less of a traveller than I, and you would have hated it."

"True," Watson agreed. "But the discomfort would have been worth it to see her once more."

"There's time, yet, for that," Holmes said. He glanced out the window and shook his head. "Look at that. The day has gone, Watson, while I've bent your ear for you." He stood and stretched.

"It has been, without doubt, one of the best days of my life." Watson stood too, and waved for the waiter to bring the bill, then carefully pocketed the emerald and the note that came with it. "I would not have predicted your confession in a thousand years, Holmes. For a while there, before you gave me this package, I guessed you were about to tell me you hadn't spoken to Mycroft at all, last night. That it was all a magnificent bluff."

Holmes grew very still. "What makes you say that?"

Watson smiled. "It is something that you would do," he said easily. Then he let his smile fade. "You don't mean. . . ?"

Holmes shrugged, and picked up the bill from the silver tray upon which the waiter proffered it. "Does it matter?" he asked. "The end result is the same. An innocent man would not have calmly followed my directions and shot himself, as Stainsbury did."

"No, he wouldn't have. But Stainsbury's final actions take the onus from you, don't they? If you were at all unsure of your guesses and lacked evidence, bluffing Stainsbury in that way would end the affair conclusively, wouldn't it?"

Holmes merely smiled, and shrugged into his overcoat while the waiter held it obligingly.

"Watson, it is good to have you back again," he said jovially.

"And you, too, Holmes. And you, too."

The two old friends departed together.

Timeline of Events Succeeding *Chronicles of the Lost Years*

1903

Holmes retires to cottage on Sussex Downs.

1914

Aug. 1 Events of "His Last Bow."*

Aug. 2 Ottoman Empire signs treaty with Germany for action against Russia, in which case Liman Von Sanders (German) would lead the Turkish army.

Aug. 15 Two German warships sold to the Turks, after Britain seconded the Turkish ships built by them. British naval mission in Constantinople officially ceased this day.

September Young Turks announce abolition of capitulation: All foreigners (*giaour*) in the empire would henceforth by subject to Ottoman civil, criminal and commercial codes of law.

Sept. 27 British ship turns back Turkish torpedo-boat trying to enter the Aegean. Turkey immediately barricades the Dardanelles.
Germany offers gold bullion if Turkey declares war against UK.

Oct. 28 Admiral Souchon (Turkish naval officer) shells Odessa, Nikolaev and Sebastopol.

November Edmund Henry Hynman Allenby, Field Marshal (1861-1936), takes command of the V Corps.

Nov. 11 Sultan Mehmed V, Ottoman Emperor, declares a Jihad.

December Thomas Edward Lawrence (1888-1935), following Turkish declaration of war, is sent back to Cairo and attached to the Arab section of the military intelligence staff.

* "His Last Bow—An Epilogue of Sherlock Holmes" in *His Last Bow* by Sir Arthur Conan Doyle © 1917

1915

Month uncertain	Enver, Turk commander, allows saboteurs to cross the frontier from Mesopotamia into southern Persia and blow up the newly constructed Anglo-Persian Oil Company refinery at Abadan.
Feb. 2-3	Sir Henry George Chauvel, Australian officer (1865-1945), commands First Australian division in Middle East during Battle of Ismailia.
February	Holmes penetrates the German high command, posing as Von Karnch, an administrative officer. He will stay there for four months, polishing his German, and carefully sowing dissension and organizational chaos while soaking up as much intelligence on German operations as possible.
Apr. 24	The Armenian genocide reaches its peak. Turkish troops attack and scatter the mainly Christian people. Reports of the atrocities will filter through to the United States and Europe for the rest of the year. Chauvel's First Australian Cavalry are landed at Gallipoli.
June	Holmes leaves Berlin.
July – Aug.	Holmes returns to London via the Balkans, gathering information on the way, which he reports back to Mycroft.
October	Allenby takes command of the Third Army. Holmes travels to the Russian front and into Russia itself.
November	Holmes reaches St. Petersburg and starts gathering information on the growing revolution.

1916

January	Defeated, the Australian troops pull out of Gallipoli. Turk confidence high. Chauvel returns to Egypt to take command of the ANZAC Cavalry Division.

September Holmes returns to London from St. Petersburg via the Russian front with grim news.

November Lawrence returns to Cairo and is appointed British liaison for the Arab revolt.

December Holmes sent to Nairobi to report on affairs in British East Africa, and to gather information on German activities. For five months, he penetrates German East Africa, roaming the plains, joins up with ad-hoc British cavalry units, and explores through the desert lands with them. Travels as Sigerson. Extremely successful mission. Uncovers a pocket of pro-German sympathizers in Mombasa who were planning to blow up the harbour, and foils their efforts.

1917

Jan. 24 Lawrence helps plan the capture of Wejh (Al Wajh) on the Red Sea Coast.

Mar. – Apr. Lawrence begins guerrilla strikes against the Hejaz railway.

Mar. 26-28 Chauvel, Allenby—first failed strike at Gaza.

Apr. 17-19 Chauvel, Allenby—second failed strike at Gaza.

May-July Lawrence organizes and leads overland expedition from Wejh.

July 6 Lawrence takes Aqaba from the undefended landward side. Vital port. Lawrence promoted to Major as a result. Lawrence uses Aqaba to support Allenby.

Apr. 9-15 Allenby fights the Battle of Arras.

June Holmes returns to London from East Africa. He awaits Mycroft's next call, his blood well stirred by the activities.

Allenby replaces Sir Archibald Murray as commander of British forces in Egypt.

October Lawrence fails to take Yarmuk River Bridge in support of Allenby's first offensive.

Oct. 31	Allenby wins victory at third battle of Gaza (surprise attack on Be'er Sheva) after three failed attempts, which were in part foiled by supreme Turkish intelligence. Allenby pushes on to Jerusalem despite stiffening Turkish resistance, water shortages, and supply problems.
Nov. 5	Holmes receives the invitation to call on Mycroft.
Nov. 13-15	Allenby routed the Turks at Junction Station. Supported by Chauvel.
Dec. 8	Allenby fights Turks in front of Jerusalem.
Dec. 10	Allenby enters Jerusalem, accompanied by Lawrence and Chauvel.

1918

Mar. 20-25	Allenby fails to capture Amman.
Apr. 30-May 3	Allenby's second failure to capture Amman.
Sept. 19-21	Allenby smashes Turkish front line at Megiddo. Lawrence uses his Arabs as extreme right-wing attack on Megiddo, supporting Allenby and Chauvel.
Sept. 27	Lawrence takes Der'aa (Dar'a).
Oct. 1	Allenby, Lawrence, and Chauvel's ANZAC mounted corps take Damascus.
Oct. 16	Allenby takes Homs (Hims).
Oct. 25	Allenby takes Aleppo (Halab).
Oct. 30	Turkey forced out of the war. Collapse of the Ottoman Empire.

Tracy Cooper-Posey's first Sherlock Holmes pastiche, *Chronicles of the Lost Years*, was awarded Best Pastiche by the Sherlock Holmes Society and met with widespread praise. Also a national award-winning romance novelist, Cooper-Posey has published e-book bestsellers and teaches over the internet. Born and raised in Australia, she now lives in Edmonton.